THE HUNTER'S GAME

BLOOD FOR BLOOD: 01

LOGAN FOX

DARK IS THE NIGHT PUBLISHERS

CONTENTS

THE HUNTER'S GAME
PLAYLIST

Red Riding Hood — ELYSIAN FIELDS
Desire — MEG MYERS
Careless Whisper — SEETHER
Inertia Creeps — MASSIVE ATTACK
Roads — PORTISHEAD
White Rabbit — EMILÍANA TORRINI
Toxic — YAEL NAIM
eyes — KING 810
Crazy in Love — SOFIA KARLBERG
Black Milk — MASSIVE ATTACK
Ready or Not — MISCHA "BOOK" CHILLAK
Paradise — MASSIVE ATTACK
Wicked Game — STONE SOUR
Sleep — THE LAST BISON
Dissolved Girl — MASSIVE ATTACK
Change — DEFTONES
Drink You Sober — BITTER:SWEET
The Hunted — SNOW GHOSTS

PART ONE

FOLLOW ME

"As Little Red Riding Hood entered the wood, a wolf met her. Red Riding Hood did not know what a wicked creature he was, and was not at all afraid of him."

LITTLE RED RIDING HOOD - THE BROTHERS GRIMM

CHAPTER ONE
CLOVER

My hands are in fists, my heart kicking hard and fast against my spine. There's no reason to be nervous, but I can't calm myself either even though the Hill Institute doesn't look as formidable as it did when I was a patient here.

Maybe it's because I have the freedom to move about, to speak to anyone I want and to leave any time I choose. I've never been one for rules, or restrictions. The fact I couldn't do what I wanted was the most difficult part of my recovery.

But now, even if I wanted to, I can't turn back—the cab driver left, effectively stranding me.

I puff a strand of red hair from my face and smooth the front of my vintage maxi dress's lace bodice. I found this beige piece of art at a thrift store and spent my last dime on it. I hike up the dress's skirt and take the stairs leading to the front entrance. Before I reach the scraped concrete entryway, my phone vibrates inside my clutch purse.

Gail: Hey hun r u safe?

Gail paid for the cab. She would have pressed even more money on me if she thought she'd have gotten away with it.

But I swore to myself that things would be different this time around. Clover Vos is clean, and I'll make something of my life, even if I'm heading into the arena later than everyone else.

I'm only twenty-three. Whatever gap there is to bridge, I'll fucking bridge it.

Clover: Y? Will let u know when done

I wait for her reply, but she must have put her phone down because I don't see her typing a response. I put my phone away and take a last, steeling breath. A breath which carries a familiar scent.

Holy shit—I was so caught up, I didn't even notice the brilliant white flowers around me. I'd never been outside the Institution at night, but I often stuck my head out of my room window to get fresh air. Now I finally know what it was I kept smelling.

I pick one of the large flowers and stick it in my hair.

Better than perfume, especially if you're not wearing any.

Strangely, the smell gives me strength.

Rehab is done.

This chapter of my life is closed. And I'm so proud that I stuck it out, I'm even willing to drive back here to get some crappy-ass certificate and my 180-day chip. I must admit, when I received my invitation to this shindig, I was back and forth for hours whether or not I'd attend.

As the glass doors open, heat and noise spill out. I follow the sounds of people laughing over low-key jazz music and turn the corner.

The Institute's foyer is a bustle of activity, but it's not the source of the animated chatter. There's a long table covered in brilliant white linen, name tags on lanyards precisely arranged on it. There are only a handful left, but there must have been more than a hundred to begin with. A bored looking girl in a crisp uniform turns disinterested eyes to me and perks up like someone just tasered her in the ass.

"Evening! Welcome to the Hill Institute. May I have your name?"

"It's Vos. Clover." I reach for my name tag the same time as the girl does, and she snatches her hand away.

"Thank you for coming, Clover." Her grin turns less sparkly— guess she doesn't have to be as nice to the patients as she does the people that footed their bills during treatment. She waves a hand to an archway leading to the Institute's formal dining hall. "The ceremony starts in fifteen minutes."

Sheesh, you'd have sworn I was half an hour late.

I'm just here for the coin, bitch. And, possibly, for a little fun. Fuck, it's been six months, I *deserve* a party.

Even one where I can't—

No. Bad thoughts. *Really* bad thoughts.

I give the girl a tight smile as I head for the dining room. She's like three years younger than me, so I have every right to call her that.

The only time I remember being in here was when I had to attend a compulsory seminar about triggers, which I slept through. Not my fault—treatment that week had been pure hell. My gaze darts to the stage. There's a podium, some expensive looking flower arrange- ments, and nothing else. No, not flower arrangements, actual pots of living plants.

Come to think about it, I've *never* seen flower arrangements in this place. I gingerly touch the flower in my hair and bump someone with my elbow.

Christ, this place is fucking packed.

The man I almost elbowed to death turns, mouth twisting with the start of a curse before his expression transforms the instant he sees me.

Yeah, the hair has that effect on people. I got it from my momma— that, and the freckles. According to her, I got my eyes from my dad. Sadly, the fact that my father had gunmetal-gray eyes is the only thing I know about him.

More bad thoughts. Dammit, you're better than this, Clover. Away, bad thoughts, away!

"Hi." The man sticks out a hand. "I'm Frank."

"Yeah you are," I say, smiling around the words as I ignore his hand. He doesn't get it, and his smile crystalizes before he pulls his hand away.

He's too old for me anyway, and that suit's gotta be a loan.

I should go into fashion. I know I have an eye for it, and I'm pretty fucking fantastic with a needle and thread. Turned this 1970s dress into something much more appropriate for picking up men, didn't I? And it only took me an hour and three YouTube videos to get it done. Although I doubt any of those top designers can thread a needle—it's all about delegating these days.

I see a handful of familiar faces, but they're so few and far between I'm wondering who in the hell everyone else is. I was in the program with nineteen other junkies, so they'd have to have brought their entire families—including second cousins—to make up this crowd.

A flash goes off. My skin prickles with ice.

Reporters? Jesus, I didn't have this in mind when I got the invite for the graduation ceremony. My gaze flashes back to the stage, which looks as enormous and barren as a desert.

What the fuck have I gotten myself into?

I should leave.

Instead, I head for the bar.

"Double jack on the rocks," I say.

The bartender—a man in his late forties with a pair of caterpillar thick eyebrows—cocks his head. "I don't serve alcohol, ma'am."

Condescending prick.

"Strange—I see a bottle of Jack right over there." I point at the offending bottle, but the barman doesn't even bother looking.

"This is a rehabilitation center." I'm not imagining it; there's a hint of contempt in his voice.

Ah, of course. Once an addict, always an addict. No smoking, no drinking, no sugar, no excessive sleeping.

"Well, then, just some orange juice. Heavy on the pulp."

"We have mocktails," the bartender says as he puts his hands on the bar and leans in a little. "Pina Colada, strawberry daiquiri—"

"Fine. Surprise me." I roll my eyes as soon as the bartender looks away and slip onto the closest empty bar stool. Only a handful of guests are sitting at the bar, the rest milling around the dining hall or seated at their tables.

Were they serving dinner tonight?

The thought makes my stomach grumble. I clench my jaw, desperate to keep my body under control. I haven't eaten today, and they had me on a horrific diet of raw food the entire fucking time I was in this place.

Wanna know a funny thing about raw broccoli? It tastes the same coming up as it did going down.

"Clover?"

I turn to the voice. Warm brown eyes study me beneath arched brows.

"You sound surprised." I give Michael a warm smile which he returns with a wide grin. Michael made sure I got enough to eat during my detox, and all the right nutrients and shit once I was clean. I made his life particularly difficult, seeing how much I fucking love broccoli.

"Delighted, actually." He takes the stool next to mine. "Can I get you a drink?"

"Thanks, but I already ordered a fake cocktail."

His grin widens as he takes a sip from his drink. It looks like cola, but I catch a whiff of brandy before he sets it down.

So unfair. *Drinking* was never my problem—my issue is heroin.

Is, Clover?

Fuck. First day out and I've forgotten my training already.

Was. Past tense. Heroin doesn't control me anymore. I'm free as a fucking bird. And as poor as a church mouse. Christ, everyone in this place is wearing some designer brand, even good ole Michael. I guess he works at the Institute out of the goodness of his heart—that, or they pay their employees really, really well.

The bartender hands me my pretend cocktail. Somehow, it's worse that it looks like the real thing.

"You look beautiful," Michael says as I reach for the drink.

I fumble, almost spill, and recover ungraciously by tackling the cocktail glass with both hands.

Where the hell did that come from? One of several hundred iron-clad rules at the Hill Institute was their strict no-fraternizing-with-employees-or-other-patients rule.

"Th—" I try, but the bartender cuts me off.

"Cash or card?"

My eyes go wide as I turn to the bartender. "This is a cash bar?"

For fuck's sake. For the price of my rehab fee, I'd have thought it included at least one complimentary fake drink at the graduation party.

"Or card," the bartender says, so smoothly that I almost don't want to be pissed at him.

"Just put it on my tab," Michael cuts in, just as smoothly.

Did their employer send them on mandatory seminars along the likes of 'Be cool, fool' or some shit?

I'm so out of my league here. Why the hell did I even come? I don't *need* a 180-day chip. I don't need a damn certificate saying I completed this course unless I can trade it in for a few bucks.

Now that's what I need: *money*.

"You don't have to—" I begin, but Michael cuts me off with another of his warm smiles.

"I did offer."

I'll give him that. "Thanks."

"So," he says through a small sigh, as if he is glad all this back-and-forth about the drink is finally over. "Where to now for Clover Vos?"

Is that some kind of pick-up line? If it was, I could've answered, 'back to your place, I guess'.

Nah, I'm not that smooth.

And I know he's actually asking me what the fuck I'm going to do with my life now that I've kicked the habit.

I stall by taking a sip of my drink.

I set my glass down and try another smile. This one doesn't come out quite as big, or quite as warm as the others. "I'll find something in the design industry."

"Design?"

"Clothes. Accessories. That kind of shit." Fuck, I swore.

Then again, Michael knows all about my swearing, doesn't he? I cringe inwardly and grimace at him.

"What's wrong?" he asks with a laugh in his voice.

"I'm sorry I threw that tray at you."

He stares at me for a second, face blank, and bursts out laughing. "That was months ago! You were two weeks into your treatment."

"Still...it looked like it hurt." I take another sip, wishing I could turn water to wine. "Plus, you had all that gunk on your face—"

"Scrambled eggs, right?" Michael smiles as he takes another sip of his drink. "I wouldn't be able to do what I do if I couldn't forgive and forget. Trust me, that's all in the past."

My smile warms up a bit, and I cast a quick eye on the audience as I think of something intelligent and witty to say. If I were still the old Clover, Michael would have been my preferred target for the night. Charming, loaded, and good looking enough I wouldn't suggest doggy style so I don't puke before he comes.

But the new Clover is in charge. And she's perfectly happy being friendly with Michael and going home alone. Gail's couch isn't the best bed, but it *is* a bed. And, hopefully, they left me some takeaways. Gail's mom makes the best fucking lasagna in the—

My clutch's clasp rattles out a tattoo against the polished wood of the bar as my phone vibrates inside.

"Sorry—" I say, cutting off when I realize I have no idea why I said that.

Michael finishes his drink and turns to the bartender to order another. I take a quick peek at my phone.

Speak of the devil.

Gail: :(

A sad face? My finger hovers over the keyboard of my old-school Nokia, but I don't know what to say.

Gail: Mom's pissed.

Pissed, or pissed off? It was a toss-up with Gail's mum.

Clover: Y
Gail: Says were not a motel

Motel? My thumb hesitates again. Fuck, is she talking about me sleeping on the couch?

Clover: Is it me?

It can't be though. I mean, I'm clean, and I didn't even—

Gail: Sorry, hun

Double fuck.

Gail: Mom says u cant stay

Clover: pls I have nowhere else 2 crash
2nite. Ill be super quiet prom—

"Everything okay?"

My gaze snaps up to Michael's face. There's a small, concerned frown between his eyebrows.

"Yup. Of course." I take a gulp from my cocktail, remember it's a mocktail, and grimace in frustration. "Just...sorting some shit out."

"Do you have any contacts in the fashion world?" he asks.

"Uh...no?" I realize my tone was a bit harsh, but I didn't expect him to look so taken aback.

"Oh. Sorry. It's just...I just thought, since you want to start working—"

"There's always Craig's List," I say, and immediately regret it. I laugh, trying to make it out to be a joke, and Michael laughs with me.

As soon as he looks away to take his new drink, reality crashes over me.

Christ, Gail, couldn't you have thrown me out of your house *before* I drove to this godforsaken place in the middle of nowhere?

Maybe she thought the further away she sent me, the less likely I was to walk back and sweet talk my way back onto her couch. Where the hell am I supposed to sleep tonight?

I'm so royally fucked.

CHAPTER TWO
HUNTER

She's late. Typical. There were twenty patients to choose from. But I chose her because she shows a history of relapse, several failed attempts at going cold turkey and DIY detoxes gone wrong.

Which is typical of almost every junkie I get in here. They set themselves up to relapse.

She was a troublemaker during her time here, but as soon as she'd detoxed, her personality stabilized.

Perhaps it's her passion, determination, and fierce pride. A pride which intrigues me, because she's broke, homeless, and hasn't had a job since she sold lemonade that one summer in Utah when things were still going well at home.

At least, that's what her file says. Admittedly, it's not one hundred percent accurate. If it were, I wouldn't have chosen her for this. The gaps interest me. Those dark holes in her timeline where anything could have happened. Things I could find no trace of.

She never knew her father.

Her mother died of cancer when she was sixteen.

She was in the foster system from the age of seventeen onward.

But there's a year unaccounted for. A year where Clover Vos disappears from the grid. If I can determine what—

"Doctor Hill?"

I snap from the thought with a grimace, and turn to Pamela, my assistant. "Yes?"

"You're on in ten minutes."

I nod at her, and she disappears like smoke.

I stay in the shadows of the stage's curtain. From here, I can see everyone in the dining hall.

Patients. Their caregivers. My staff.

Through the process of elimination, I know exactly who I'm looking at.

Vos has too much pride to give up a chance to have a room full of people acknowledge her success—even if she knows it will be fleeting. It's more reasonable to assume she's tardy than to assume she's not coming.

I glance down at my Patek Philippe watch, positioning it parallel to my wrist and the hem of my suit jacket.

Seven minutes, and still no Vos.

I look up as she enters the dining hall. She's impossible to miss with her red hair and an outfit meticulously selected to highlight not only her hair's brazen color, but every curve on her body. She even has lipstick on—something I didn't expect to see. Although she's far from a shrinking violet, I assumed she would hang back tonight as she gradually adjusted to the concept of a party that doesn't involve her firing up some china white.

She takes a few seconds to scan the room before she moves to the bar—as I anticipated she would.

My apologies, Vos. There will be no alcohol for you tonight. I need you to have a clear head.

CHAPTER THREE
CLOVER

"I guess we should go to our tables, right?"

I look up at Michael. I'd almost forgotten he was sitting beside me, that's how busy I was trying to sort out my train wreck of a life. I'd been going through my phone book, hoping to find a name on my contact list that wasn't a dealer or a fellow junkie. See, I don't *just* need a couch, I need a couch in a house without drugs.

I'm strong, but fuck my life, I don't want to risk everything just to catch some shuteye. I'd rather sleep under a piece of cardboard. Or a bridge. Both, preferably. It's fall, so the nights can get pretty—

"Which table are you sitting at?"

Fuck, now I'm zoning out. What's wrong with me? Oh, yeah—my life is fucked. I almost forgot.

"I have no idea."

Michael's hand zooms toward me. I watch it coming. Brave man, wanting to fondle my tits in the middle of—

Nope, he's going for my lanyard. He lifts it up, turns it over. "Table five." His eyes flash up to mine. "Me too."

That's odd. Or is it? I can count the times I've been to rehab graduations on one finger. Maybe it's standard procedure to be paired with one of your caretakers, despite the fact that he's handsome, and sweet, and is willing to look past the fact that you called him a moth-erfucking cumdumpster and threw a tray of scrambled eggs at his head.

"Lead the way," I say, sounding a fuck load cheerier than I'm feeling.

As I wait for him to get up—seems there's this whole ritual surrounding the buttoning of a suit before and after sitting that I wasn't aware of—movement catches my eye. The guy next to Michael walks away from the bar, leaving behind a folded fifty-dollar bill.

I'd like to think that I struggled with myself for longer than like one second. I didn't. That crisp bill found a new home in my clutch.

A girl's gotta eat.

Michael walks straight to our table without looking around. I guess he scoped it out before—okay, who cares? I'm starving, and I blame him entirely. I never used to have anything approaching an appetite until I started my program at the Hill Institute. Before I began rehab, I was stick thin and used to eat maybe twice a week. True, on those days I'd pig out, but that's beside the point. Michael thought it would be good to introduce me to the concept of good nutrition. Green things. Fresh things. Raw things. He tutored me on how bad processed food was. Sugar. Caffeine. All the things I loved, he took away from me.

Including heroin. Grass. Barbies.

Which just about sums up my entire six months in this hell hole. Everything good in my life was stripped away from me. I was led to believe everything I'd thought good in the world was an evil equal to Lucifer himself.

Guess I'm a convert. Go figure.

And now, at a time of night where I'd usually be in orbit around our blue marble, I'm ravenous. Seriously, I could eat a small goat. Raw, if necessary.

Michael unexpectedly pulls out my chair for me, which means I end up perching on the edge like a moron before he can push it in again.

Yeah, real smooth, Clover. Go wait in the back with the staff. You have more in common with them than these hand-tailored twenty-thousand dollar suits and Armani gowns.

I down the rest of my mocktail, hoping its demonic dose of glucose will send dopamine to my brain so I can stop stressing the fuck out.

I hate Michael for that too. I didn't even know about dopamine or what the fuck glucose was until I met him.

I glance in his direction. He's watching the stage with a faint smile on his face, all expectant like. Is this his first graduation, or does he know what's coming?

"Do I have to go on stage?" I ask, leaning in so I don't have to raise my voice. I don't want the old biddies across the table to hear what I'm saying. A teenager with bad skin and vacant eyes is sitting next to them—one of the girls I was in rehab with.

Juliet? Julia? Eloise?

Personally, I don't think she's gonna make it. The relapse demon is breathing over her goddamn shoulder, and no surprise with two uppity parents like hers. The mother's even wearing pearls, for fuck's sake. No kid can handle—

"Just to collect your chip." Michael's hand slides onto my leg. Or am I imagining it? After all, I imagined plenty of shit when I was detoxing—that's the official name for this place getting you off of heroin—and it was much more erotic than Michael's hand up my leg.

Between my legs, sure. And not just his hand, either.

I shift in my chair, torn between politely pushing him away and tugging his hand higher.

And here I thought he was this reserved guy, possibly even someone who went to church every Sunday. Maybe the four shots of brandy he has in him are breaking down his brick wall of inhibitions.

"It'll be over in no time." He turns to me, brown eyes as inviting as chocolate fondue. "You don't have stage fright, do you?"

I laugh too loud and cover my mouth with my hand. "Me? Never," I lie.

If there were fifty people here, then yeah, no problem. But there's like a thousand and I feel like I'm on display even though no one's looking my way. And, pretty soon, I'm gonna be *all* they're looking at.

I pick up my glass, but it's empty.

Shit.

"Can I get you another?"

"Not unless it has something stronger in it," I say.

"Clover..."

"I'm not a fucking drunk," I mutter, glancing around to see if they have waiters in this joint, or if I have to walk back to the bar to get a refill. I have money now. Maybe Mr. Holier Than Thou Bartender will slip me a shot.

If not, then I'll get a soda. Fuck, the sugar or the caffeine will get me through this. Maybe I can sneak outside and find someone with a smoke. I would literally decapitate Michael for a cigarette.

Fun fact: six months in rehab for heroin addiction does nothing for craving nicotine. Just so you know.

"What do you drink?"

I jump. Michael whispered that question right in my fucking ear. If I turn, I could kiss him. Instead, I stay still for a second. "Double Jack on ice."

"You promise you'll behave?"

Again, I almost turn. I give my lips a quick swipe with my tongue. "Promise," I mumble.

He stands up, buttons up his suit—I think it's a Tom Ford or something, but I'm not hundreds—and weaves his way through the crowd as he heads for the bar.

Well, fuck. That was unexpected.

I sit back, both relieved and suddenly anxious that I'll finally get something to drink. It's only been what, six months? Pfft.

"Excuse me, Clover Vos?"

I put a crick in my neck as I spin to face a waitress bending over me, a hand on my shoulder. "Yes?" I manage, although the word barely makes it past my throat.

In reply, the girl hands me an envelope. I take it with numb fingers and watch her depart as a deep frown pulls on my eyebrows.

I look down at the envelope. It's an off-white color, thick card

CHAPTER FIVE
CLOVER

Something akin to an army trampling over my future grave rattles up my spine. I keep rereading the words, thinking they'll make sense the fourth, fifth, twenty-seventh time around.

Why the hell would Dr. Hill want to meet me? I'm assuming he's the owner of this rehab facility—it would be a fucking hilarious coincidence if this place is called 'The Hill Institute' and it has nothing to do with him. Does he want to thank me for enrolling in the program? It was a fuck load of money, sure, but I never paid a red cent.

I swallow a throat full of guilt and, luckily, Michael arrives as I feel a gag come on.

Snatching the drink from his hand, I down it. He pauses as if he's reconsidering every decision leading up to this point. What is it, Michael? Worried you're gonna get fired because you got a 180-day-chipper drunk as a skunk?

"Sorry," I mumble as I set the empty glass on the table. The ice cubes rattle, and the sound makes Dead Eyes look up in longing.

And now I feel like shit. Thank you, Dr. H. Fucking Hill.

"What's that?" Michael asks, pointing to the note as he takes his seat.

"Nothing." I shove the note back into its envelope, fold it in half, and ram it into my clutch.

Michael lets out an awkward little laugh, and I know I've blown it with him. If anything's going to happen tonight, it might be a fuck against the back wall where they bring in deliveries and shit, but there's no way this guy is taking me back to his place.

My phone is too heavy in my hand as I take it out and stealthily go through my messages.

Nothing from Gail. Guess I won't be wearing out her couch tonight.

Fuck!

I guess I could try to find a shelter somewhere? Wouldn't be the worst thing I've had to do.

I shudder and hastily push the thought away.

Now I want another drink if only so I've got something other than my goddamn phone to fiddle with.

"So, Michael, you seeing anyone?"

And, of course, he changes the subject as if he hasn't even heard me. "I think they're starting."

I slump in my chair, pout, and press a hand against my stomach when it lets out a nasty little growl.

Fuck you, Michael. My metabolism was fine before you came along.

True enough, the lights in the dining hall dim, and everyone heads for their seats. Another two parent-kid parties crowd our table, one as dead-eyed as the girl who's been here all along, the other looking like they've just found Jesus.

Fuck, that was me this morning. Clover Vos, ready to take on the world.

Now I don't even know where the hell I'll sleep tonight.

Your presence is required in the den.

I won't lie, I'm a little creeped out. Not only because I've never met this Hill guy, but because who the fuck does that? I shiver, and Michael sends a smile my way as if he wants to warm me up with it. It almost works, but then I remember the expression on his face when I downed my drink.

time. Gone are the shadows normally smudged under hollow eyes. My eyes shine, my hair is lustrous.

When was the last time I looked so fucking healthy? I haven't worn makeup in six months, and I was in such a rush to leave Gail's place that I almost took out an eye putting on mascara.

It could have been the Jack Daniels I downed, but Hill also threw me off guard.

I guess I have the Hill Institute to thank for all this—and Hill himself, if he's the one that really came up with the program.

Smug prick.

I straighten my shoulders, adjust my bustier, and haul in a deep breath before touching up my lipstick. Gail loves red, and this one almost matches my hair. Looking in the mirror, I'm not sure if that's a good thing or not, but at least I feel better than when I came in here.

When I march out of the bathroom, there's some kind of commotion happening. Shit, have they moved onto the award ceremony already?

True enough, when I arrive in the dining room, there's an ex-junkie on stage and another on their way up. I collapse into my chair beside Michael.

"Did they call me?"

"Not yet," he replies. He's got a new drink, and I see he ordered for me. Another Jack, surprisingly. Then again, if anyone knows the history of my six months of rehab, it's Michael. He's got to realize my addiction stops at heroin.

Immediately, my counselor's droning voice cuts through my head.

Don't substitute one addiction for another.

There was no smoking at the Institute because too many addicts transposed their addiction for hard drugs onto something just as bad for them if legal: cigarettes.

My phone vibrates.

Sneaking it out, I scan through the notifications. Of the five people I texted, only two replied. Neither of them has a place for me to crash tonight.

Shit.

I force myself to sip my drink although the urge to down it is intense. It would soothe my nerves, but it would make Michael second guess himself and I might need him tonight.

"So...I don't think you heard me earlier?"

Michael turns, glass against his lips and a frown on his brow. "Sorry?"

"You seeing someone?"

He shrugs.

Shrugs! What the fuck am I supposed to do with a shrug?

"Handsome guy like you?" I ask, curling a chunk of hair around my finger. I'm assuming he's single, or it's complicated, but I'm desperate over here. Sleeping under bridges was never my thing. "Come on."

"There's..." He trails off, glancing at me from the corner of his eye before he carries on. "It's complicated."

Nailed it.

"God, I'm sorry," I say, oozing fake sympathy. "Relationships can be so tough."

Which is why I'm not looking for one; take the hint, retard.

He smiles at me. "What about you? You going back to that guy?"

That *guy*...? Oh, right. Spencer. The one that paid for my rehab. *Pfft*. Fine, he was a sweetheart and whatnot, but way too bald for me. Then again, I think he realized we weren't a match after I OD'd on his five-thousand-dollar sofa and left permanent sick up stains on the fabric. He threw me in this institute so fast I was still high as fuck when I woke up here. They told me I'd died for a while.

Spencer had everything: tons of money, his own company, and a job that required ninety percent of his available time. All I had to endure was the odd dinner, seven hours of intense snoring, and a quickie every three days—if he wasn't out of town on business.

In return, I was rewarded with the unholy trinity of addiction—boredom, drugs, and money.

I'm surprised it lasted as long as it did, really.

"No..." I drop my head, hiding behind my hair because I'm not sure I can pull off the expression he's expecting to see. "He didn't sign up for dating an addict."

CHAPTER SEVEN
CLOVER

"Congratulations, graduates. Let's give them another hand." Hill claps loudly, but he steps away from the microphone like a pro before he does.

I watch him from behind my glass, taking tiny sips that can't wash the taste of shame from my mouth.

Something happened up there, and I don't have a fucking clue what it was. It's like we had this whole conversation, but didn't say a word.

He knows me. He knows everything there is to know about me. But how?

I'm not a recluse, but I'm secretive. I go to parties, I mingle, I sleep around. But I'm not on social media. Mainly 'cos I'd need a cellphone that cost more than a few bucks to engage on that shit. But also because I've never liked people *knowing* about me. The only thing I want to share with the world is what I consider a good time.

But he *knows* me. He found out stuff, and for some reason that makes him interested in me.

But why? I'm a fucking nobody.

"…later tonight?"

I jerk back to the present and give Michael an apologetic smile. "What?"

"Where you headed after this?"

Ah, fuck. A bridge, Mike, don't you know? If I'm lucky, I might even have a piece of cardboard handy to ward off the cold.

"Wherever you're going," I say, my lips perking into a smile.

He looks down, and a shy little smile plays on his mouth. "Yeah?"

"If you want. I don't know about you, but I got some celebrating to do." I hoist the glass of Jack to my lips and drain it.

A flicker of doubt flashes across his eyes, but then I give his thigh muscle a squeeze and it disappears like it never was.

Good boy.

"Lamb or pork, ma'am?"

I start, spinning to face a dead-faced server standing behind my chair. "Uh...lamb's fine, thanks."

Je-sus! I thought Hill would let me starve.

The server gives a dry little nod and moves on to Michael. He orders the pork, but I won't judge him for that. As long as he has a bed for me to crash in, I'm gonna be pretty lax in the whole judgment department tonight.

The server notices my drink's empty and then realizes it had alcohol in it. This makes him seize up like he's having a stroke, and I chuckle before I can get my hand up to stop the sound.

Even Michael suppresses a smile and gives the waiter a little wink. "Another round, please. Put it on my tab."

The server gives an awkward little bow and leaves while Michael and I are still chuckling at him.

"You gonna get into trouble for this?" I ask, tapping my nail against the edge of the glass. In his haste to leave, the server left it behind.

Michael shakes his head. "Nah. Long as Dr. Hill doesn't find out."

I realize I'm twining my bracelet around my finger, cutting the metal chain into my wrist. What, does he expect the waiters to report back to Hill on what I'm drinking? Who the fuck cares?

He cares, Clover.

I find him a few seconds later. He's seated at one of the larger tables, surrounded by ten intellectuals in suits. Three of them are women, the others resolutely male. Spectacles and officious chuckles abound.

Gah. I hard-swallow my last mouthful of broccoli and push away the plate before I can puke.

"Another round?" I ask, peeking out at Michael through my hair as I tap a nail against my nearly empty tumbler.

He gives a big nod, his mouth still full of pork, and looks around for a passing waiter.

I happen to glance in Dr. Hill's direction as I bring the glass to my lips.

He's staring at me. He's sitting straight up in his chair and smelling whatever the fuck people that drink wine think they can smell. Oak, cranberries, cotton-candy—fuck knows.

I raise my glass, give him a grim smile, and toss back everything except the ice cubes. They bump against my lips, hard and cold, before I set down the glass. I wipe my lips with the back of my hand, making sure the gesture is something he can't miss over the intervening space.

He takes a tiny sip of his wine and breaks eye contact as someone leans across the table to talk to him.

Clover: 1.
Hunter: 0.

"HOW WAS YOUR MEAL?"

I jerk, turning to Michael with what must have been a guilty look on my face. I'd been staring so hard at Hill, I hadn't noticed the waiter setting a new drink in front of me, or clearing away our empty plates.

Even my garnish hadn't survived the onslaught.

"Uh...Good. Good." But my heart isn't in it. For one, Hill trumps Michael at looks any day.

And Clover Vos has never stood down from a challenge. Well,

except if it involved heroin or coke, of course. Everyone has their vices. Mine just happen to be illegal, dangerous, and as addictive as fuck.

Hill has vices, I know it. If you have warm red blood flowing in your veins, then you have a vice.

What's his?

My phone vibrates, but I already know it's only notifying me of more disappointment.

Face it, Clover—you have no friends. You've got no place to stay. Tomorrow, this time, you're gonna be nothing more than a starving rat unless you can find someone to take you in like a stray.

'Cos that's all you are—a stray. You chose heroin over college. You chose heroin over a job. And you chose heroin over every single fucking pseudo relationship you've ever had.

If only you'd been a more caring lover, you might have made out okay.

Instead, you're fucked. If this were a marriage, you'd be the divorcee with no custody who still has to pay alimony.

I hear myself say, "I'll be right back," without any intention of keeping my word.

News flash: Clover tells fibs.

She scoffs as she drains her glass and looks to her lackeys for support; a troublemaker, just like Clover.

"You see, Susanna, rehabilitation cannot succeed if the traumas which create an addict's triggers aren't fully explored."

She looks surprised that I know her name. Why wouldn't I? She's a member of the medical research community, just like me. Would an Olympic athlete not study his competition to determine their weaknesses and strengths?

"So why don't you counsel them?" Susanna asks.

"Psychological counseling is an integral part of the program." The glass in my hand grows heavy as a server tops me up. I almost ask him for a better vintage, but I doubt anyone at the table would truly appreciate it.

I abhor waste.

"So they shouldn't relapse then, should they?" Her voice holds a tone of triumph.

"Some patients don't respond to counseling." I test the wine and find it wanting. But I drink it anyway because this woman is getting on my nerves. "Especially those that have repressed past trauma."

Mathers leans forward, his eyes aglitter with intrigue. "And those are the ones that relapse?"

"Undoubtedly," I answer, taking another sip of wine. "You see, although my detoxification program overcomes their physical addiction, the subject remains susceptible to their psychological addiction. A single trigger will…"

A flare of red catches my eye. I set down my wine glass as Clover approaches our table.

She looks determined, furious, and intoxicated.

Where on earth did she obtain alcohol?

The colleagues around my table turn to see what I'm staring at. Susanna's face turns back, a twist on her mouth. Mathers gives me a quick, knowing smile before turning back to his meal.

Clover stops across the table from me, at the only empty seat. Professor White of Mallhaven University should have been in attendance tonight, but one of his children contracted measles or some other contagious disease, and he retracted his RSVP earlier today.

I'm about to stand, but Clover pulls out the empty chair and flops down in it for all the world like she has a rightful claim to a seat amongst studied professors.

"Well?" she asks in that voice I've come to know so well over the past six months. "You wanted me over for dinner." She spreads her arms. "Here I am, Doctor Hill."

CHAPTER ELEVEN
CLOVER

My heart's gonna pound right through my ribs. What a bloody mess it'll make of this dress, right?

But it's worth it, oh yes. Hill looks like there's a frog stuck in his throat, and his enlightened friends in their fancy suits and feministic hairstyles are foaming at the mouth.

Thank you, Jack. I owe you an eternal debt. Because nothing puts the fight in Clover Vos like a few shots of whiskey.

If it weren't for the jazz playing in the background, the sound of crickets would have been loud as fuck.

A chick at the end of the table leans in—she's had one too many, just like me—and says, "I'm sorry, and you are?"

I wave. "Clover." Then I point at Hill. "I'm one of his."

I didn't mean for the sentence to come out quite like it did, but what's done is done, right?

"A patient?" asks a strangled voice beside me.

A nerd with glasses looks shell-shocked, and more than a little inebriated.

Fuck, if I'd known intellectuals partied so hard, I'd have gone to college.

"Not anymore," I quip, and grab an empty wine glass. There's a server across the table from me, and he sees me lift my glass but doesn't make a move to come over and fill it.

Wanker.

"Ms. Vos." Hill rises to his feet. "I think you misunderstood my earlier invitation." He sounds like he's talking through his teeth. The fury in his eyes is a good look on him. Broody, filthy rich maniac. I like it.

"Ohhhh." I nod and put down my glass again. "'Dinner.'" Yup, air quotes and everything. I laugh and give the girl at the other end of the table a knowing smile. "Silly me."

I stand, blatantly adjust my bustier to increase cleavage, and point out the hall. "After you, Doctor Hill." I drop my voice a few octaves.

A guy at the table drops his fork.

Hill's lips go into a thin line. "If you'll excuse me," he mutters, buttoning up his suit jacket with white-knuckled hands.

No reply from his friends.

He stalks from the table, and I grab a slice of French Bread from the basket in the table's middle. I send a wink in Dr. Geek's direction and hoist up the slice of bread. "Think I'm gonna need my stamina."

His lips part, but he seems unable to produce words.

Hill is waiting outside the dining room for me, but off to one side so I don't notice him. He grabs my elbow, spinning me to face him.

Intentionally or not, I crash into him. This close, a circle of green is visible in his eyes, pressing against the brown.

"Hey!" I push back, feeling hard muscles under my palms before I swipe my hands away like he scorched them.

"What are you doing?" he whispers furiously at me. "You can't just—"

"What the hell do you want from me, huh?" My voice is too loud, but I don't bother lowering it. Hill tries to grab my arm, perhaps to drag me somewhere quieter, but I've only just begun. "I was your fucking lab rat for six months. What more could you possibly want to know?"

"Lab rat?" His eyes crinkle with incredulity.

Her expression turns to stone. "You know what? I just remembered: I *do* have somewhere better to be."

"Ms. Vos, I merely—"

"You merely nothing, you freak." She tugs at her door handle and throws me a furious scowl. "Let me out. Now."

I watch her yank my Jaguar's door handle, and it's all I can do to remain calm. "We had a deal."

She stops trying to open the door, but her hands stay on the handle. "I stayed at a relative's house, then I went into foster care."

"A relative?"

"Yeah, family." She throws a frown my way. "Do you even know what that is?"

I laugh. The sound is far from a mirthful one. "Oh yes, unfortunately I do."

My driver halts in front of the gates leading to my home. "We're here," I say, and Clover's fingers slip from the handle.

A familiar expression crosses her delicate face.

Resignation.

CHAPTER THIRTEEN
CLOVER

An orange glow peeks through the thickly clustered pine trees. Hunter's Jaguar stops in front of a black, ornate gate that opens as incrementally as a glacier. Tires crunch over gravel an eternity later, and my stomach twists tighter the closer we draw to the structure ahead.

Compared to the Institute, Hunter's house is night versus day. The Institute is all sharp angles, concrete, glass, steel. This house looks like a log cabin designed by an architect with an inexhaustible budget.

My door unlocks with a quiet *snick*. I scramble from the car so fast that when I slam the door shut behind me, my dress gets trapped in the jamb.

Hunter comes around the back of the sleek, black Jag, his smile growing from faint to smug as he sees me trying to open what's now a very locked car door.

I look away, taking in his house as he walks past and instructs the driver to unlock my door again so I can be free.

A hand slides down my side, and I jerk at the unexpected touch.

Hunter is standing less than a foot away, the incriminating hand dangling at his side.

"Don't touch me," I snap, taking a big step to the side in case he tries his luck again.

"Your dress was—"

"Forty minutes, Hill." I refuse to call him Hunter—it humanizes him too much.

He ducks his head, watching me through dark lashes as he passes me and heads for the front door. The Jag drives away, and it feels as if my stomach leaves with it.

Fuck, it's a beautiful house, but I refuse to retract my claws just because this guy has nice digs. Beautiful? This place is fucking stunning.

He's at the door, and I slow down, expecting him to take out keys or a keycard or something, but it opens for him as if he never even bothered locking it.

Well, if I have to run, at least I know I won't have to break through one of those massive glass walls to get out.

I step inside, trying to keep my eyes to myself and failing miserably. Natural materials abound—reclaimed wooden beams in a vaulted ceiling, exposed stone trimmings, a fur throw on the leather sofa, antlers as decoration bedecked by a wreath of tiny dried flowers.

And then there's the silence.

Utter silence.

"Where is everyone?" My voice sounds hollow in the space between us.

Hunter pauses beside the leather sofa and shrugs off his suit jacket. He turns to me wearing the first relatable expression I've seen on his face all night—relief. His tie comes off next as he steps out of his shoes.

Jesus Christ, whatever happened to foreplay?

My hand tightens around my clutch. I'd have to be an idiot not to know this was coming, but sometimes it's fun to pretend I'm naïve.

Laughable, I know. But a girl can dream, can't she?

"It's just me and the staff." He's in his shirt and suit pants, face the most relaxed I've seen it all night as he loosens the strap on his antique-looking watch. He glances at the watch face before letting it drop on the table. "Who've left by now."

Alone.

Something tells me the front doors will be locked if I happen to try it.

But why, Clover? Why would you want to run?

Because there's something I'm not seeing. I know how to read people, and I can't read Hunter's face for shit. I can see nothing in his eyes about his intentions with me. He doesn't look horny, doesn't look tired; but he does look relieved to be home.

"Thirty-five minutes," I say, but my heart really isn't in it.

He cocks his head. "I only need ten."

My eyes go wide before I can stop them. His lips perk up and then he crosses the floor and stops in front of me. "Would you like a drink?"

"Is that a rhetorical question?"

His smile fades as he heads for the kitchen.

He didn't even ask what I wanted. Maybe I don't have a choice in the matter. I follow him if only because I don't like him being out of my sight.

A bottle of port rattles on a granite countertop. He pours two fingers in a pair of tumblers. "Ice?"

"Thanks." Look, maybe this is the extent of his civility. Not everyone can be as charming as me.

He hands me the glass. Our fingers brush. Exactly like it happened in the Jag on the way over here, the hair on my arms stands up in a rush. I pluck the glass away and swipe a hand over my skin. "It's cold in here," I mumble into my glass. "I thought log cabins were supposed to be warm?"

"There's no heat to retain," he says.

Wait, was that a diss?

He returns to the living room on silent feet. He even took off his socks, but fuck knows when. Which is how I can see that his feet are slightly grubby underneath.

Hunter Hill, barefoot stroller. I snort quietly into my port as I take another sip. Weirdo.

Instead of sitting on the sofa, Hill crouches in front of the fireplace. It's in the space where a flat screen television would normally go, but I guess Netflix and chill doesn't form part of Hunter's schedule.

I sip at my drink, twisting left and right as I hug my free arm around my stomach. I'm still in the kitchen, but the design is open plan so I can keep an eye on Hunter while I try to locate something to defend myself with just in case.

He's acting like a gentleman now, but I've known evenings like this to turn rather unpleasant. Then again, drugs were usually involved in those—I sincerely doubt that'll be the case here.

"What's so funny?" Hunter asks.

Does he have superhero hearing or something?

"Nothing." I go closer, watching as he packs logs into a triangle.

"Have you built a fire before?" he asks, but his eyes are solely on his task as if my reply is kinda irrelevant.

"I live in this century." I know it's a silly comment to make, but he's got my guard up again. I mean, how does someone who wears a billion-dollar suit know how to make a fire?

I go sit on the sofa. The port is delicious, of course, but as much as I want to down it and just lose the rest of tonight in a haze of alcohol-induced amnesia, something tells me to stay alert.

Outside, what little light beams from the cabin reaches only the closest pines where they press against the house's driveway. Everything beyond those first trees is utter darkness.

I shudder, unable to tear my eyes away from the inky nothingness brooding out there.

Fuck, imagine getting lost in those woods. Scared, alone, utterly disorientated. I'm the furthest thing from a hippy—I prefer concrete sidewalks and alleyways reeking of piss. Yeah, it's fucking gross, but it's familiar. Alleyways always end. Someone's always around—even if they're not the type you necessarily want around you.

You can get lost in the city, but you'll never, ever be alone.

Not for long.

Something thuds on the fireplace's grate, and I almost jump halfway out of my fucking skin.

Hunter stretches out a hand to reposition the fallen log, and I notice a mark on his wrist. It's small, something he'd easily covered with his watch's strap, but for some reason I can't look away.

I expect him to pull out a lighter or turn a switch that'll magically ignite the fire…

He doesn't. He takes a piece of dark stone from a container on the mantel and a pocket knife from his belt.

I'll admit, the knife scares me. Who the hell wears a knife with their suit? He scrapes at the stone, letting a few shards fall onto a bundle of fluff that could be cotton or wool, who the hell knows?

"See, the trick is to ensure your tinder is as dry as possible."

"Like the app," I say.

Hunter pauses in his fire starting duties to glance at me over his shoulder. "Excuse me?" There's frustration in his eyes, as if not understanding me makes him uneasy.

Get ready, Hunter—there's gonna be a lot of that coming your way if you still intend on grilling me tonight.

"Strange—random hookups seem to be your thing."

Hunter turns back to the fire, adjusts a log, and flicks the edge of his knife against the stone. This time, the only thing that comes off it are sparks. A second later, the cotton glows. He crouches lower, blowing over the pile of fluffy stuff until it smokes and, eventually, catches flame.

It's fascinating to watch, but I'm focusing more on him than the fire. His hair is long in the back—it curls rebelliously over the collar of his button-up shirt. It's a shaggier cut than you'd expect to see on someone wearing a suit.

Maybe it's a long drive to the hairdresser.

But what about those grubby feet?

The tattoo on his wrist.

Who are you, Hunter Hill?

He gets to his feet, and the new angle of his arm throws light over the mark.

No...not a tattoo.

A *scar*.

And the type I recognize. The ones you create when your body is screaming for mercy, but you ignore and try to find a vein anyway.

My, my, Doctor Hill...I do believe you're living a double life.

"What was your vice of choice?" I ask, sipping at my glass of port.

Hunter stands, dusting his hands against his suit pants without looking at me. The few sparks he produced have set the tinder aflame. Bright tongues caress his pyramid of logs; a ravenous dog licking blood from its master's fingers.

His voice is quiet and strangely distant. "Heroin."

Heat flashes through me, but it's not coming from the fire. That's still in its infancy and this heat is dangerously primal.

There's a reason my dress has long sleeves—it'll take a while for my scars to heal. And there are others on my body I know will never go away.

When my love affair with H was new and bright as Hunter's fire, I was careful. I chipped so I could never become addicted and my tolerance would remain low. The cravings would then be psychological, not physical.

When I lost my first job—the boss tried to grope me, so entirely unrelated to my addiction—my life didn't have structure anymore. Weekends merged into weekdays, and I found it impossible to keep track of when I was supposed to be up and when I was supposed to be down. And because being down sucked donkey balls, I chose up.

I chose up *way* too many times.

He comes to sit beside me, downs his glass, and turns to the side table. I hear something opening, and an invisible ice cube slides down my spine.

I throw back the rest of my port.

I have so many questions but I can't ask them. This is a dangerous topic—Hunter knows it, I know it.

Why the fuck didn't he lie?

You know what, I shouldn't be here. Not an epiphany, sure, but I just realized why this guy is so fucking wrong.

I hurry after her, catching up as she sets foot on the landing. I grab her elbow, and she tears it free with a low growl.

"You got me, okay?" she spits out as she throws her hands up. "I *don't* have anywhere to go." She storms up to me and stabs a finger in my chest. "But I'm not some charity case you get to brag about to your stuck up friends. Yes, I need a place to sleep tonight. I'll give you what you want, but don't you dare think you're doing me a fucking favor."

Her fingers flash between us. "*Quid pro quid,*" she snaps.

My mind goes blank. All I can manage is a murmured, "*Quid pro quo,*" but the correction is completely automatic.

I stick the joint between numb lips and light it. Who knows, maybe this will all make sense when my mind isn't so crowded anymore. I draw long and hard, filling my lungs with itchy-sweet smoke.

Her eyes flicker to the joint, back to me. A slow realization washes over her face, and a touch of color paints her cheeks.

I don't often become angry. Irritated, frustrated, yes. But pure anger is something that usually has to accumulate over time. Layer upon layer of sediment.

I take another drag of the joint and then hold it out to her. Smoke coils between us before I exhale.

"Since you insist..." I say, pushing the words through my teeth.

CHAPTER SEVENTEEN
CLOVER

The joint feels warm and brittle in my fingertips. A flicker of flame ignites the paper, and I draw deep at it. I cough, take another pull, and push it away from me. Hunter takes it, draws deep, and crushes it out under his bare sole.

I'm transfixed on that foot until fingers grasp my chin and turn my face upward.

Fuck it, I'm done fighting this.

I thought I'd grown a fucking spine after six months of rehab. Turns out, I was just playing hard to get.

It's his self-confidence. His aura. Hunter Hill is heading somewhere with the speed and determination of a jet plane. And me? I'm walking barefoot through the desert. I would have found my own footprints again by now—but the desert wind keeps blowing them away. I don't realize I'm going in circles and the whole while the sun bakes on me, scorching my flesh.

I stand on tiptoes, leaning into Hunter's touch.

He studies me, but even in this moment I can't read anything in his eyes. I like to know what I'm dealing with, but this man is an enigma. No, I don't like to know. I *have* to know. It's the only fucking compass I have in this godforsaken desert I'm stranded in.

"Can you trust me?" Hunter asks.

His pulse exudes like electricity from his fingertips, thrumming against my jaw bone.

"No."

"Will you?"

"Yes." My mouth feels numb around the word, and I have no idea if it's my response or the weed's.

My body relaxes. My mind breaks apart like driftwood in a storm. My anger drains away. My fear relinquishes to curiosity.

And even the dark doesn't press as hard against the glass anymore.

How does he stand living out here by himself? Can't he sense those eyes on him, watching his every move? Unseen but as physical as an unwanted caress.

I can.

Ever since my mother died, I always can.

But those aren't her eyes—that much I know. Those eyes belong to someone who's still alive. Not a human, but a demon wrapped in human flesh. Those eyes watch me even now. As if that demon tracked me here over uncountable miles. Perhaps my fluttering heart was its beacon, my racing mind a signal fire burning bright.

"I am going to fix you, Clover." Hunter's breath washes over my lips and it feels as blissful as the sun peeking out after a week of drizzle.

Warm.

Comforting.

Real.

"I'm not broken."

"And because you think that, you'll never be whole." Hunter presses his thumb to my bottom lip. A current surges through me, forcing my lips to part with an inaudible gasp.

What the fuck was in that weed? My heart races as I consider the possibilities.

Meth. Cocaine.

Heroin.

He wouldn't.

He wouldn't.

He *fucking* wouldn't.

Tears fill my eyes, and I squeeze them free.

"No," I whisper.

"It's the only way."

"No...please..." My voice is reduced to a mewl.

My body responds like a moonflower touched by starlight. My eyes roll back, breath whispering past lips tingling with pleasure.

"Enjoy it, Clover." A warm puff of weed-scented breath accompanies each word. "Because this is the last time heroin will *ever* have control over you again."

CHAPTER EIGHTEEN
HUNTER

I've strayed so far from my script, I'm not sure I can ever get back to it. I try not to think of the wasted time I spent preparing tonight's events. Instead, I focus on what is coming.

But I'm distracted, and I despise the feeling. My thoughts should be on the research trial, but instead I'm fixating on the feel of this girl's lips against the pad of my thumb.

So soft.

So *warm*.

Why didn't I choose a sativa? I can't think straight with all this dopamine in my brain. Can't concentrate.

I'm saving this girl's life, but for some reason I'm riddled with guilt.

Guilt, of all things!

Is it because there was no warning, Clover? You look as if you feel betrayed.

I was your priest, you my altar boy. I broke the trust. Now you're overwhelmed with self-loathing, blaming yourself for falling into my trap.

"There's no other way." It takes me a few seconds to realize those words are mine. "I'm sorry."

She brushes against me.

Her lips are bright as loganberries.

I'm a man of science. I should have been able to resist her mouth, but I can't. I'm a bee drawn to a blossom, its ultraviolet nectar guides speaking to something in my very DNA.

Our lips meet in a warm rush of mingled breaths.

She relaxes into me and crushes her mouth against mine in sheer desperation.

CHAPTER NINETEEN
CLOVER

Hunter tastes of weed and port and intoxicatingly sweet saliva.
I know this is wrong.

I know this is fucked up.

I don't care.

My body wants release. Why can't Hunter provide it? Doctor Hunter fucking most eligible bachelor of the year Hill wants me to trust him?

I give you my cunt. Now tell me I don't trust you, asshole.

But this isn't vindictiveness flowing through me. It's not revenge.

It's lust.

And that's all it is. He's the first piece of decent meat I've laid eyes on in six months. Sure, I think he's a condescending prick, but when has that ever stopped me from fucking someone?

He thinks he's noble? He's not. He's a man, and he has a dick, and he has needs just like me. He might not acknowledge them like an ordinary person, but they're still there.

Why does he want me to trust him?

Haven't I trusted him for the past six months? Sure, not *him*. Not *Hunter* fucking Hill. But I've been putting my trust in the Hill Institute, believing their six-month program will cleave this fucking monkey from my back and cast it back into the hellfire from whence it came.

I'd love to think this is all beyond my control. I want to relinquish responsibility—like I always do—but I'd be kidding myself.

I want him.

I *need* him.

And I don't even care if the dark watches us—I want him to end my suffering and soothe my soul.

Even just for one night.

Because maybe, tomorrow, I'd wake without this craving clawing away at my brain like a feral animal too long contained.

Because even if there hadn't been anything in that joint...

If I'd landed on the street tonight, I'd have woken up in a crack den tomorrow morning with no fucking clue how I got there.

Fun fact: Clover Vos has a shitty fucking life.

Six months of rehab didn't change that—I know a night with Dr. H. Hill won't change it either.

But I'm buying myself some time.

Twenty-four hours.

I've sold myself for much less before.

PART TWO

OBEY ME

"The wolf thought to himself: 'What a tender young creature! what a nice plump mouthful!'"

LITTLE RED RIDING HOOD - THE BROTHERS GRIMM

CHAPTER TWENTY
HUNTER

Despite my meticulous plans, something wholly unforeseen is happening. For one, I have a one Ms. Vos in my arms.

I'm kissing her.

And I want more.

I will be the first to admit that I'm a recluse, a hermit more at home with my research at my isolated home in the mountains than at any fine dining establishment in Mallhaven. Sex is something I have little time, or patience, for. I can deal with my most primal urges more efficiently by myself than having to endure a game of cat and mouse with a complete stranger.

But this is something else entirely.

And I have only one vague hypothesis to explain it.

I've studied Clover closely these past few months. There is a chance I may have become enamored with her, transferring my obsession with her into something else.

I guess the time for analytic study has passed. I fumble our kiss, and she draws back with wide eyes.

No surprise; I'm acting like a virgin on his first date.

Am I panting? I must sound like an animal. Who wants that? I suppress my furious breathing and swipe the back of my hand over my mouth when I notice that I've smeared her lipstick.

In the landing's low light, it looks like blood. I taste my teeth with my tongue to make sure it isn't.

I lost myself there for a moment.

"Ms. Vos, I must apologize." My voice sounds strangely thick.

Hers is barely a whisper. "You must?"

"This...this is most inappropriate."

"It is?"

My teeth grit. She's being unhelpful, and I suspect she knows it. I'm sure I'm not imagining a certain smugness under that faintly surprised expression of hers.

I want to push her away, but the hand in her hair tightens instead. Her head tips back a little, and stray light gleams from her lips.

She lets out a tiny gasp when I barrel into her. As I surge forward, she's forced back. I stick out my hand and shove open my bedroom door. No wood in this house is varnished, but everything's been polished to a luxurious sheen. The wood feels like wet clay under my fingers as it slides away and slams into the wall.

I trip over something—a sandal?—and our legs tangle. I have just enough momentum to lift her and toss her on the bed before I collapse on top of her a moment later.

Her breath washes over my face. She squirms under me, her livid eyes so wide, so spectacular.

Our legs are hanging over the side. I shove a hand under the small of her back and lift her, forcing her higher up the bed. Her dress is between us, twisting around her legs and mine.

I kiss her, trap her, make her mine.

She's struggling, but whether to get out from under me or to untangle from her dress, I can't say.

Right now, I couldn't care. If she wants out, she'll have to scream or kick or bite.

This is her fault. She stole inside me when I wasn't paying attention and lodged herself deep in my brain, in a part I don't ever take notice of. In a single encounter, she's torn apart whatever flimsy barriers I had erected.

I grope my way down her body until I find the hem of her dress, which I hike up to her hips.

There's an ambient glow in my room that casts a sensual haze over her face, her hair, the pale stretches of her legs. My fingers graze over her thighs and encounter a ridge of flesh.

I look down and catch sight of a thick scar on Clover's inner thigh.

But that's all I can see before Clover grabs my straining cock through my pants.

CHAPTER TWENTY-ONE
CLOVER

I'm Dorothy. I was in Kansas, and now I'm on the way to fuck knows where. The tornado that sweeps me up got hold of every-thing else; my emotions, thoughts, desires.

As I'm spinning, it's tearing me to pieces.

His strength terrifies me. I've been under heavy men, men who spend more time in the gym than they do sleeping at night, but this is different.

He doesn't just pin me with his weight, he's keeping me here with some kind of force of will.

I want out, but not as badly as I want to remain his captive. I'm aching for him, my body crooning from the memory of his lips. When he pulls up my dress, so intent on fucking me that he doesn't seem to want to bother with more foreplay than our few rough kisses, my core contracts in hedonistic expectation.

But then he finds a scar and looks down.

Brief anger flares like a newly struck match inside me. I shift, but he's already seen it. There's a frown on his face, and he opens his mouth as if to ask—

I grab his dick. It brings him back to the present, but it sends me out of my mind with desire.

Fuck, I had no idea he was this turned on. My body responds instantly—my legs twine together and my nipples bunch into tight little buds through the fabric of my dress.

Hunter shoves a blade of a hand between my legs, trying to pry me open. I want him to touch me, but I don't want to give up the delicious thrumming my thighs are pressing into my cunt, either. He leans on an elbow, grasping roughly at my breast, weighing it in his hand as his thumb and forefinger tweak my nipple.

He kisses me again, hard, as if he's threatening pain if I don't open to him.

Doesn't he get it yet? I don't take well to command.

I twist my hips, dislodging his hand.

My punishment is another hard grope of my breast, another painfully tweaked nipple.

This is what happens when you don't get laid for six months—the smallest thing turns you on.

It's the only explanation I have for the fire splashing over my core at this man's brutal touch. I squeeze his dick again, trying to bite back with some of my own punishment.

I'm rewarded with a groan.

Deep, low, primal as fuck.

Goosebumps break out on my skin. He dips his hips, forcing his erect cock over my pelvic mound. The sensation thrills through me, and it's all I can do to catch my breath as his mouth descends on mine.

I taste blood in my mouth.

Somehow, I know it's mine.

I guess he was holding himself back before because shit just got real.

CHAPTER TWENTY-TWO
HUNTER

What has this woman done to me? I consider myself a gentleman, but there's nothing gentle or manly about the way I'm treating her.

Filthy. Brutal. Savage.

Those are the only words I can summon to describe the things I want to do to her.

How will these unchecked desires of mine affect the trial? What if I contaminate my own data? What if—?

"Fuck, woman, open your goddamn legs!" I don't recognize my own voice, or the obscenities flowing over my tongue.

She laughs.

The fucking harpy *laughs* at me.

Fabric tears as fibers give way under my fingers. The delicate lace of her bodice is in tatters.

I can't kiss her anymore—I think I tore her lip—so I bite at her breasts instead. She gasps, writhing under me like a fish. I get my hand between her legs, but she's clamping her thighs closed with such determination that I can't even touch her.

And fuck, how I want to wet my fingertips with her.

I lift myself, wedge my knee between her thighs, and drive down so hard that she has no choice but to open. Her shocked gasp tears through me. My head darts up, catching the tail end of that sound with my lips. She moans, and I realize I'm hurting her bruised lips. I draw back, our lips barely brushing now as I rake my nails up the inside of her thigh.

She's not wearing underwear.

I stop an inch from her cunt, grasping roughly at her thigh to control myself.

She grabs my belt buckle and fumbles with it. Her breath becomes a furious pant that paints sweet warmth over my lips. I run my tongue over her bottom lip, then the top. She mewls, and finally pops open my pants button.

My muscles contract when her hand dives behind my silk underwear. She grabs my cock and gives me a hard pump. Her legs come up, heels hooking at my waistband and tugging my pants down over my ass.

My boxers are next.

Now there's nothing between us but warm air.

Despite the dim light in my room, I can see she's watching me. I lean on one hand, our gazes locking as I wrap my hand over hers.

Clover arches under me, bringing her slit in contact with my knuckles.

She's soaked through.

I go down on an elbow, grip a handful of her soft, silky hair, and guide the tip of my cock to her cunt. She squirms, goes quiet. Her panting breath slows in anticipation.

I tighten the grip in her hair, earning another arch of her slender back, and then I'm inside her.

CHAPTER TWENTY-THREE
CLOVER

Christ, this man knows how to fuck. I stretch deliciously warm around him as he fills me. My legs hook around his waist so when he thrusts into me, I'm at the perfect angle.

Ready, waiting.

And thrust he does. Hard and fast.

I cry out, grab his shoulders, sink my nails into his skin.

He doesn't notice.

I arch when he tightens the fist in my hair, and grind against him to urge every single inch of his cock inside me. His breath changes into a hard pant that sends tingles of pleasure over lips throbbing with abuse.

Our mouths brush, but not for a kiss—he whispers my name. It should have sounded sexy, desperate, wild. Instead, it sounds like a curse.

Like he hates the fact that I've unraveled him.

He eases out of me, leaving a trail of sparks and a dull fire in his wake. I have a chance for one breath, such a brief respite, before he fucks me again. I can't go anywhere—he has me pinned. He's still wearing his shirt and his pants are still around his legs.

I struggle, wanting out of a dress that's chafing my skin. Skin against skin, sweat. That's what I want to feel. But the buttons for this dress are on my back, and Hunter doesn't seem interested in undressing me.

Writhing furiously, I whip my head away from his accidental kisses. "Take my dress off."

"Quiet." His voice is a growl, and as punishing me for interrupting him, his fingertips sink dimples into my thighs as he yanks me against his cock.

"Please, Hunter, my..." The words trail away.

At the mention of his name, his breath hitches.

"Hunter," I say again.

He groans, forehead pressing hard against mine as he struggles for breath.

Fuck you, Dr. Hill, you're not coming yet. I'm still far from done.

I twist my legs and drive my knee into Hunter's stomach. It's a move I've pulled before, so I know I won't hurt too—

He grunts as air leaves his lungs. There's a moment where we're both scrambling for purchase on each other's bodies. I manage to sit up, and work furiously at my buttons while Hunter's trying to pin me down again. My shoulders are free—the dress is around my hips now.

Hidden lights in Hunter's room cast a low light over everything.

He stops trying to fuck me when he sees my dress around my hips. His tongue swipes over his lips as he grabs my breasts, urging me up the bed and against the headboard.

I squirm furiously along the way, trying to wriggle out of my dress.

I think he finally realizes what I was trying to accomplish.

Hunter sits back on his heels, cock standing proud from his narrow waist as he studies me for an agonizingly long moment. Then he starts unbuttoning his shirt, for all the world like we've gone straight back to foreplay.

CHAPTER TWENTY-FIVE
CLOVER

I don't know what's wrong with me. I should have come after getting such a pounding. Maybe it was the position—there was zero clit action with my legs up like this.

It was fucking delicious, but delicious doesn't make for coming.

My legs slide down when Hunter releases me. He sits back on his heels.

I don't like the look in his eyes. He's pissed off—mouth a line, eyes flashing.

"Hunter?"

He grabs my legs, forces them open, and shoves his fingers inside me. I gasp, sitting up dead straight as a wave of furious pleasure crashes through me.

"You don't have to—" I begin, but the sentence strangles itself in a gasp when he grinds the heel of his palm into my clit.

Fuck. Oh, sweet, fucking, Christ.

He shoves my legs wider apart as he glares at me as if daring me not to come.

Really, Hunter?

Challenge accepted.

I ride his fingers, bucking my hips in time with his furious arm pumps. But I'm also dislodging him from my clit, which means I'm not getting any closer to coming.

But he doesn't realize this.

I'm smiling, and I think he's wondering why because his anger is turning to confusion.

Maybe he thinks I'm broken. Ruined by years of sexual slavery at the hands of other rich men.

I laugh.

Something I already know he doesn't like.

He yanks his hand away—much the pity—grabs my hips and turns me over so fast my head's still spinning by the time I land on all fours.

What the fuck—?

His cock spears into me, and I yell out half in surprise and half in pleasure. Sweet Jesus, talk about a short recovery time. What the fuck?

I'm still trying to get into position when he drives his hand between my shoulder-blades and forces my head into the mattress.

Now he's fucking me like he wants to break me and doesn't care if I tear apart and bleed all over his bed.

For some sick, twisted reason, the thought leaves flames over my psyche. I moan and gasp and writhe as much for air as to just make his life a living hell.

He grabs my neck, pinning me to the mattress as he folds over my back. We're sweat-slick against each other—him grunting like a wild animal and me moaning like a wounded kitten.

Hunter uses his knee to push open my legs and wedges himself between them. He begins strumming my clit, and I shriek at him, furious that I can't get away with my game any longer.

My struggles intensify, but he doesn't respond to me scraping the skin from his wrist.

So I clamp my fingers around his cock as hard as I can and begin to fuck him back.

I'm still far away from a climax, but him? I'm sure he's—

"This hard enough for you?" comes his strained voice.

I shudder hard, and let out a spluttered, "As if."

He loses rhythm, and I laugh hysterically because of it, which earns me a stinging slap to my rump.

Fuck. If this was a race, I just overtook him and the finish line's in sight.

As if he can read my mind, he slaps me again.

Christ, I can't—

He stops fucking me. Buried balls deep, he suddenly stops.

He's coming again, isn't he? I squirm, so close I want to start sobbing.

The vicious fingers over my clit begin stroking me instead, barely touching me.

Ah, fuck. My body trembles as I unsuccessfully suppress a deep groan. He draws out but an inch before sliding back inside me again. Again. Harder. Harder. But still just an inch.

I can't even.

I moan his name, beg him to end me, start to struggle. He slaps me again.

Seconds later, when the furious tingling where he's stroking my clit overwhelms all reason, I come with a hoarse yell.

He pulls out, thrusts back once, twice, and comes inside me again. I ride out an excruciating orgasm, gasping and writhing on his bed like I'm dying of cyanide poisoning.

He grabs my hair, wrenches my head up, and presses his lips to the side of my neck as he lets his weight slowly push me down.

He's still inside me, pulsing. I bring a hand up to touch his face, to feel his jaw. It's hard, his lips quivering. I twist my head for a kiss.

It's as soft as the brush of a butterfly's wing.

Seconds later, he rolls off me. I stay where I am, mentally and physically drained, and watch him move around his room. He takes a robe and throws it over his shoulders. Then he leaves without a word or a look in my direction.

Still panting, I roll onto my back. Slowly, I come up to my elbows.

I didn't even have a chance to see his room.

It's as immaculate as the rest of the place.

Color catches my eye.

There's a bright red hoody on a hanger on the outside of his dresser.

It's too small for him.

My thundering heart does a strange galloping twist. I swallow hard and try to will myself to get off the bed before he comes back.

But my body is lame, my mind numb and useless.

He eclipses the doorway, pausing before coming closer. He has a glass of water in his hand and sets it down on the nightstand. Two white pills click onto the wood. "Sugar water and aspirin," he says, sitting on the mattress beside me. "Take them. You won't wake up with alcohol poisoning."

I barely get a hand to my mouth in time to cover a burst of laughter. "Alcohol poisoning?" I take the glass of water and pills, grinning at him over the rim. "I had like four drinks."

Instead of replying, he moves a section of hair from my face with the side of his finger. His face is in shadow, and for some reason that disturbs me.

My eyes flash down to the pills cupped in my palm.

"I don't want you to wake up with a headache."

Oh really? How fucking dapper of you, Dr. Hunter. His finger trails the outer edge of my earlobe, and I shiver. I toss back the pills and swallow them down. I gag theatrically at the nasty tasting water.

He watches, head tilting slowly to the side. I expected a smile, even a small one, but I'm disappointed. I take another sip of water, rub my tummy, and let out a sarcastic, "Mmm!"

Still nothing. Crap, did I just fuck the sense of humor out of this man?

"You okay?" I ask, trying to make my voice light. I take another sip and move to put the glass down.

"What happened tonight doesn't change anything," he says, with the solemnity of a priest at a gravesite.

"What?" The glass rattles, and I look down. I'd almost set it on the edge. I fumble, lose my grip, and watch distantly as the glass falls on the floor. There's a woven carpet under the bed, so it doesn't break, but the rest of the water splashes over his nightstand. "Sorry," I try to say, but it comes out, "Sowwy."

"It's time for you to leave," Hunter says, getting to his feet.

He's wearing clothes. Which is strange because I could have sworn he was wearing a robe.

Now a shapeless long-sleeved shirt, sleeves rolled up.

Lines of white on his arm. More scars. Not from popping or missing veins. Those look like defensive wounds.

I would know.

On impulse, I try to squeeze my thighs together.

They don't move.

I can't move.

I'm paralyzed.

The thought alone has my heart racing, but there's no surge of adrenaline.

No fight, no flight.

I lie here, breathing shallowly as the light begins to fade around me.

My gaze flies to the windows, and if I could have moved, I would have recoiled.

The darkness is pushing in.

It oozed through the joints where the windows meet the wood.

Black tar-thick liquid drips to the floor and edges closer as determinedly as a blood spill.

"Help," I moan.

"Quiet," a voice murmurs. "It's almost over."

The dark swarms over everything. It collapses on me as a cold, heavy weight. I struggle, and hands pin me down.

Whatever strength remained in me leeches out, siphoned by the pulsing throat of midnight. A dark that's been watching me since I can remember.

Watching.

Waiting.

Biding its time.

CHAPTER TWENTY-SIX
HUNTER

The only sound in my office is the quiet hum of my computer's fan.

I don't keep any paper files. All my research, my notes, every paper I've ever written—it's all on my computer. Backed up to the cloud—several storage sites for redundancy—and on three different external hard drives, one of which I keep off-site.

Three monitors face me, the outer two turned slightly in for a better viewing angle.

Clover fills all three screens. In the center monitor, she's curled in a fetal position as she sleeps. She braids her hair at night, and it lays behind her on the pillow like a dark snake. There is no color to this video—I have to use my UF cameras to watch her in the dark.

Half an hour ago, the room was much brighter. She was one of only two patients who insisted on a night light. I insist the light is turned off as soon as she is asleep, of course.

Deep sleep, delta sleep, is a crucial remedy for broken minds.

On the monitor to the left, Clover hunches over a bowl of fresh fruit. She picks idly at the food, her skin lackluster and her eyes dull.

That was week two of her detox. She lost four pounds before her appetite eventually returned.

On the monitor to the right, Clover stands by a floor-to-ceiling window, staring out over the Institute's landscape.

I will be the first to admit that the H.I.'s panoramic view is far superior to my own cabin's, mostly because much of the surrounding forest had to be removed to make way for a parking lot and recreational areas.

As I watch Clover sleeping, my thumb caresses the scar on my inner wrist. The sensation is a comforting one—one I never allow myself outside these four walls. An abscess of its size should have been a blatant wake-up call. It wasn't. If my sister Holly hadn't seen the wound, I wouldn't be here today.

Now that everything's in place, I almost feel anxious.

If last night was a yardstick for the success of my trial, then I should prepare for more surprises.

However, where Clover was in her element last night, now I'm in mine.

The success of my entire thesis revolves around this next phase.

A success which depends, in some part, on Clover. On her ability to open up to me.

To *trust* me.

She did last night. She will again.

On the center console, Clover shifts and rolls onto her back. One hand splays to the pillow beside her head, the other falls in her lap.

A reverie of last night blasts through my mind like a DMT hallucination.

Clover's back arching as I fuck her, drawing a rough gasp through wide parted lips.

Hunter.

I shift in my seat and force the memory from my mind with vicious determination.

Clover sleeps undisturbed, chest rising and falling.

None of these feeds are live, of course. I'm simply double-checking the notes I made on Clover's sleeping and eating patterns during the first stages of her recovery.

Passing the time really.

I exit the center monitor's feed and glance at the time.

Dawn broke an hour ago.

Clover will be waking soon.

———————

"ESLI?"

I pause at the front door of my cabin, waiting for Esli to answer.

A few seconds later, the serving woman hurries into the living area, wiping her hands on a dish towel. "Yes, Mr. Hill?" She's sixty-eight, Salvadoran, and I doubt she even has a green card—but her husband is dead and she doesn't ask any questions. I'm not sure why she came to America, but I've never felt the need to ask, either. I won't say I trust her, but I don't lose any sleep over the things she might have seen in my home.

She has no one to tell about them, to my knowledge. And the only affiliations she appears to hold is to whichever Pope holds the papacy these days.

"Lock up when you leave. I'll see you on Friday."

"Friday?" She pauses, wrinkled hands clutching hard at the dish-cloth. "You don't need me?"

"Not until Friday."

Her eyes dart over my outfit, and she gives me a toothy smile. "Ah, *pescar!*"

I dip my head. "You got me."

"*¡Excelente!* You work too hard." She nods emphatically. Then she shrugs. "You tell, I make tea bread."

"I'm fasting," I say, patting my stomach. "But thank you, Esli."

She nods, twisting the rag between her hands as I turn and head for the front door.

The fishing rod goes straight back in the storage shed tucked in the back of my property.

I grab the edge of my baseball cap and tug it lower over my forehead.

Seconds later, I disappear into the inviting green bosom of Shadow Fox Grove.

CHAPTER TWENTY-SEVEN
CLOVER

I'm woken by the furious trilling of a bird. I open my eye a crack and squeeze it closed again. It's too bright for my dry, grainy eyes. I shift a little, lips twitching as something sticks in my side.

Fuck—I remember Hunter's bed being more comfortable than this.

Hunter.

I lose myself in a blissful wave of erotic memories.

"Mmm," I murmur, rolling onto my back.

The air moving over my legs feels cool, but damp.

Strange. I bring a heavy hand to my chest where it touches something warm and soft. A sweater or something? My fingertips trail down.

My legs are bare.

And they're freezing. I run my hand down my body, hunting for a sheet or a coverlet—something to draw over myself so can warm the fuck up. I can't even feel my toes.

I find nothing but strange, sticky things that plaster themselves on my palms.

"Hunter?" I croak.

I feel beside me.

Finally, the sensations my fingertips have been submitting via my nerves are cleared by customs and my brain receives a thousand bazil-lion teragigs of information.

I scramble up, a scream trapped in my throat.

I slap at my legs, trying to swipe damp, rotting leaves from my skin. A swarm of thoughts flood through my head.

I'm dreaming.

This is a dream.

The dark is waiting for me, and the hands that always come in the dark.

I spin around, and then I *do* scream because I finally have control of my voice.

The forest whirls around me like we're dancing.

I stagger, barely noticing as my bare feet crunch over more molding leaves and sharp twigs.

The smell of earth and my own sweat fills my nose.

Something tickles the nape of my neck and I scream again, brushing my hands furiously in my hair.

A beetle falls out, rolling into a little ball before opening and scurrying away. It disappears into my bed—a patch of damp-dark leaves piled in a heap beside the trunk of a fallen pine tree.

My arms strangle me as I hold on to myself. Color catches my eye, holding it like a neon sign.

A bright yellow arrow is painted on a nearby tree. It points to the right. I force myself to look away.

Wake up. Wake up. Wake up!

I spin again, and this time I topple to the earth. Sticks bite into my flesh, and I shoot up again, swiping damp hands over my ass.

I'm wearing a pair of boxers.

Silk.

There's something overwhelmingly familiar about them.

"Wake up!" I yell.

But there's no waking from this nightmare.

Something is trying to get my attention, and as I haul in a breath for another frustrated scream, it finally flags my brain.

I look down.

A piece of string dangled from my neck. It's threaded through the corner of an envelope.

I recognize that Celtic seal. My finger is halfway through tearing open the envelope when I feel something moving in my hair.

I stick both hands in there, letting out a hoarse scream as I try to find whatever the fuck's burrowing its way toward my brain.

A millipede.

Its legs tangle in my hair. I grab it in a fist and yank it out, taking out some of my hair in the process.

I stumble forward, a new yell in my throat.

Calm the fuck down!

But this nightmare isn't ending.

And the pain is too fucking real.

"Help!" There's a raw note to my desperate plea.

The note.

My hands shake as I tear open the envelope. I rip the string from around my neck, not wanting to confuse it for all the other creepy crawlies that are surely biding their sweet time in my mess of hair.

A piece of paper, folded once.

Hunter's handwriting, and a perfect geometric shape.

Follow me

>

My gaze flashes up and fixes on that neon-yellow arrow.

I spin around, trying to pierce the dark shadows between the close-knit trunks of this gnarly forest.

Run!

The command comes from somewhere deep inside me. Neanderthal me is freaking the fuck out, and it's choosing flight.

But why? What am I not seeing?

Creepy overgrown forest—check.

Bugs in hair—fucking check.

A message from Hunter.

The man who dumped me here.

And then I feel eyes on me. I've been feeling them for a while, actually, but I distracted myself by flipping out about the bugs in my hair.

I spin around again, trying to find the owner of those eyes.

I expected to find Hunter.

Fucking hippy prankster.

Instead…

The hair on the back of my arms, neck and fuck it my entire body stand up at once as I see something moving there in the dark. Something big. Hunched. Monstrous.

I whirl around, facing away from the creature skulking in the dark.

The yellow arrow blurs as I lunge into a run.

I crash through moss and leaves, biting my lip so I don't scream when I stub my toe on a rock buried under a drift of leaves.

I must be *quiet*.

Then the dark can't chase me.

A nonsense thought of course, for someone hurtling through a forest without a care for the noise they make. Even my breath sounds like a steam engine. My heart a thundering army all dressed in armor.

A root trips me. I fall hard enough that stars sparkle behind my eyelids.

And just like that, what little fight I have dissolves.

I rock back on my heels, gulping for air through a lip that tastes of copper.

Get a grip!

I'm holding onto myself a second later, but it doesn't help. I squeeze my eyes shut, but when I open them again, I'm still here. Still stuck in this nightmare.

I hear a whisper of a noise behind me.

The dark.

It's found me.

I'm up a second later, throat too constricted for a scream as I plow through snaggle-clawed foliage desperate to trap me.

A beacon. Yellow, bright, precise.

Another arrow.

I don't know which part of me decided it would be a good idea to turn in the direction it was pointing, my brain, my body, my soul.

But turn I did.

CHAPTER TWENTY-EIGHT
HUNTER

It's humid out, and no surprise—this forest has more than its fair share of bogs and streams. Despite the vegetation growing here, this place reminds me more of a jungle than a forest—the lianas strung from pine to pine like Samhain decorations, the mossy trunks, the liberal heaps of decomposing plant matter that make up the forest floor.

It's any botanists wet dream.

A city slicker's worst nightmare.

My nightmare. I was twenty when I got lost in this mesh of green and brown and black. Still had no idea what direction my life would take, or even that it needed one.

My family had enough money and too much power.

My father's tyrannical rule was the thing of legends.

There's a saying in Mallhaven that dates back three generations:

The Hills don't make friends. They acquire people.

A warbler trills nearby, and I try to spot it through the trees. Shadow Fox is deceptive at best—sounds echo in strange ways through its living, beating heart of green. It distorts space and time like a black hole...and it's just as thirsty.

But it welcomes me as I step into it, and for the first time in close to a week, I feel complete again.

———————

I PAUSE for a sip of water, closing my eyes and letting the forest in. The sounds, the smells—even the feel of the air against my skin—feels like a homecoming.

A flying beetle lands on my arm, and I urge it off onto a nearby leaf.

Unfortunately, there's precious little time for me to drink in the scenery.

I have to remain focused—something I would never have found difficult to do if it hadn't been for the fact that I'm surrounded by such a vast ecosystem. I've spent years cataloging the botanical species in this forest, and I always find more on each trip.

But this isn't one of those excursions.

I cap my water bottle, slide it into my backpack, and hoist the straps over my shoulders.

I've hunted in these woods before. Mammals are just as intricate a part of this unique ecosystem—the elk, the squirrels, the foxes.

And the wolves that pass through here.

No—this forest belongs to its namesake—the fox.

Highly intelligent. Superbly evolved. And this place is their home. Their playground.

Their feeding ground.

This time of year, they should be well fed. Songbirds are working on their clutches, and foxes can loot their nests once a day for eggs.

They don't feed if they're not hungry. They're not greedy.

But they do like their little games, don't they?

CHAPTER TWENTY-NINE
CLOVER

Another arrow. Then another. Soon my eyes are already hunting for the next as soon as I've raced past the last. My way through the forest becomes clear—a rough path with less overhanging branches and things to scrape and scratch.

My lungs ache for release, my legs are rubbery, my hips feel too loose.

I take stock of myself as much as I can while I sprint through the woods toward some indefinable destination.

That red hoody I saw on Hunter's dresser? Turns out I'm wearing it. That, and his silk boxers.

Nothing else. Granted, I wasn't wearing underwear when I arrived at his house, but it still means he dressed me. I don't know how I feel about that. Violated? Not quite. But definitely pissed off.

Right, so what happened last night? What can I remember?

His cabin. The joint. The *heroin* in the joint. The sex.

Nothing unusual for Clover Vos, I'm afraid to say.

Leaves slap into my face because I'm looking back like a right fucking idiot instead of looking ahead.

It's still chasing me.

Can I really outrun the dark? It's the middle of the day—it should have been a fucking piece of cake—but in this forest, day just makes the shadows seem darker.

After the sex, Clover? What then?

Sugar water.

Aspirin.

I stop running, the last two lunging steps clicking my teeth together. My entire body feels wrung out like a dish rag.

Sweet forest air churns like fire in my lungs. My throat is dry, my lips feel cracked.

At least they stopped bleeding. I look up. There's another arrow nearby.

Follow me.

I'm fucking done. Either I break my neck or I have a heart attack—fifty-fifty.

I swing around. My gaze darts to every shadow clinging between the trees.

It's gone.

I sink to my knees in relief, desperately hauling air into my lungs.

Follow me.

"Shut up," I wheeze to myself.

A tiny sound—a twig cracking, maybe a crunch of leaves, who the fuck knows?—and my head snaps up. My eyes narrow as I scan the dark pools around me.

I find it seconds later. An indefinable, sentient shape lurking in the darkness beneath an overgrown bough.

My skin tries to crawl off my body, and I wish I could let it. I wish *I* could crawl away—but my body's gone into shock.

Heroin and gym don't mix well; the most exercise I think I've ever gotten was when I ran from the cops a few years ago.

Funny story—they weren't even after me. They just happened to put their siren on a few seconds after I'd bought and my paranoia did the rest.

My gaze drops to the forest floor, and I see a mossy stone nudged up against an exposed root. I grab it, hoist it, hurl it.

Pretty fucking accurate shot if you ask me—but the darkness doesn't budge. Either my eyes are fucking with me, or the darkness can't be hurt by throwing stones.

Women hunted by darkness shouldn't—

"Burn in hell, you motherfucking cocksucker!" I scream. My voice is hoarse, and the yell burns like acid in my throat.

The darkness watches, impassive as all shit.

"You hear me? Do you fucking hear me?" I hunt for another stone, find one, throw it.

It misses the darkness by a mile. I'm too wiped out by my sprint, so angry I'm shaking. I couldn't hit the wide side of a barn with a tank right now.

I want to keep fighting—I burn to keep up this charade—but my spine collapses. I thump onto the floor, and for a second I want to start bawling like a baby who's just filled up their diaper.

The squishy leaves under me feel just like shit. I run my hands down my face, laugh bitterly, and let my arms fall into the mulch underneath me.

Bugs. Beetles. Worms.

I don't give a shit.

Above, the sun peeks through the leaves. It's pretty. This forest is so fucking pretty.

But not the damp, rotting leaves under my ass. Not my stinging, aching soles. Not the crawling sensation I *still* have in my hair from those fucking horrible creatures who'd decided to build a nest in it.

Not the darkness.

It waits.

Silent.

Patient.

I manage to push myself into a sit.

"What do you want?" I put a hand on my throat, squeezing my eyes shut as tears prick against my lids. I can't keep yelling. Can't keep running. I'm thirsty as fuck, exhausted, scared out of my mind.

I draw my legs up, put my head on my knees, and try to cry.

It doesn't work.

I'm too fucking pissed off to feel sorry for myself.

For now, the darkness can't touch me—there are too many gaps in the canopy above me.

But what if I don't get out of here before night?

CHAPTER THIRTY
HUNTER

When I find her, it takes everything I have to control the burst of anger that floods me.

Clover may have followed the arrows, but she's at least an hour behind schedule. I'd placed her IQ at around 115, which is on the high end of average. Her adjustment period is taking longer than I'd anticipated.

Or perhaps she's just not the test subject I expected her to be.

I was only expecting to catch up to her in another two or three hours, yet here she is, stumbling through the forest like a drunkard. I pause in the shadows, willing myself to calm down as I watch her pick her way through the undergrowth.

Clover spins around as if she's looking for something. Seconds later, she stares straight at me. I know she can't see me. The woods only get darker the deeper in we go, and my clothing was precisely chosen for its camouflage properties.

Regardless, her gaze locks onto me.

She freezes, eyes widening, and then she starts looking at the ground.

A stone comes hurtling in my direction, and it's all I can do not to move or make a sound when it strikes my cheekbone.

"Burn in hell, you motherfucking cocksucker!" she yells in a broken voice. "You hear me? Do you fucking hear me?"

She throws another stone, but this one misses.

Clover collapses to the ground, washing her hands over her face and muttering to herself.

Is she delusional, or just infuriated with her position? She huddles into herself as if she's crying, but I don't hear any sobs.

I take a moment to bring a finger to the tickle on my cheek.

She drew blood with that stone. I rub the liquid between my fingertips and then smear it off on my pants. Retaliation is to be expected. Fatigue, resignation. I had this all planned out but only in a few hours.

No...this is too soon. She has such a far path still to travel. My trial will be ruined if she gives up this soon.

Minutes later, Clover slowly falls to the forest floor. It's more of a gradual unfolding than a faint, but it's clear she's fast asleep before that red head touches the floor.

It's a trap. It must be. She saw me, and now she's trying to lure me from the shadows.

Silently, I crouch.

And wait.

MY PATIENCE IS SPREAD TOO thin for me to endure this anymore. I consult my watch and twitch my wrist in irritation.

Forty minutes have passed, and she sleeps like the dead. Her back is to me—I can see her shoulders rising and falling in that unmistakable rhythm.

Perhaps the dose of heroin she imbibed last night took a toll on her nervous system. After being clean for six months, it may have come as a greater shock to her body than I'd anticipated.

So many variables—and here I thought I'd calculated them all.

She has to get moving. She must understand how important this is.

But I refuse to show myself. I refuse to veer from my plan more than she's already forced me to.

I grit my teeth, glancing around the forest as if in search of an answer.

And, as always, the forest provides.

Lured by the quiet, a cottontail rabbit jumps gingerly into a pool of light. It studies the girl, grabs a small clump of clovers, and chews it almost thoughtfully as it watches her unmoving body.

My hunting knife is in my hand. A second later, it's between the rabbit's ribs. There's a wet, renting sound and a dull thump as it strikes the tree trunk where it was grazing. My gaze flickers to Clover, but the sound wasn't enough to wake her.

I obviously haven't impressed the importance of this journey onto her.

Was it because we fucked yesterday? Does she somehow think me softened because I was inside her?

It's time to remind her just how little control she has, since she keeps forgetting who the fuck is in charge.

CHAPTER THIRTY-ONE
CLOVER

I wake up, and the fact that I fell asleep scares me so much that I scramble up with a frantic yelp. I immediately check myself for bugs and don't find any.

But then I see the blood.

I back up a few steps until the trunk of a nearby tree stops me. I feel behind me, clinging with desperate hands to the rough bark.

It's a bunny. Or a hare. I don't even know the difference.

Correction: it *was* a bunny.

Now it's a pile of fur and innards nearly black with flies.

And it fell from my lap as I shot to my feet.

I look down. Wished I hadn't.

I spin around, puking into the leaves as I hold onto the trunk for support.

Blood shines wetly on the bottom of my hoody and Hunter's silk boxers. Blood runs down the inside of my thighs.

I puke some more, until there's nothing left, and even then I can't seem to stop.

Honestly, I want to rip my clothes off, but there's nothing around here for me to clean myself with. I mean, the first plant I pick will probably be poison ivy.

News flash: Clover Vos can't tell the difference between a rabbit and a hare and knows even less about plants.

Follow me.

Or what, you sick fuck?

I'll end up looking like that rabb—animal? All inside out and shit?

My head reels as I stand, and I hold onto the tree for a bit.

Tree hugger. If Gail could see me now.

I want to laugh, but I can barely summon a smile.

Follow me.

"Fuck you."

I push away from the tree, sway a little, and force myself to ignore everything—the blood, the trickles down my legs, the darkness—everything except the arrow.

I stare at it for the longest time. I want to stop, but I can't.

That wasn't there earlier. I would know because all the arrows up till this point have been immaculate, stenciled designs.

This one is angry. Rushed.

And red.

I stumble closer like a drunk on legs that curse me for ever taking that first wobbly step at age two.

When I touch the paint, I already know what I'm going to see when I turn my hand around.

It's still wet.

And it's not paint. It's blood.

––––––––––

I'M SUPPOSED TO RUN, but instead I walk. It's all I'm capable of, right now.

I know Hunter wrote the note. He must have painted the arrows—both new and old.

He planned this, obviously, but for how long? A week, a month... half a fucking year?

The thought sends a cold shudder through me.

Hunter was trouble—I knew it the moment I laid fucking eyes on him, but I ignored the warning signs because he intrigued me.

His wealth. His intelligence. His strange charm. I didn't admit it to myself back then, but I was curious.

I played hard to get, but Hunter was patient. He waited me out. And now I'm trapped in whatever the fuck this is—his science experiment, his world, his fucking game.

The dark watches me. It stalks me as I weave through the forest, making barely audible sounds that disappear as soon as I spin around.

What does it want?

What does *he* want?

Tears? Resignation? Surrender?

No.

It wouldn't be that easy.

Hunter dumped me in this forest after dressing me in a hoody that was ready and waiting to go before I'd even arrived at his house. Which meant he knew I'd come home with him.

How much of last night had he anticipated or predicted?

Did he know I'd let him fuck me?

Somehow I can't believe he predicted that. It was too intense. Too *real*.

So he's not a fucking psychic. I can still surprise him.

But if I plan to do something he doesn't expect, I first need to figure out what the fuck he's *expecting* me to do.

There's another arrow—there always is. He's forced me back onto his path with a warning painted in bunny blood. My brain barely registers as I turn in the new direction it points to.

And then my feet are wet.

I look down, hurriedly squeeze my eyes shut, and try to eviscerate the sight of those dark runnels tracing sinuous lines of dried blood down my legs.

Water.

I can wash.

My eyes open, and I splash forward, nearly falling on my face when my foot slips on a slimy rock.

It's a little stream I could easily step over if I wanted to, but instead I crouch in it and go to my knees. The rocky bed has been worn down, and the moss makes it a little softer but it's not exactly pleasant kneeling there with things drifting against my skin as I wash the blood from me with shaking hands.

The water running from me turns a dark pink. I try not to look, but I also want to make sure that I'm getting everything off.

The water's only a few inches deep—it doesn't even reach the bottom of the hoody unless I sit down. Which I do.

It's ice cold, but it brings me such a sense of relief to be clean that I disregard the chills working their way through my body.

Instead, I forcefully ignore the feel of the dark's eyes on me and yank off the hoody so I can wash it properly. There're all kinds of gunk on it—leaves and bits of twigs and even a squashed bug that almost makes me puke again.

If I had something in my stomach, I would have puked.

After a moment's hesitation—fuck it, he's already seen me naked—I yank off the boxers and give them a good wash too.

Some water splashes on my cheek by accident, and I feel compelled to wash my face.

I lick my lips and freeze in sudden terror.

Can I drink this water?

My mouth turns bone dry.

I swipe the back of my hand over my mouth, looking down at the water. It runs clear now. There's no more blood on my legs, and just a stain on the boxers.

Flowing water's safe right?

But I can't imagine adding cholera or whatever the fuck you get from drinking dirty water to my list of issues right now. I'm sure it'll take a few days before I die of thirst—I'll worry about drinking water when I'm down to the last day or two.

Yeah, fine, I know fuck all about survival, but that's the point, right?

"Right?" I parrot, throwing the word at the water as it streams innocently past me. "Isn't that right, you sick fuck?"

There's no answer, of course. Why would there be? It's just me and the darkness out here.

Night is coming. It's stalking me along with the dark, trailing that obscene monster like the shadow of a shadow.

I'm shivering, and it's not just because of the icy water swirling around me. I squeeze out the bottom of the hoody—I tried to keep as much of it dry as possible—and yank it over my head.

Dark floods over me, but it disappears an instant later.

I'm not sure, but I think it's late afternoon from the slant of the light. The sunlight coming through the trees looks more yellow than white, and the shadows are starting to blur a little.

There's got to be an end to this godforsaken forest.

I stand, wincing when my legs complain, and crack my back. Across the way, a yellow arrow beams at me like a street lamp.

I cross the stream to follow it.

I will make it out before dark. I know that much. No person in their right mind would expect me to get anywhere in a forest at night.

But I don't think Hunter *is* in his right mind. In fact, I'm starting to suspect he's bat shit fucking crazy.

He probably used glow-in-the-dark paint, didn't he? The thought makes me hesitate, and then I force my legs to speed up.

Fuck it—I refuse to find out.

I CAN'T TELL if it's because I'm walking slower, or because the arrows are further apart, but I'm starting to panic. I trudge through the woods for what feels like minutes on end before I see another arrow. The next? Fifteen minutes, easy.

The path isn't always as noticeable as before, either. In fact—and this is pure fucking conjecture—but I have a feeling I'm being led deeper into the forest.

While my starting point was messy and overgrown...this? This is insane. If it weren't for those arrows—now very few and far between —I'd be convinced I was the first human being gracing this place.

And it's not just because of how overgrown this area is—it's the animals.

I hear them, but I never see them. They scatter before I get near.

There are larger things moving around, too. Things I also can't see.

Things I sincerely fucking hope are gentle, Bambi-like deer and not savage bears.

Christ, are there bears in these woods?

Wolves?

Shit.

My ambling walk speeds to a slow jog.

Where's the next fucking arrow? Did I wander off the path? How am I supposed to keep track of where I'm walking? I can barely see where the sun is, the canopy is so thick here. I mean, at least if I had a compass...

Then I'd just have to figure out how to use a fucking compass and I wouldn't be lost anymore.

I let out a bitter laugh, but I don't like the sound of it out here in the woods.

It sounds alien, desperate, insane.

Makes two of us, Hunter.

There's one thing I *do* know—I don't think there are many daylight hours left. Three, maybe four. Twilight will probably be like midnight between these trees.

So am I going deeper or is this the way out?

Deeper.

I stop walking.

Follow me.

"No," I murmur, taking a moment to look around and scrutinize every hollow, every shadow, every snarled bush.

I've been following these arrows blindly, hoping they would lead me to freedom but that doesn't make any sense, does it? Why would Hunter dump me in the middle of the forest and then show me the way out?

That accomplishes nothing.

And from what I know of the sick fuck that is Dr. Hunter Hill, not accomplishing something isn't part of his vocabulary.

Which means he's leading me toward something but it's not the outside. It's not freedom. Not yet.

Maybe not ever.

"Why?"

The dark isn't as constant as it used to be. I can feel it going away now and then. It watches, and then it doesn't. I'm not sure if it's because my brain can't focus on more than one thing at the moment, or because it grows bored with my slow progress and wanders off.

Right now, it's not here.

My heart starts a slow drumbeat in my chest.

But for how long?

I glance at the arrow pointing to my right. It screams at me to follow it, but the thought of going deeper into the forest makes my skin crawl.

I turn around and start walking back.

At least, I *think* I'm heading back. I'm not sure I can remember which direction I was heading—

I see a familiar tangle, a pretty vine throttling a nearby tree trunk.

Okay. I can do this. Pay attention Clover: you gotta ace this test. Your fucking life depends on it.

A few minutes later, I see another arrow.

Thank *fucking* God.

But then I see the note beneath it, and my blood runs ice cold.

———————

MY FINGERS TREMBLE as I reach for the note. It's been nailed against a tree trunk right beneath an arrow. Another new arrow—red runnels bleed into the bark.

Fresh bunny blood.

I open the note, but I know what it's going to say.

Obey me.

I drop the note and take a step back. I swing around, hugging myself hard as I interrogate the shadows with wide eyes.

It's not the dark. It never was. I fucking knew it.

Hunter's *here*.

And he's watching me.

CHAPTER THIRTY-TWO
HUNTER

This time, she doesn't see me in the shadows. Perhaps she's tiring—I know I was perfectly concealed the last time she looked in my direction.

I've had setbacks, and to be perfectly honest, I wasn't expecting them this soon in the trial. But I've come this far, and I refuse to abandon everything I've worked so hard for the past few months just because of Clover's stubbornness.

All she has to do is follow the goddamn arrows.

It's not rocket science.

I think the note worked—she looks suitably terrified.

Perhaps she's finally realized that the only way through this is complete obedience.

If she doesn't surrender to me, to the trial, then there's no point in her living any longer.

No one wants to live with addiction.

And this is the *only* way to cure it.

CHAPTER THIRTY-THREE
CLOVER

I follow the arrows. I don't want to, but what the fuck else is there to do?

My mouth feels gummy. My lungs are on fire. I can't run anymore, but I'm stumbling as fast as I can in a half-jog, half-limp.

Please, God, let it be fast enough. I don't want any more notes. I don't want to feel Hunter's eyes on me.

At the moment, I don't. I feel alone—so *very* fucking alone—in a forest that, if not evil, is at least so impassive it's the same fucking thing.

I'm thirsty. I'm exhausted. And I'm starting to get hungry, too.

Is there food, water, or shelter in my distant future, or is this just some sick game for Hunter's amusement? A game where he herds me along a nightmare path until my mortal body succumbs?

I've heard of snuff films. Hell, there was a rumor going around the Hill Institute that there was some big police investigation into a bunch of pricks that were filming real live snuff films right here in Mallhaven.

What if Hunter's one of them?

Hunter.

I laugh, but to myself.

Was his mother psychic or something? Or have family names—

along with cruel traditions like human hunting—been passed down generation after generation?

I bark out a laugh, and it sends me into a coughing fit.

I catch hold of a tree trunk, leaning against it as I try to catch my breath. When my breathing is back to its now normal heavy rasping, I hear something else. Something once hidden by my own crashing footsteps and bellow-like breathing.

Water.

I swallow, but my mouth is so dry nothing goes down my throat. I wipe the gunk from my lips and listen as attentively as I can.

Definitely water. Rushing, pouring water.

If I can't drink that shit, then I don't know how Neanderthal man ever got this far.

Fuck the arrows.

Fuck *Hunter.*

This is not me turning back—I'm turning aside.

And boy, do I know it seconds later when I'm suddenly trying to force my way through the brush that could have doubled as a drafty wall.

And not just that—those eyes are back on me.

Hunter.

He's seen that I've veered off his path.

And I have no doubt his punishment will be swift and brutal.

Gritting my teeth, I hold my arms in front of me like a shield, and charge through the forest with a battle cry spilling from my cracked lips.

CHAPTER THIRTY-FOUR
HUNTER

What the hell is Clover doing? I had to take a piss, and when I come back, she's gone.

Gone, but not lost. I can hear her crashing through the forest. Why do I keep getting the feeling she knows every move I make?

I force out a laugh and pick up my pace.

Maybe I shouldn't be taking her reactions so lightly. After all, she could be slipping into flight or fight mode. Our physiology changes drastically as soon as enough adrenaline is introduced to our nervous system. For one, her senses will seem heightened. Actually, it's just a kind of mental focus, but she's probably feeling like she's on some kind of high right now.

The adrenaline will wear off, of course. In an hour, she'll be docile as a deer.

Why did she leave the trail? Another rebellious stint, or—?

Despite her distant, crashing footfalls, another sound piques my interest.

The river.

She heard the river.

Damn it, Clover—do you really think I'd let you go thirsty much longer? Stupid, *stupid* girl.

My jaw clenches so hard that tooth enamel squeaks together. I fall into a light jog, tracing Clover's breakneck path through the forest with ease.

I guess I shouldn't be that surprised anymore, but I recognize this path she's taking.

CHAPTER THIRTY-FIVE
CLOVER

Brambles snatch at my hair. Twigs snag my hoody. My legs sting and burn from multiple wounds.

I don't care.

I *refuse* to care.

He can kill me if he wants.

But I know he won't.

He's planned this for months. Either he's anal—and I'm not ruling that out just yet—or someone like me doesn't come around that often.

Come around. Ha! I bet he's *never* made anyone like me come.

What the fuck's wrong with me? God, this monster is hunting me like I'm a fucking bunny rabbit—*bad, bad comparison, Clover*—and I'm thinking about the motion of his fucking ocean?

Maybe I'm delirious. Hell, I last ate yesterday. My last drink was that sugar-water-poison he fed me last night. Since then, I've run several marathons—probably—and been scared half to death.

I'm surprised I'm still alive.

And I have a feeling that's only because he wants me to be.

He could have killed me when I was drugged. If he'd covered me up with those leaves instead of stacking them under me, no one would have found me for days, weeks, months?

Jesus Christ, no one's going to find my body when he's done with me, are they?

The thought drains my willpower.

My legs crumple.

My hands go out automatically—thanks, instinct—and my palms are ripped apart by a particularly nasty bramble-kinda-bush.

I yelp in pain. I'm already scrambling up, but the intense agony in my hands stops me from moving forward.

Why does it hurt so goddamn much? I've always been a bit gangly, so my extremities were in constant danger of being scraped, banged, and abused since I could remember. I've scraped a knee before. Chipped a tooth.

This fucking *hurts*.

I shake my hands—which only makes it worse—and attempt to ignore the stinging pain as I follow the sound of the water again.

It doesn't seem to be getting any closer.

Why?

I suddenly wished I'd paid more attention in Geography.

There it is. I tip my head and then look down at my hands.

Ah, that's why it hurts so much. I have several nasty tears through my palms, and bits of grit are lodged in there.

And there's not a first aid kit in sight.

Great.

Now I have a vast selection of things to die from: exhaustion, dehydration, malnutrition, and dirt.

Oh, and don't forget Hunter.

As if just thinking his name summons the demon, I feel eyes on me again.

But I don't look back this time.

I don't know if it's supposed to give me some infinitesimal advantage over this sick fuck, but I'm going to stop letting *him* know when *I* know that *he* knows...fuck it, I won't give myself away anymore.

My hands dangle at my side.

I grit my teeth through the insistent throbbing of my wounds.

And then I forge the fuck ahead.

Goddamnit, that river has to be up ahead somewhere.

Water. Clean hands. Hell, I might even drown myself just to spite Dr. Hunter fucking Hill.

Put that in your pipe and smoke it, you sick hippy fuck.

PART THREE

DRINK ME

"When she went into the room, Red Riding Hood had such a strange feeling that she said to herself: 'Oh dear! how uneasy I feel today.'"

LITTLE RED RIDING HOOD - THE BROTHERS GRIMM

CHAPTER THIRTY-SIX
HUNTER

I shouldn't be making this much noise, but it's that or I lose sight of her. Clover is heading straight into danger—something *I'm* particularly aware of, but she doesn't have a clue.

This river is so far off her course, I never even thought she'd reach it. Thus, I'd never considered the fact that she might actually drown during her trial.

For some reason, I'm more concerned with the fact that Clover might die than with the fact that my research will be rendered null and void if my subject were to perish during the trial.

What the hell has she done to me?

When did I start to care?

Water rages ahead. Clover has never seen the rapids, but I have.

I've *been* in them, spitting and coughing and fighting for my life.

And I can't help but wonder at the serendipity of this moment. I am a man of science, but don't think for one fucking second I haven't noticed how Clover's experiences mirror my own.

Even now, as I'm crashing through the underbrush, déjà vu slams into me.

It derails my mind, my sense, all reason.

This test is hers, and yet *ours*.

I passed...but will she?

EIGHT YEARS earlier

THE FOREST SHIFTS around me as I race for the only thing I recognize in this vast wilderness—running water.

To say I am entitled does little to explain just how wealthy and fortunate I am.

But I was never a happy child.

My sister, Holly? She's the happy one. She's the one that builds rainbows from storm clouds with no effort. I just bring hail, and lightning, and floods.

Her spirit never seems dampened by mine—although it should. I'm a serious child. Devoted to my studies. Earnest in proving to my father that I deserve the luxury he bestows on me.

But still, I'm aimless. In a world that has so very much to offer, how could I possibly choose a single direction? A single area to focus my studies? I want to cherry pick from every vocation the world has to offer. I want to know about ancient relics, and plants, and industry. I want to follow mankind through the ages, making assumptions about their thinking based on the manuscripts they themselves penned while knowing to an inarguable degree exactly which elements constitute the perfect compound.

And why can't I?

If my lust for knowledge is this deep, this voracious, why must I substitute my love for the entire world by choosing but one of its many children as a favorite.?

I can't.

I couldn't.

My father saw this as a weakness. The man with iron focus can't understand that his first-born son was a dreamer—if an intellectual one.

In his eyes, I had to excel. I could never be a jack of all trades—with him it was always master of one.

I chose botany. If only because of the vast knowledge the plant kingdom had to bestow on me. But even that wasn't enough for Father. He wanted letters behind my name. A doctorate, a Ph.D.—something concrete for him to hang his legacy on.

I had no interest in grades. I wanted to know everything, but I didn't feel the need to prove that to anyone.

Over the years, I realized it was one or the other.

He would pay for my studies, but only if I excelled.

Excel I did. I pursued my doctorate in Botany, got my Ph.D. and immediately went on to obtain a Masters in Clinical Psychology. If I hadn't, he would have deprived me of the only thing that drove me from sleep every morning—knowledge.

They say, when you have enough money, you want power.

What they don't tell you is that knowledge—*higher* knowledge—can only be attained through power.

Money buys power. Without money, the knowledge I so sorely sought would have been denied.

A rushing noise fills my ear.

I'm getting close to the source.

Suspended in the air, water particles condense on my face as I crash through the forest's tangled embrace.

Too close.

I'm going too fast.

The moss floor is treacherous. When I see the drop ahead, water misting like fog in an attempt to partially obscure it, I already know I won't be able to stop in time.

Momentum, you see?

My body battles the inevitable.

I grab hold of a passing branch, willing it to root me.

Instead, it snaps in two, and I thump down onto my ass.

I'm not prone to fear. Horror. Terror.

But speed? I don't fancy it.

Free falling? For idiots.

I'm not dissuaded by the fact that I'm compelled to remain Earth-borne by gravity.

Gravity is my friend. It's kept me grounded all these years, after all. So I have no intention of fighting it. Flaunting it. Or disrespecting it.

The last few feet go by in a blur, and then I'm free falling.

But not for long.

The churning white waters of the river claim me less than a second later.

Ice water closes over me. It's just deep enough for my head to bob under the surface before my bare feet strike the slimy river bed.

Spluttering and coughing, I surface. I spend desperate minutes fighting my way to the bank. Several times, I think I'm not going to make it. In fact, I almost resign myself to the fact that this may be my last few moments on Earth.

Any normal person might consider the afterlife. Religion. If this is it and if so, what a waste.

All I kept thinking was how much I still had to learn. And how pissed off I was at myself for doing something as foolish as this.

I drag myself out of the water, wet and spent. Rolling onto my back, I stare up at the sky. Purple twilight glows and fades in time with my pounding heart, and I wonder if that means I'm close to death.

But no...it just means I've finally reached the starting point of my journey.

The thought terrifies me more than anything in the world. I let out a wild howl, scramble up, and dart into the woods.

Please, protect me.

Please, don't let me lose myself.

But Shadow Fox Grove would show me no mercy. This journey was meant to test me, and test me it did.

They say Ayahuasca is the mother plant. Maternal, yet strict. Her loving embrace can swiftly turn to punishment if you don't heed her words.

That was one of several lessons I learned during my journey through the forest.

Lessons Clover must learn if she's to survive this.

If she's to break free from her addiction.

CHAPTER THIRTY-SEVEN
CLOVER

There's so much noise surrounding me that I feel like I'm having a goddamn panic attack. Water ahead. Green things snapping and breaking around me. And from behind the sound of furious pursuit.

I've pissed him off by directly disobeying his arrows.

What'll my punishment be?

Death? Something worse?

The sinister thought spurs me on.

Moist air flows over my legs. The forest floor becomes spongy underfoot with moss. It flourishes here, turning bark and rocks an emerald green.

Too late, I see the path ahead is suddenly clear. No more trees. No more branches.

Just a precipitous drop where a fine mist hangs in the air.

I try to stop. My feet slip. I throw out a desperate arm—fingers grasping—with a scream trapped in a throat too tight to let it escape.

Someone grabs my hand.

But it's not enough.

My legs slide over the edge. My hips are next. The hoody hikes up my back, and a jutting stone scrapes over my spine and shoulder blades.

A shock jars my body. I dangle an inch above a churning river that starts licking at my toes.

I twist, tipping back my head.

Hunter is halfway over the side of the small cliff, teeth gritted in a face painted with stripes of brown and dark green.

I've never noticed before, but his eyes are almost the color of tree bark.

"Don't let go!" he yells.

But *I'm* not the one letting go. Gravity's doing all the work. Our hands are both damp, slippery with sweat and this mist.

I throw my other arm up, trying to grab hold of his wrist.

Then I realize he's slipping too. I get a hold of his wrist, but he slides nearly a foot over the lip of the river bank.

I was going to pull him in.

And he doesn't have enough leverage to pull me out.

Both conclusions slammed into my brain at the same time.

Hunter's eyes widen.

"No!" The word is desperate and commanding at the same time.

Doesn't he get it by now? I *hate* being bossed around.

We were holding onto each other, fingers locked around each other's wrists. But when I release my grip on him, I slide out of his hand like a wet fish.

Look, we can't *both* die out here. That's just fucking stupid. But if his plan was for me to make it out of this thing alive, then he can always come to rescue me, right?

See, I'm not a vindictive bitch. I should be, but things start clarifying moments before your death.

It's quite an enlightening experience.

You should try it sometime.

FRAGMENTS of a violent dream force me awake. I'm on my stomach, my body an ice effigy covered in hair-line fractures. I squirm, and even that small movement sends a contraction through me like I'm giving birth—I assume, okay?

I spew out a lake's worth of briny water and bile.

When my head stops spinning, I open my eyes. I'm on a strip of riverbank populated by rough, dark stones and various bits of slimy, damp, forest debris. The smell is absolutely wonderful—part swamp, part seven-day-old fish.

I get my arms under me and push back onto my heels. My brain does a quick scramble to gather some context to this strange new world I've found myself in, and I must say I'm disappointed by the results.

At least I'm not dead.

But, if I *were* dead, this would all be over.

Right now, I'm not sure which of those things are a blessing or a curse.

The river is quiet here. Judging from the slant of the light, I must have washed up here a few minutes ago. I remember fighting invisible hands that kept trying to crack my skull against rocks. Growing tired. Water going down my throat.

And then this.

At least I don't have a dead rabbit in my lap.

Where is Hunter? Did he lose sight of me?

What if he jumped in after me and wasn't lucky enough to survive?

I want to cry out hallelujah, but I know instinctively that he's my only shot of getting out of this godforsaken wilderness alive. I mean, I know I won't survive a single night in this place. I'll become bear fodder or die of hypothermia or some shit.

And, judging from the light, I have maybe an hour before dark.

I crush my palms over my eyes, and then whip away my hands.

"You win, okay?" I yell. Fuck, that hurt. I grab my throat, swallow hard, and try again. "You win, I lose. Now can we stop this? Whatever you want, you have it. But I'm done playing."

To cement my statement, I sit on my ass and draw my legs up. Resting my chin in my knees, I stare around at the deepening shadows between the trees. From the way my voice echoed up and down the river bank, if Hunter was in a mile radius I'm sure he would have heard me.

I'm good at the waiting game.

A shiver tears through me, and I grip myself a little harder.

But I'm no good at the dying game.

CHAPTER THIRTY-EIGHT
HUNTER

My feet drag under me, and I'm having a difficult time getting them to stop. I know this isn't physical strain—I keep fit as a rule—but rather a mental drain.

The experiment is a failure.

I revealed myself to her.

Even if she suspected I've been following her, she didn't have concrete evidence. But I've just changed the scope of this trial, and I'm still trying to calculate how that will affect the grander scheme of things.

My intention had always been to replicate my own experience in these woods. For a hypothesis to be ratified, you must first duplicate the results. Of course, she's *not* me—but at least if I made sure that her experiences were just like my own, then I could have begun the arduous process of cross-testing for variables.

I must start again. A new subject, a new trial. A new, confined environment.

That was my mistake. Attempting a clinical trial in an environment that in its very nature is constantly changing. Day and night, spring and fall. Nature doesn't lie, but it's not exactly a constant, either. It's a fickle thing, and that's something I should have considered before initiating this trial.

Now I've lost her. For a while, I was tracking her through the trees, along the river bank.

Then she went under, and I couldn't find her again.

I'm still searching—I would prefer not to leave her body out here for someone to find. Although I made certain no one saw us leaving the graduation party last night, she could still be linked to the Institute.

I can't have anyone investigating the Institute or my private affairs.

I also refuse to believe she's dead until I've found her corpse.

It's been almost an hour since I lost sight of her. The day is slipping away as is any chance of me redeeming this study.

A distant voice. Cursing.

Cursing me.

I allow myself a grim smile and change direction.

I'm glad you're not dead, Clover, but you've certainly fucked up my plans, haven't you?

CHAPTER THIRTY-NINE
CLOVER

Well, I managed to wait a whole ten minutes—I'm guessing here—and it felt like hours. If Hunter were close enough to hear me, then he'd have made his presence known. After all—what could he possibly gain in hiding from me?

My shivers are getting worse, and I have a sneaking suspicion that if I don't dry and warm myself, I'll be dead come morning.

Right. Nothing to it, Clover. You got to start yourself a fire.

I think back on Hunter's fireplace—how perfectly he positioned the logs, that dark stone he used to light the tinder, right? That's what he called it.

Wood. Tinder. Something to make a spark.

If a fucking Neanderthal can figure this shit out, then so can I.

They just had more time to practice, of course.

———

I HAVE WOOD. I have tinder. I found two really dark rocks. I piled everything into the same shape Hunter had in his luxury fucking wood cabin, and I'm ready to go.

Let's make fire, human!

I sit cross-legged, trying my best to get my shivering body under control as I hit the rocks against each other.

I won't lie—I'm disappointed. Not only do said rocks make an incredibly sad *thwack* sound every time I hit them against each other, I keep hitting myself on the knuckles.

Me thinks stones damp with my own blood aren't going to make good fire starters.

Fuck it.

I pause, shake out arms lame from hitting two stones together, and try again.

There's a breeze picking up—honestly, I'm not even surprised at this point anymore—and I huddle over myself in an effort to ward off the cold. Maybe I should move deeper into the woods.

No.

Fuck no.

Deeper forest means deep shadows.

I may have lost Hunter, but I sure as fuck haven't lost the dark. That shit's everywhere.

Am I losing my mind?

Ha.

Would I even know?

No, I can't think like that.

Fire. Sparks. Embers. That's what I should be thinking about now. I'm willing these two rocks to produce a spark. That, or a random lightning strike.

Shivers wrack my body.

Question—would I be warmer if I took off my wet clothes?

Bear in mind—there's only one right answer, and the wrong one's gonna get me fucking killed.

I have to stop laughing. I need to conserve energy.

Oh, fuck…a spark!

In my shock, I stop hitting the two rocks together.

Was it my imagination?

I start hitting the rocks together with—if not renewed vigor then at least with some extra enthusiasm—but it seems that was just a fluke.

I'm destined to die, cold and alone, in this horrible forest.

Maybe I should have gone to church.

At least I would have had someone to pray to in my final hours.

CHAPTER FORTY
HUNTER

She's using the wrong type of stone, of course, and I doubt her kindling is dry enough to catch flame from a flame thrower.

But she keeps trying.

It's pitiful, watching her.

And yet, somehow, inspiring.

Was this how prehistoric man felt? How long did they spend trying to recreate the fire they'd witnessed?

Clover slumps.

Has she given up already? She's barely been going for ten minutes.

How long was I at work trying to breathe life into a heap of the driest tinder I could find? An hour, two?

I guess Clover and I aren't that similar after all. For one, I don't give up after the first—

She made a spark.

If I hadn't seen it with my own eyes, I'd have called bullshit. But I saw it.

And so did she.

But it's not enough, Clover. One spark is never enough. You have to keep trying, you have to keep—

She throws her stones away from her with an outraged scream and then falls into a bundle.

I sink onto my heels, watching her through the descending darkness.

Maybe it's a mercy that she'll be asleep before full dark—she seems to have an aversion to it.

But she'll never live to morning. She's wet, shivering. From where I'm crouching, I can see a blue tinge around her lips.

Strange—she still has a smear of lipstick on her lips. I'd have thought the rapids would have erased those traces of promiscuity from her.

Lipstick won't do her any good out here.

Survival depends on intelligence. Common sense. A yearning for life.

If Clover doesn't have any of those things, she won't live.

And I'd be corrupting my own data if I stepped in to help.

I turn away, smudging paint over my skin as I graze nails over my face.

This study is already fucked—why do I keep trying to salvage it?

Could it be sympathy?

A tangle of memories lights up my mind. This wasn't the exact spot, but it's close enough.

The chase, the river, no fire.

It's like she's tracing my own journey through this forest. My own journey to discovery—to freedom.

Despite everything, this is more than I could ever have hoped for. Is that why I can't give this up?

Everyone must walk their own path. No one knows the way, but...

I never had a guide. I came to this journey like a newborn child, still wet with amniotic fluid.

And I barely came out of the experience with my mind intact. What if she doesn't have the mental fortitude to deal with this?

I chose the forest because of the many lessons it has taught me over the years, but I've just put Clover through a crash course.

And what if it comes for her like it did for me? I haven't seen tracks, but I didn't that night either.

It will come for her too.

Eight years earlier

I'VE LOST TIME. I don't know how, but it's full dark already, and I'm still wet. Shivering now. I can barely keep my feet moving, let alone find my way in the dark.

I should never have run. My experience was supposed to take place in a clearing close to home.

Why did I run?

Because something frightened me.

In a forest I knew so well, something moved in the shadows, and my body switched off all reasoning. It took control out of a desperate need for self-preservation and it made me run.

If I had stayed where I was, then I could have been at home already. I could have been warm and dry and—

And in the presence of my father.

He wasn't around that much—he worked in the city and for long stretches he'd only be home one night a week.

But mother had informed us that his therapist had scheduled him three days off. And he'd decided to spend it with his family.

Instead of taking the Ayahuasca three weeks from now, I moved up my schedule.

I didn't want to see him.

Didn't want him to see me.

If he did, then he'd undoubtedly find something to criticize. My grades, perhaps. The fact that I hadn't yet grown to his height—would I ever? How I wasn't home enough to look after Mother.

And then he'd start comparing me with Holly, and that I couldn't take.

That's why I'm here now. In the woods. Mind poisoned with a brew that's supposed to show me the way through a mind that's become as tangled as this forest.

I've tried to get clean so many times. Mother secretly paid for more visits to rehab clinics than I can keep track of.

They never work.

It'll be a day, a week, a month. As soon as I hear my father is coming home, I relapse.

I make it easy for myself too. There's a part of me that hides just enough stash for me to get off and escape.

I never remember hiding it.

But I can always find it when I need to.

That alone scares me more than anything. I don't want to be part of a collective consciousness where decisions are out of my control.

Father would disapprove.

The thought sends a shudder through me. I pause, trying to make sense of the dark, twisted forest around me.

And that's when I see those eyes in the dark.

So the hallucinations have begun.

But no...

This was the same creature that's been hiding in the shadows all along.

It followed me, even after I'd fallen and nearly drowned in the river.

And now it's come to claim its prize.

A wolf steps from the shadows, silver fur radiant in a stray moonbeam that manages to pierce the canopy above.

It snarls at me and lets out a sound that turns the marrow of my bones to ice.

Again, I run.

CHAPTER FORTY-ONE
CLOVER

I wake up, and I don't know why. I mean, I should have been dead. I know this on some molecular fucking level. I was too cold to survive.

I shift, my eyes narrowing at a brilliant flash of light.

No, not a flash. A pulse.

A fire.

There's a fire burning less than two feet away from me.

Hunter.

I scramble to a sit, whipping my head around as I search the shadows.

It's night, so he could be anywhere. I'm a few yards away from the river, but the forest is a snarling mess around me. Animals whoop and trill in the distance, and the sound is less than calming.

I feel bugs on me. Spiders, millipedes, beetles. But when I jump to my feet, a red cloak falls onto the ground by my feet. I'm still wearing the hoody and boxers, but there's nothing on me. Nothing crawling in my hair, ready to burrow into my brain.

Fuck off, I'm sure as shit something like that can happen. I don't want no fucking spider eggs in my brain.

I calm down, but only because it's pointless freaking out when there's no one around to calm you down.

And I *am* alone—there are no eyes watching me from the shadows.

Why would Hunter save me and then disappear?

I sit back down, crowding against the fire. I haven't died of cold, true, but that doesn't mean I'm not still damp and shivering. I wrap the red cloak around my shoulders, my eyes darting here and there as I interrogate the shadows.

Where were you last night at 3am? Who were you with? Had you been taking drugs prior to that?

Fuck, Clover—sanity is rather fucking important right now. Hold on, bitch. *Hold. On.*

I do, but to the cloak. Sanity is a bit of an abstract concept anyhow. But this cloak? It's thick. It's warm.

It smells like him.

Why? Why would it smell like him?

Because he doesn't smell like cologne, or aftershave. Hunter smells like the forest.

I hadn't realized that last night. I was high on life. Clean. Free.

Until he drugged me.

The thought's a bitter one. But not just that. I haven't even processed the fact that I've gotten high for the first time in six months.

And I hardly noticed.

Why?

Because Hunter was fucking me at the time.

What kind of sick—?

A twig cracks behind me. I let out a tiny shriek and spin around. I'm holding a stick, but fuck knows what I plan to do with it. Beat the dark to death? This stick will probably snap before I even do damage.

Maybe the forest is settling, like houses do. I mean, it's old. Houses are old.

The house I lived in with my uncle was ancient. The sounds it would make—

I force the thought away so violently that my head spins.

Flames.

I focus on them with the determination of a drowning man and empty my mind.

It's worked before. Once or twice.

Heroin, of course, works much fucking better.

The flames are hypnotic. Sensual.

I'm starting to understand why our ancestors would sit around a fire and tell stories. Well, besides the obvious lack of binge-on-demand entertainment, a fire is an entrancing thing. As the logs turn to embers, I can see things in those glowing lines.

Faces.

Animals.

Hands.

I squeeze my eyes shut. My stomach turns over, and I'm not sure if it's from hunger or nausea.

Time to take stock. You're stuck in a forest in the middle of nowhere Mallhaven. The only person that knows you are here is the same person that put you here in the first place. Let's not count him as an ally just yet.

Enemy? Possibly.

Nemesis? Most definitely.

So is this a game? A test? An experiment?

Is there even a fucking difference?

Not really. But in each instance, there's a winner. A goal. A conclusion.

Which is what, exactly?

I survive the forest and that proves what? That I'm a descendant of Neanderthal man?

Or is there more to come?

Jesus fucking Christ.

What if all of this was just the first round?

Maybe I haven't even reached the actual test yet.

My stomach makes an unhappy sound.

Suck it up. You've had worse. Remember the binge of '16? Ain't nothing went into your stomach except chewing gum for over seventy-two hours.

Hunger, dear Clover, is the least of your fucking concerns right now.

The dark? That's something you should be worrying about.

This fire isn't going to last forever unless you keep feeding it.

Shit! It's burning out. The logs are almost spent, and if I don't get something dry and crackly in there in the next few moments, I'll be spending the rest of tonight alone and damp.

I get to my feet. Around me, the forest goes silent.

A glance back at the fire confirms my fear—I have ten, maybe fifteen minutes to find more wood. If I wander too far off, I might never find this fire again.

And then I'd be dead because, for some reason, Hunter gave me a reprieve. He brought me fire, saving me from death.

Will he do it again? Who the fuck knows.

I'm not taking a chance that he will.

I have to find wood. Dry wood.

My hoody is still damp, but at least it's not cold anymore. In fact, it feels more like a Floridian summer than anything.

I wouldn't know—I've never been there. But fuck—alligators couldn't be worse than this, right?

THE FIRE'S BLAZING AGAIN.

I have time—perhaps even till the break of dawn. Hey, isn't that a song? I dunno—my brain's mush.

My body's pumped with adrenaline from my frantic search for dry wood, so I can't sleep. But staring at the fire is starting to do eldritch things to my brain.

My past is starting to seep through cracks in those walls I took so much time plastering up.

The dark.

It presses against my shrine of light like a physical presence.

It *was* a physical presence, you fucking dolt.

I was sixteen. Maybe I didn't have the mental fortitude to handle shit like that. I guess I might have done some weird, psychological shit in my brain to cope.

After all, I know the dark doesn't have hands. It can't touch. Feel. Invade.

But still I attribute those violations to every dark shadow, every closet, the space under every bed I've ever slept on.

Does that mean I'm delusional? Or simply trying to make sense of something that could never make sense to anyone...ever?

An owl hoots in a distant tree and the present claws me back.

The forest is strangely quiet this late at night if you don't take into account the crickets and their orchestra of chirps.

I close my eyes and lose myself to their song. The rhythm is intoxicating, soothing.

My eyes flicker open on the edge of sleep, and I spot a familiar shape in the shadows.

Hunter.

He's here—watching me.

I guess I should be used to that by now.

He's been watching me all along. None of this was random.

Oh no.

Hunter Hill had a plan.

And as soon as I was booked into his facility, he had a subject primed for his research.

Doesn't he get it?

I'm not a fucking addict anymore.

"I'm clean, motherfucker!" My yell echoes in the trees, and for a long moment I can't get over how disparate it sounds to the forest's breathing.

"I'm clean," I mumble, but the words are lost in my knees, my face pressed into my defensive huddle.

Fuck it, I *know* I'm clean. No one could endure six months of rehab and not have addiction out of their system.

Fuck that.

But still, the dark reaches for me.

How am I supposed to keep it at bay?

Heroin was always the answer to that, but now?

I'm not sure sheer force of will's going to cut it.

I need something stronger.

For a demon like this, I need a fucking exorcism.

CHAPTER FORTY-TWO
HUNTER

At this point, I am unsure if any data from this trial can provide anything worthwhile to my research. But if I hadn't meddled, she would be dead. And then she would be absolutely no use to me. At least now, I can study her from the dark. She seems anxious, fidgety.

It's not fear.

I recognize those micro expressions crossing her face.

She's craving.

I should be victorious. Instead, I'm weighed down. Giving her body a taste of the compound it had been addicted to for the past five years was essential to my experiment, and I've just confirmed it.

Only an addict could crave again after such a small dose. She was never clean, she was just—

"I'm clean, motherfucker!"

I start. She's staring right at me again, face a picture of wrath. But then her eyes flicker, flicker, drop. She hugs herself and begins rocking.

That was uncanny—and I don't use the word lightly. Mass hysteria is a well-documented phenomenon. A misleading term, too. You don't need a mass, all you need is more than one person. Shared experiences create an ephemeral, psychic bond between humans capable of relaying information. Like a school of fish outmaneuvering a shark.

Odd, that something like that has happened so soon though. An element of Clover's near-death experience? It could be anything...and another variable to add to the exhaustive list of things this study needs to establish.

The rocking ceases. Clover slumps even more. And then she's on her side, that bright red cloak a blanket.

We're running behind schedule, girl. But you're useless to me if you're exhausted. You must understand how I am going to save your life.

The fire beckons me, but I refuse to let it lure me from the shadows. My clothing will protect me, and I brought along a windproof jacket. The night might not be comfortable, but I will survive it.

Clover *will* survive it.

And, in the morning, we'll begin.

CHAPTER FORTY-THREE
CLOVER

A bird trills urgently nearby, jolting me awake. I sit up in a rush, clutching my cloak-blanket to my chest. The little clearing doesn't show signs of life and, after my abrupt waking, it's silent too.

I swallow hard—fuck, I'm thirsty—and stretch out stiff limbs and a sore neck.

This is the second night I've slept on a forest floor. I should be used to it by now.

I snort at the thought and get to my feet. The fire's gone gray, but strangely I can still feel the warmth coming from it. Compared with the breath-misting cold of morning, it's most welcome.

Fuck, I need to pee. I need to eat. Water. Clean clothes.

God, Clover, you're alive. Bask for a moment, you entitled bitch.

Okay, done basking. Still need all that shit.

Seriously, how did we ever get this far? I mean, we got to space, for fuck's sake, and I can't even handle two days in the forest.

Admittedly, astronauts go through training. The closest I've been to roughing it was that one time I fell asleep at a bus shelter waiting for a dealer who never came.

I shake out my hair, making sure I'm not nesting a host of creepy crawlies. Fuck, I have a feeling I will have to cut this mess off at the scalp. Ain't no hairdresser gonna get these knots out.

Separating my rat's nest of a hairdo into three hanks, I braid it. It works, kind of, and I use the hoody's drawstring to tie it off.

There. Good to go.

The river runs nearby and fuck it, I'm drinking that water.

I mean, I'll probably be mauled by a bear before I die of cholera, right?

Right?

I wince as my bare feet crunch over the forest's gritty floor. I have several cuts down there, and the ball of my left foot feels so tender I must have bruised it. But, eventually, I make it to the river bank.

I stoop and cup some water to my mouth, glancing around as I slurp it through a lip that's still tender where it split.

You know, if I wasn't barefoot, starving, and being chased by a homicidal maniac, I might have been able to appreciate the beauty of this place a little more.

But I have more important things to consider.

I scrub my face with the river's icy water and splash some on the back of my neck. When I'm done rinsing out my mouth, I almost feel like I'm going to make it through this.

Almost.

As I'm walking back to my impromptu campsite, the sun dims. I look up, but it's impossible to see more than a few dappled slices of the morning sky.

A cloud passing over the sun, or is the day becoming overcast?

Mallhaven got a lot of rain the past six months I was at rehab. I thought it was their rainy season, but I passed through two different seasons altogether. Mallhaven just likes rainy days, I guess.

Christ, don't let it rain.

At the campsite, I scoop up the cloak I was using for a blanket and take a last look around the place for something I may be leaving behind. You know, like a Happy Meal or a pint of ice cream.

Ugh, just the thought makes me salivate.

A flash of color catches my eye.

An arrow.

Freshly painted.

My skin begins to crawl.

There's a note beneath it.

Fucking hell—I don't know how much more of this I can take.

CHAPTER FORTY-FOUR
HUNTER

Disobeying me again. Clover doesn't take the note, and although she's heading in roughly the right direction, her rebellious attitude is near palpable.

What in the name of damnation is so difficult for you to understand, girl? There's only one way out of this maze, and that's the way I'm showing you.

I suppose I can't fault her too greatly. In fact, I almost feel a sense of simpatico. Eight years ago, that was me—taunting authority, rebelling against anything that even hinted at rules.

But rules are there to protect us, Clover. To sustain us. A lawless society is the worst kind of nightmare.

I can't cure you if you won't let me guide you. I know it's a difficult lesson to learn, but learn it you must.

You will.

I trail her for a few more minutes, and then up my pace so I'm ahead of her.

Last chance, Clover. Best you take it.

CHAPTER FORTY-FIVE
CLOVER

The sun is definitely not as strong as it was yesterday. Under the forest's thick canopy, it feels like a winter's day. I hug myself as I walk, trying to stop shivering. Trying to stop wondering where the hell I'm going.

I should turn back to the river. After all, it eventually reaches Mallhaven—I remember driving over the bridge to reach the Institute for my graduation ceremony. Admittedly, I don't remember the first trip here—I think I was still high as fuck.

Bad thoughts.

Bad, *bad* thoughts.

I wish the sun would come out again. I can't stand how fuzzy the shadows are. It's like they're leeching into the day from whatever dimension spawns them. As if the barrier between night and day is failing.

I was exhausted last night, and the fire repelled the dark. If it hadn't been for that...

My next shiver turns into a shudder. I pause to get my bearings— ha!—and I hear a noise.

I whirl around, but there's nothing to see except those undefined shadows everywhere.

Hunter.

I grit my teeth, tempted as shit to yell out his name so he knows. But instead I shrug those invisible spiders from my shoulders and forge ahead.

Ahead? I could be going in circles for all I know. I mean, it's not as if I have a sense of—

I come to a dead stop.

Red arrow.

Holy shit, there's even gunk on it now. Bits of pulpy, flesh-like globs. I swallow down pre-emptive bile and squeeze my eyes shut.

Another note. This one is stained with a fingerprint.

Evidence.

If I keep it, and if I make it out alive, I could have Dr. Hill's ass locked up.

No, fuck that—they'll send him straight to the electric chair. If they still do that.

Actually, I think I'll just kill him myself. Vigilante style.

I hear myself laughing and clamp a hand over my mouth to still the noise. He's following me, so I know he—

Thoughts collide in my brain like a bad traffic accident.

I hurry up to the arrow, to the note. This close, I can see just how wet it still is. In fact, there's a chunk of—Jesus fucking Christ, skin?—sliding down the bark.

How could he be *behind* me if he had to be in *front* of me to make this arrow?

I spin around, hunting the shadows.

There are two of them.

Oh fucking God, there're two of them.

CHAPTER FORTY-SIX
HUNTER

You know how this works, Clover. I leave a note, you read the note, you obey the note. I realize I'm gritting my teeth and have to force myself to stop. This woman is working on every one of my nerves.

She's busy looking around as if she's trying to find me again, but she's not even looking in the right direction this time. See? Adrenaline only lasts so long—she's no longer superhuman.

The light around us fades, and I hazard a quick glance up through the canopy. The temperature's dropping, and it's not even mid-morning yet.

This is why I wanted to avoid delays, Ms. Vos. Don't you get it? You don't want to be out here in a few hours's time. I would go on at length about low-pressure systems, but I doubt you'd care.

Follow the goddamn arrow!

As if she feels that psychic pressure from my thought, she turns back to the tree and rips the note from its nail.

God, you'd think she was scared of contracting a disease, how she treats everything around her.

She shivers visibly and folds open the note. Reads it.

Her hand drops to her side, and the paper falls from her fingers.

And, finally, she sees it.

I've already made a mental note to leave something more visible—perhaps a bottle I've painted with that same neon-yellow paint. I'd thought she'd pointedly ignored the previous water bottle, but perhaps she hadn't noticed it at all.

She crouches, picks up the bottle, and gives it a shake.

There's a noise somewhere behind her, something moving through the trees. I turn the same instant she does and glimpse what's very possibly the flank of an inquisitive deer.

Clover lets out a throttled yell, steps back, and walks straight into the tree where I painted the arrow. She yelps, spinning around and swiping furiously at the arm of her hoody where blood now stains the fabric. Another strangled sound, and she drops to her knees.

She never struck me as an emotional creature. Of course, during her rehabilitation program, she went through the entire spectrum of human emotions. But that was to be expected. This?

Why is she so terrified? Does she have a phobia I wasn't aware of? I'd have spotted agoraphobia a long time ago, possibly during the first week of the program.

No.

This is something else.

If it's a phobia, then it's a very specific one.

That, or...

Has she already accessed her trigger?

I reel at the thought. Bark scrapes my fingertips and I realize I've caught hold of the closest tree.

How is that even possible? If she's locked down those parts of her mind containing her triggers, could such a short time in a harsh environment be enough to force her to look inside that locked chest?

Is she crying?

No, she's shivering.

Why? Her clothes should be dry. Has she contracted something? But how?

I press my eyes closed, and massage them with my fingers. I must focus on the here and now. I can't expend my entire mental energy on trying to calculate every single variable right now. That I will do later.

Right now, I must observe, and guide.

If she'll even let me.

If she won't, then what's coming is going to be a terrifyingly unpleasant experience.

CHAPTER FORTY-SEVEN
CLOVER

I thought I could stand up to him. I thought I could outsmart him. But every time I've disobeyed him, I've only fucked myself up the ass with a prickly pear.

Two of them?

I don't stand a chance.

Now I understand how he always knew where I was. I thought he might have put a tracker or something on me, but it looks like he has a crony to help him out with things like gutting rabbits and painting bloody arrows everywhere.

Hunter and Friend: 1

Clover: 0

I tear the note from the tree, grimacing when my hand touches the blood on that white paper.

Drink me.

I stare at that command for the longest time.

I don't understand. It seems so familiar, but it makes no fucking sense.

Drink me.

What? Where? I can't—

I turn a little, and a stray beam of light flashes from something that's not the forest.

A water bottle, propped at the base of the tree.

If it were a snake, it would have bitten me.

I pick up the bottle and give it a shake. Inside, brackish water swirls. My mouth salivates, and I realize my body is one fucked up piece of equipment for me to—

A twig cracks.

Fuck! I let out a squeal and slam into the tree.

Double fuck! There's blood on my sleeve. It went straight through —I can feel its dampness on my arm.

Off, get off!

Eyes.

I can feel eyes on me.

Two sets from different directions.

They're both here, aren't they? Surrounding me. Watching me.

The forest spins as I fall to my knees. Something's wrong. My head's stuffed with cotton wool. The dim shadows are stretching, reaching for me. The dark is so eager to consume me I can smell its rotting breath.

Drink me.

Oh, of course.

One pill makes you larger, one pill makes you small.

But the one that momma gives you, don't do anything at all.

I screw open the water bottle, swallow hard, and put it to my lips.

I gag as soon as the liquid touches my tongue. Water splashes over my face as I splutter. I lean forward, convinced I'm going to puke out my stomach, but then my mouth goes dry.

What did I do to deserve this?

I force the rest of that foul drink down my throat, clamp a hand over my mouth, and retch. Luckily, nothing more than a little saliva escapes my lips.

I won't upset Hunter anymore.

I don't want the next arrow to be painted with my blood.

CHAPTER FORTY-EIGHT
HUNTER

Good girl.

I watch from the shadows as Clover gets to her feet and starts heading in the direction of the arrow. In a few minutes, she'll be back on course.

A day late, but on course.

I trail her. After all, she's making so much noise anything in a one-mile radius knows she's here.

I, on the other hand, can move as silently as that deer.

In fact, I don't think I've made a single sound to rouse her suspicions.

The sun fades, and this time, it doesn't reappear.

I grit my teeth as I glance up through the canopy.

It's coming.

Faster, Clover.

Faster!

CHAPTER FORTY-NINE
CLOVER

I'm trying not to lose my shit. I have no idea what I drank, but its foul taste refuses to leave my mouth. I've spit more times than I can count, but my mouth just waters and brings the taste back from the bowels of my stomach.

The sun's gone for good, and even with the cloak wrapped around me, I'm a shivering mess.

What *the fuck* did I drink?

I'm starting to wonder if I did the right thing. I mean, is poison a better way to die than hypothermia or starvation? Don't forget the bear.

Was that what this was all about? Hunter came up with some kind of poison, and he wants to see how long it takes me to succumb?

Dude...*cyanide*. I mean, we've been using it for ages. Why waste your time on something new? Go and cure cancer, you fucking freak.

I blink hard and pause. Christ, it's getting dark in here. I've known overcast days, but this is something else. It's like the leaves are drinking in every ounce of sunlight that's still bouncing around out here.

Drink me.

Which I did.

There's a reason I stopped blindly following orders.

Bad, bad thought.

The ground is spongy. The air damp and cool. I'm warming up, as if I'm jogging—

Wait. I *am* jogging.

When did that happen? My bare feet thump down at every step, my breasts bounce, my jaw tightens.

I'm not running from something anymore, I'm running toward something.

But what? What does my body know that my brain is so fucking clueless about?

He's following me again. I'm not sure if they both are, but I know one is.

Is it Hunter, or his friend? The only reason it would be Hunter is if he's up to no good, somewhere up ahead.

Another message?

Another command?

Unlock the door, Clover.

"No!" The word is a rough shout, and I lose rhythm in surprise.

I stop, put out a hand, and lean against a tree as I catch my breath. The world settles, but not entirely. I've never been on a boat but, somehow, I imagine this is how it must feel as the world dips and flows around me.

Heart attack?

Stroke?

Or is the poison finally beginning to work its death-dealing magic?

Up ahead, an arrow.

It's yellow, precise, dry—that much I can see from here.

The skin on my legs shivers as I break into a cold sweat. Holy fucking mackerel, I'm unfit. I hike up the long sleeves of my hoody, adjust the cloak as a rough scarf—something tells me I might need it again, so I'll be fucked before I leave it behind somewhere—and I start forward again.

I touch the arrow, just to make sure.

Bone dry.

Let me in, Clover.

"No." Not a shout, but still a vehement protest. What the fuck's wrong with my mouth? Stay shut, motherfucker. I need to concentrate over here.

The dark.

It's closer now.

I can feel it breathing down my neck.

I spin around, but there's nothing behind me. Just a breeze, Clover. A cool breeze against your sweaty neck. Felt like a breath.

Get a fucking grip.

Bitterness washes my mouth. God, I thought I'd gotten rid of that—

I crash to my knees and retch long and hard. There's barely anything to puke up, but I keep going for an eternity.

The purging finally stops. There's soft moss on my cheek. I've fallen over.

It takes more strength than I ever thought I'd need to get up, but up I fucking get.

My mind is suddenly, terrifying clear.

Follow me.

Obey me.

Unlock the door, Clover.

AS I FOLLOW THE ARROWS, darkness slowly engulfs the forest. Every sound is amplified as if the world is dissolving around me and there's nothing left to muffle my progress through this alien place.

My fingertips tingle. I look to the right. My hand reaches out for the closest tree. I grab at the rough bark and haul myself forward.

Christ, the ground is flat, but it feels like I'm trying to summit Everest. My legs are heavy, awkward, stubborn. I weigh a ton, and my breath heaves as I haul my fat slug of a body forward.

My hand grabs another tree, and something sinister slides away from my grasping fingers.

I stumble away, hand pressed to my chest where my heart's thud-thud-thudding away like a bass drum.

A snake appears between the shadowy bark like an optical illusion. I scream and gasp, somehow at the same time, and back into a tree.

If it was a snake—

It *is* a snake, and it almost bit me.

I bolt away into the trees and, seconds later, I realize I've gone off the trail.

Not good.

I swing around, but too far, and tumble over when my balance fucks off. Now I have no way of knowing which way I was going, which way—

A snake slithers over my leg. It's gone before I have a chance to scream, leaving behind a ghostly caress that makes my hair stand on end.

A second later, I'm plunging through the slowly darkening forest.

Branches reach for me. Leaves slap my face. Roots grab my feet at every chance, and I end up on my knees, howling in pain.

Something lands on my head.

A snake.

It slithers down the nape of my neck and into my hoody. I yell, stick my hands under the thick fabric, and try to haul it out.

It's already gone.

I can't. I just can't do this anymore.

I run.

I run until I see a blood-red arrow slashed into a tree, and then I turn and follow it. Another. Another.

My path becomes less tangled. The way ahead, clear.

Arrow after arrow, angry, dripping triangles stab out my direction.

Hot air dries my lungs. I'm sweating and ice cold at the same time.

Still, the dark comes. It's nipping at my heels. I plunge through shallow pools of it, whimpering when fingers brush the bare soles of my—

Don't you dare disobey me, Love.

"Please," I mewl, tears blurring my vision.

She left me in charge, Love.

You will obey me.

Obey me.

Something bobs up ahead through the close-knit trunks of pine trees and tangling bushes.

Yellow.

An arrow?

No...it's glowing.

Light.

Light!

There's someone out here. Someone who can help me, who can—

My foot strikes something soft that splits open under my heel. I slip, pitch backward, land so hard on my ass that I don't have air to scream with.

The dark—the snakes—slither over my hands, my ankles.

I haul in a breath and scream, shoving myself up from the mulch forest floor. A snake encircles my arm, and I shake it furiously as I surge forward.

Please, help.

Help me.

Something lands on my face. I wipe it away before I can register what it is. Then another. Another.

Fat drops of rain.

Cold. Wet.

Not striking me directly, but filtering through the canopy above.

I can't believe how dark it is. The shadows are melding together. Midnight can't be far off, and the things birthed into the world at the stroke of twelve.

Unlock the door, Love.

The path turns muddy underfoot. I have to slow down, but if I do, then the dark will surely catch me, snatch me, scratch me.

Like those nails. Those dirty nails.

Nausea wells inside me, and I bend over, hurling while I'm running.

Can't stop.

It'll get me.

He'll get me.

In the dark.

At night.

Every night.

I clear the trees. Drops of rain shatter against my face, too hard to be just water. Biting my cheeks.

I run through puddles and reach out for the shape rearing up ahead.

A cabin.

Light flickering in its single window.

Stout, but small, but so solid in a forest that's whipped into a frenzy by a howling wind and stinging, driving rain.

I slip. My teeth crack together as I land on my belly.

Warm breath on my neck.

A hand holds me down.

A weight pins me.

Nails scrape, scrape up my legs.

"No!"

There's a perfect rectangle of white on the cabin door, and another arrow—

No, not an arrow. A cross. Dry, slightly weathered.

I crash into the door, and rip at the handle.

It's locked.

It's *fucking* locked.

"Let me in!" I bang a palm on the rough wood.

Obey me.

Drink me.

Open up, Love.

I spin around, expecting to see a teeming fog of hands and claws reaching for me.

But I ran too fast. The darkness is still leaking from the trees. It skips over the sodden ground, covering the puddles so not a trace of light shines on their surfaces.

Unlock the door, Love.

"Please," I whisper, my words shaking as hard as my hands.

I spin around again, slam my fists into the door. It rattles, but doesn't open.

"Please!"

Wind whips around me, and the square of white turns into a thin bird. It flutters, heading for the heavens, but it's been nailed to the wood.

Tearing.

It's tearing—

I snatch the piece of paper. Fold it open against the door so I can read it before the wind tugs it from my hands.

The paper is damp. The ink, running.

Tr...st me

What might have been words dissolve into nothing but a black smear.

I squeeze my eyes shut.

"Please..."

The rain has turned into a torrential downpour. Water splashes against my bare legs. Debris sticks to my skin, kicked up by those splashes.

It's charging me now, the dark.

I've lost, it's won.

Pitter patter. Pitter patter. It has substance now. I hear it approach.

I press my forehead to the wooden door, inhale its scent.

I'm sobbing like a little girl, because I still am one. I never grew up. I never changed. I've always been this kid. I grew boobs and got my period and did tons of grown-up stuff, but I've always just been a scared little girl.

Frightened of the dark.

Terrified of what waits beyond it.

Fuck this shit.

I spin around, teeth gritted in defiance.

Rain creates a halo around the hunched figure making its way toward me.

Walking slowly, carefully. There's no rush, when your prey has run out of hiding places. Why run, when she can't?

You always knew where to find me. You knew I couldn't run, and you knew I'd never say a word.

Because this is my karma. This is my life.

I wished she was dead, and then she was.

I deserve everything coming to me.

Even you, *Dark*.

Even you.

Rain clatters from the Dark. It reaches out a shapeless arm as if to touch me.

My body goes rigid. I want to shut my eyes because I don't want to see what's coming. I want to die because that's better than feeling.

Water pours down my face, obscuring the Dark, making it impossible to see anything more than three feet away.

I'm a coward, and a thief. I stole a life, and I must pay with my own.

"Trust me."

I let out a shivering, spluttering gasp.

"Trust me, Clover."

Another command, and I'm so good at obeying, aren't?

Unlock the door, Love.

Get on the bed, Love.

Keep quiet, Love.

Open up, Love.

A strangled sob escapes me. I try to press myself through the door as that hand comes closer and closer.

It's different now, that hand. The nails neatly manicured. The skin sun dark, not withered.

"Wha...?"

It reaches past me, and I see it's holding a key.

I tumble aside, barely catching myself against the door jamb.

The door swings open. A hand clutches my arm, hard, tight. My legs are wooden under me, like they don't belong.

The Dark shoves me inside, and I trip over my useless, pathetic legs. I sprawl on a rough floor the same instant the Dark sweeps into the room and snatches every last molecule of light from the air.

Midnight falls on me like a lead blanket.

I go into a huddle because I don't want to see what's coming. I don't want to feel anything anymore.

Ever.

The fury of the storm abates as soon as the door is closed.

The key turns.

The Dark descends on me again.

CHAPTER FIFTY
HUNTER

S he's a shivering wretch. Her sobs fill the small cabin, the warmth of our bodies evaporating the rainwater we brought inside and turning the air humid. A gust of wind has snuffed out the candle standing on the window sill—my last beacon to call her in from the dark.

I shrug out of my black rain jacket and hang it up on the back of the door. I must get light back in this place, but first, I need to get her off the floor.

She recoils when I touch her.

"Quiet," I murmur. Her body stiffens as she wails. She's not fighting me, but it's obvious she's not encouraging my touch.

If I could explain this to you, I would, Clover. But this is something you need to understand for yourself. Only you can walk this maze. I can be there for support—a light that beckons at the end of a dark, twisting road—but you must make the trip.

You have to stumble. You have to fall. You have to get up.

I can't do it for you.

I lead her to the bed. She makes a pitiful sound as she collapses onto the mattress and goes back into her little huddle. The storm rages outside, but I think she's muttering something under her breath.

Or is that the sound of her teeth chattering?

She's soaked through from the rain, her hair a wet rope down her back.

I need to undress her.

The thought lingers in my mind like the remnants of a dream on waking.

What is wrong with me?

"Light. Light. Light."

The night light.

The way she kept searching the shadows...

Darkness. Is that her phobia?

It might not be a full-blown phobia—*yet*—but if left untreated...

Perhaps two miracles will be accomplished here tonight. But not if I'm going to keep having impure thoughts.

I'm a scientist. My only passion should be to deepen mankind's knowledge, not to...not to undress her.

At the same time, however, I realize she might be going into shock from the cold. I didn't give her a big dose of Ayahuasca, but it treats everyone different. One dose could be sufficient—other people need three to four times the regular volume.

It all depends on how hefty you built the barriers in your mind.

"Light. Light. Light." Her chant sounds like a desperate mantra.

I climb on the bed, and fumble with the snuffed candle. Outside, light glances from the slanting rain. It's late afternoon, but you'd swear it's twilight how dark it is. Especially in here where there's only this small window to let in any ambiance.

The candle sputters to life.

I'm kneeling beside her, my thigh but an inch from hers.

I can feel cold pulsing from her skin.

Is she going into hypothermia? It's possible I underestimated her resistance to the elements.

I grab her shoulder and turn her onto her back.

Her eyes are squeezed shut, her mouth a trembling line. I don't know what she's seeing in her mind, but it can't be pretty.

I should sympathize with her. After all, I remember how this feels. But my mind is on my subject's body. If her core temperature has dropped as drastically as I assume it has, then she won't be able to warm herself even if I layer blankets over her. With zero body heat of her own, she'll just fade out like a candle starved of oxygen.

"Do you trust me, Clover?"

Her eyes fly wide open. They are the color of a brewing storm, and they pull at me like a magnetic current.

"Hunter." She's breathless, surprised.

I grab one of her trembling hands, and place it on my breast. Can she feel my heart beating?

"Do you trust me, Clover?"

Her eyes search mine. Her mouth becomes a hard line.

"No!" she spits out, wrenching her hand free. "You're a fucking monster."

Did I mishear her?

But then she's scrambling off the bed, and I barely catch her in time to stop her from reaching the door. I locked it, obviously, but she could hurt herself trying to get free.

"Clover."

"Let me go!" she yells, and in this tiny cabin the sound reverberates. "Help!"

Why are you being so cruel to her, Mother Ayahuasca? Why won't you let her know I'm here to help?

I'm struggling with her, trying to contain her wrath, when I hear the answer. I'm not on anything—my mind is clear, if a little distracted —but that doesn't make the voice any less real.

Any less *correct*.

I'm not trying to help her, am I? I'm trying to *prove my theory*. This is nothing but a test for me. If she fails, I'll find someone else. If she passes, I'll mark it a success and set up another trial.

But the Mother knows.

Clover needs my help.

I must be her guide in the most unselfish of ways.

I release her, and she falls to the floor. I land on my ass a few feet away and watch as she gets her bearing. She swings around, face wild with terror, and then stops.

We're both breathing hard; panting like animals.

"Let me help you," I whisper.

CHAPTER FIFTY-ONE
CLOVER

A brilliant surge of light destroys the dark, embracing me. I surface from black, muddy waters, choking for air. I'm on a bed, Hunter kneeling over me.

I'm frozen to my very core.

"Do you trust me, Clover?"

"Hunter?"

It's a trick of the light. It must be. There's only one person in this world as decrepit and cruel to drag me into this isolated cabin.

I know what he wants to do to me. It's the same thing he did all those nights he was supposed to be my protector. My caretaker.

I had to call him Father.

He *insisted* on it.

It was the sick game he played with me. I'd lock the door, but he'd always have a key. And then he'd punish me for keeping him out.

I tried to tell someone. But the words would never come. Mortification gagged me every time.

And guilt.

He would tell me every night why he came into my room. What I'd done to deserve his punishments.

I killed my mother.

Not physically. I didn't smother her in my sleep or poison her water.

I wished her dead, and she died.

The mind is a powerful, powerful thing.

Father would always remind me of the fact. On the nights he didn't come to my room, I would stay awake waiting for him to arrive.

I dropped out of school. Knowledge was something I wanted no part of.

I suppose I already knew there was nothing that could explain Father's punishments.

All I knew back then was that I deserved them.

He was simply showing me the light.

Every night.

In the dark.

PART FOUR

TRUST ME

"With one bound, the wolf was out of bed and swallowed up Red Riding Hood."

LITTLE RED RIDING HOOD - THE BROTHERS GRIMM

CHAPTER FIFTY-TWO
HUNTER

I lift a hand to her. She watches me as intently as a trapped deer, eyes wide and wet with fear.

"You can trust me, Clover."

Dangerous words.

I've been treating addicts for many years. I know almost all of them have triggers.

Trust is always a trigger.

Asking someone for it.

Gaining it.

Breaking it.

I'm asking much of her, but I'm hoping I have Mother Ayahuasca on my side. If any entity can guide Clover to the light, it's her.

She showed me the light.

And I opened to her like a flower.

Can't Clover see I'm doing the same? Guiding her. Showing her the light?

Without light, you can't banish the darkness.

CHAPTER FIFTY-THREE
CLOVER

Around us, the forest turns pitch black. The walls breathe along with me—but at least I'm not panting anymore. But I am cold, and my breath shivers out of me at every exhale.

Too cold.

My body is numb.

Brain turning to sludge.

Hunter is still holding out his hand.

He's washed his face. He looks like he did the night I first saw him on that stage.

Charismatic.

Intelligent.

Kind.

How could I have been so very, very wrong?

Another shiver, this one worse than the last—it clicks my teeth together.

His eyes search mine, and that study is so intrusive I want to look away. But, at the same time, I'm hypnotized. It's like he's calling to me on some unconscious level. Begging my psyche to let him in.

Open up, Love.

I kick away from him, a scream bursting from my mouth. He's on top of me a second later, clamping a hand over my lips.

"No." He's calm, collected, but annoyed. "You have to trust me."

I struggle furiously and manage to graze my nails over his cheek. He recoils, grimacing at me, and then rips at my clothes like a wild animal.

I scream. Fight. Lose breath and whimper. My fingertips are so numb, I don't know when I'm making contact with him or grasping at thin air.

All around me, the room grows smaller, darker. The air, thicker. I gasp, unable to breathe the dark soup surrounding me.

My hoodie is off.

Those silk boxers next. I'm naked, shivering. Hunter's body is too heavy to shift.

I can't—I won't—resign myself to this fate.

Not again.

I've paid my fucking dues.

If I killed her, then I've already been sent to death row more times than I can count. I've lived hundreds of lives as a sex slave, and that has to count for something.

But he's not. He's just lying there.

Catching his breath?

Waiting?

The walls close around me. Tighter.

What happened to the candle? It's snuffed out.

Darkness shrouds me. Invades me.

I'm crying.

But still he doesn't move.

My naked back is pressed to the rough floor. A heavy breath escapes me, shivering my body—maybe it's just the cold—and I relax fully.

There's no fighting this.

There never was.

I've tried before. Failed before.

Fighting makes time slow down. With resignation, an hour

becomes minutes, easily forgotten the next time you shove a needle into your vein.

So easy to stop fighting.

So easy to forget.

Except you never forget, do you?

Never.

CHAPTER FIFTY-FOUR
HUNTER

She's still under me. The occasional shiver bursts through her, but on a tangent it's slowing down.

That is not a good sign. She's out of her wet clothes, but she's not warming up. If her body's own survival mechanisms fail, there's not much energy left to fight.

Her body goes limp, and for a heart wrenching second, I think she's comatose.

I thumb back her closed eyes, and there's no response from her pupils to the light.

No. Clover.

"Don't you dare give up on me." The words are out before I even realize I'm going to speak.

She's a dead weight in my arms. I drag her over to the bed and haul her onto the mattress.

The edges of her lips have turned blue.

How could I have been so wrong?

Instinct takes over.

Instinct or muscle memory?

EIGHT YEARS AGO

EXHAUSTED, wet, drained. At first I think the light that beckons me from between the trees is just another hallucination.

I've spent months studying Ayahuasca. I read over a hundred frank journals detailing its effects on people across the world.

Yet nothing could have prepared me for this.

Nothing.

My mind is a terrifying, alien place. A forest as familiar as my home has turned against me. I have enemies everywhere, and my only friend—the sun—left me behind hours ago.

The stars might be out by now—I have no idea. The canopy above is too thick for me to see the sky.

I step into a tiny clearing, its only feature a log cabin, newly erected.

There's a pagan symbol painted on the door, and a candle in the window.

It flickers as if to beckon me near, but as eager as I was to reach this safe harbor, now I'm reluctant to go near.

I know the forest.

I know its moods, its intricacies.

I've never seen this cabin before, and that bothers me on so many levels. A construction like this—crude as it is—would have taken several days to complete. How could I not have known it was being built?

More importantly, *who* built it?

I should be able to warm myself. If I take off these wet clothes, find enough leaves to cover myself with, my body heat...

Orange light blooms from the cabin.

A hallucination?

I've had so many tonight, I can't tell what's real anymore.

Pale smoke coils from a stub of a chimney, and a warm glow suffuses the inside of the cabin. I see a figure inside, but the angle is wrong for me to make out much more than that.

Fire.

Shelter.

Someone to assist me.

I stumble forward, gripping myself with shaking arms.

I sense another presence, and it's not the person inside the cabin.

No. I know this soul as well as I know the forest.

I'm tempted to start running, but I know that would be the worst thing to do. Some animals wouldn't care if their prey began running. Others wouldn't be able to prevent themselves from giving chase.

In my condition, the wolf will win. I don't have the strength or mental fortitude to fight it off.

He'll have torn into something vital before I make it to that window of light.

Shelter I may have, but I would die a slow death inside those warm walls.

So I force myself to keep walking.

I don't look back. Even when I know it's following, I keep my eyes straight ahead and hope like hell I'll make it.

I keep my composure for all but the last few yards. Then I bolt forward, self-preservation overriding every ounce of my remaining logic.

I skid the last foot, and bang a fist against the door. Again. Again. Harder, until it drowns out the sound of the wolf racing up behind me.

The door opens, and I'm faced with the gaping maw of a double-barrel shotgun.

"Move!" a thick, guttural voice growls.

But I'm frozen in terror.

A burly arm swipes me out of the way, sending me sprawling.

Boom.

Boom.

Chaching.

Boom.

The shots echo in the forest like a bad dream. I whip my head from the protective huddle I've collapsed into.

What's left of the wolf lies in a bloody heap a yard from the doorway. A filament of smoke coils up from one of the shotgun's muzzles before the man lets his arm sink to his side.

He turns to me, grubby face slack. "Cold?" he asks.

I'm still too shocked to move. I'm not even sure if I'm out of danger yet—this potato sack of a man could knock my head clean off my shoulders. A ham-sized hand grabs me by the scruff of my neck and hauls me inside.

"Sit."

He releases me, and I barely manage to scramble into a nearby chair.

My teeth chatter but not as hard as they were outside.

Thank God. I might actually live to—

The man tosses a log on the small coal stove, making me jerk in surprise. He comes over to me—in this tiny house, it only takes three of his big steps—and presses his knuckles to my cheek. I recoil, but not before he's touched me.

"Cold."

I just nod dumbly. He reaches again, grabbing the neckline of my jumper between thumb and finger. "Wet."

Oh, monosyllabic brute, what are you going to do to me?

The thought has hysterical overtones. Just like that, I break into gales of laughter.

The man watches as impassively as he'd stared at the wolf's corpse outside. I eventually tire of my mirth, and hug myself hard in an effort to claw back some shred of control.

At least my teeth aren't chattering anymore.

The room darkens a little. Is his candle going out? I slide off the chair, and land in a heap by the brute's feet.

What the hell's wrong with me?

I fell looking toward that solitary candle. The beacon I'd followed so faithfully to this refuge in the middle of the forest.

"Dry."

I don't understand him. I don't understand this cabin, or the candle, or the way the forest echoed back the shotgun's crack.

The floor is consuming me. I couldn't have stood up if I tried and as it is, I'm terrified that I'm going to fall through into the depths of hell.

The brute grabs me by the back of my neck again and hauls me up. Thick, scarred fingers dig between my pants and the hem of my sodden jumper.

I watch him like he watches me—impassive, docile, dumb.

He eases my shirt and jumper over my head in a surprisingly gentle gesture. I sway a little before I can steady myself.

My nerve endings aren't working anymore. I should have felt something. Warmth, cold, air moving over my skin.

Nothing.

I fear I've disassociated from this moment; My brain's clever way of getting the hell out of dodge before this got more serious.

The brute turns away from me and grabs a filthy blanket from a heap in the corner I can only assume must be where he sleeps like a dog at night. He swings it over my shoulders and wraps it tight. Then he crouches in front of me and yanks off my shoes—one after the other.

Socks.

Pants.

Underwear.

They all come off.

The brute brings another blanket. He scoops me up and takes me to the crackling fire. Swaddling me like a babe, he encircles me, my face stinging as the first wave of heat touches my cheeks.

I'm crying.

I don't know how long ago it began, but I can't seem to stop.

My tears evaporate from the fire's heat before they reach my jaw. Before they can drip on the brute's hands. Yet, somehow, he seems to know.

He holds me tighter, and rocks me.

Then he starts to hum some wordless melody.

My body aches and begins to tremble. But there's another pain too. Something ephemeral. Something I can't define or locate.

It's everywhere, and it's been there all along.

How could it have hidden from me all these years?

Or had I simply mastered the art of forgetting?

I'd left home because I couldn't stand the thought of seeing my father. I'd left Holly and Mother behind because then I could return and pretend nothing had happened.

We could *all* pretend.

Mother and I, at least. Holly never had anything to fear from Father. Holly was His Little Girl.

But Mother and I could never live up to Holly. We always fell short, one way or the other.

When I was seven, I told the doctor I'd been riding a bike. He didn't say anything. He simply put my arm in a cast and prescribed me painkillers.

When I was nine, my tutor listened reluctantly to the tale of how I fell out of the tree. She sympathized at the time—said that's how she broke her leg when she was a kid too.

I've always been an excellent liar. It's a skill I taught myself in order to survive.

At age thirteen, I'd had enough. No one at my private school bought my bullshit story about a ski accident. So I went home and confronted Father.

It was exhilarating. Freeing.

The biggest mistake of my life.

The next morning, Mother didn't come downstairs for breakfast. When Holly asked, Father said she wasn't feeling well.

The doctor made a house call later that day and left looking grim. When we finally saw mother again, two days later, her hand was still in a cast, and the bruises on her face were only barely starting to heal.

That night, Father sent for me. He never told me that what he'd done to Mother was my punishment. He didn't have to.

Since that day, I bore every slap, kick, and punch like a man. When I couldn't stand the thought of him laying his hands on me, I'd make sure I wasn't in sight when he arrived home.

Those times, I worried he'd turn to Mother or Holly to fulfill his sadistic needs. But he never did. And, the older he got, the longer his trips in the city would last.

It's been almost a month since I've seen him.

Almost a month since I've last used.

I was clean.

But when I heard, I went to go find the stash the other part of me had hidden away for emergencies.

I couldn't find it.

I took that journey sooner than I'd anticipated, and yet it was too late. My eyes should have been opened years ago, not now. Father is old and decrepit now. No one would believe I'd survived under his cruel intentions for so long without saying anything.

I couldn't even believe it.

I cried a decade's worth of tears. I howled out Father's name and accused him of every crime he'd ever committed against me. I spat out his sentence, became judge and juror.

Of course, when I return home, he'll be there. Waiting.

Except if I never return home again. Then there might be hope for me.

The brute rocked me till I was spent, until my tears ran dry and the aching pain inside me subsided. And then he hummed me to sleep.

The first full night's sleep I'd had in years.

CHAPTER FIFTY-FIVE
CLOVER

Hunter undresses me while I try summoning enough energy to fight him off. He's the Dark, then he's himself, then he's a monster from the pits of hell. Morphing between states too quickly for me to focus on which one he really is.

Maybe he always was a demon. Always the dark.

The Dark.

The Dark.

I squeeze my eyes shut, but it follows me inside. Hands on my skin.

Unlock the door, Love.

But I don't want to.

Go to bed, Love.

But I'm not sleepy yet.

Don't make a sound, Love.

Why would I when I don't ever want anyone to hear?

He's holding me now. No, there's a blanket around me. It's soft and smells of fabric softener. Wool? Chenille? I force my eyes open and grab a handful of the sensually soft weaves.

I breathe in the scent of it, and huddle into the tightest little ball I can.

My body pulses, but more than that I can't feel. There is no sensation of heat or cold—just this slow pulse.

Slow, and becoming slower.

"You're too cold."

My eyes snap open—when had I closed them again?—and Hunter's face is inches from mine. Brown eyes crinkle with concern, and I realize he has his fingers against my neck, that he's burrowed his way in between the blanket I'm huddling under.

Trust me, Clover.

Hunter slips away, dissolving into the light, and I jerk in shock at being alone. Then I see movement and turn my head with difficulty to watch him building a fire.

Just like he built one for me the other night. The same precise structure, near perfectly sized logs.

Sparks.

A billow of smoke.

He blows, and a gale of wind rattles against the cabin.

Hunter is twenty-foot tall; a giant crouching at the foot of a volcano. He pours fiery breath into its core as every snake in the forest congregates at his feet. I squirm, try to move, but I can't.

I'm trapped inside my own body.

Trapped as that pulsing grows slower. Weaker.

The fire takes, but I don't feel its warmth. Light blooms, but my vision is dimming.

I guess the Dark won't have to wait any longer.

CHAPTER FIFTY-SIX
HUNTER

Clover isn't going to make it. She was too weak to take this journey, yet I forced her to. The thought is a resigned one which is why I can't understand the flash of emotional pain that accompanies it.

This was a possibility, starting out. On some level I knew it.

But, back then, I'd only ever seen Clover on a video feed.

I'd never met her.

I'd never fucked her.

The brute made sure I was dry. He made sure I was warm, and he soothed me as I found the psychological release I'd been so desperate for and hadn't even known I needed.

Most people don't.

Mental illness is stigmatized at every turn. Families would rather you remained silent than bring them disrepute. You suffered abuse? At whose hands? That's all in the past now.

Forgive and forget.

Blood is thicker than water.

The ones closest to us are usually the ones that win most of our trust. The closer they are, the easier it is for them to slip into our rooms at night, to raise a fist, to belittle and demean us.

I don't doubt for a moment Clover was the subject of abuse. Whether physical, emotional, or verbal, the trauma is just as real. The scars, just as deep. Sticks and stones...but words can slice me straight through.

A broken bone, a broken hymen, a broken family, a broken marriage—the wounds heal, but the scars remain.

If you can accept your scars, then you will no longer feel the need to hide them in shame.

Warm.

Dry.

She's begun her journey. I will ensure she finishes it.

"Trust me, Clover." I make it a command, not a request, because her life depends on it. Whether she gives me consent or not, I won't stand idly by and watch her succumb to the cold.

I don't think she's here right now.

Her eyes are fixed on the fire I started, but with an intensity that makes me think she's purposefully avoiding looking at me.

I take off my sweater as a surge of anger flashes through me. Who could hurt someone like Clover? Crude and sarcastic she may be, but there's not a bone of bad in her. Her bitterness comes from whoever thought they had the right to take what wasn't theirs. Her happiness, her confidence, her mind, her body.

Thieves took what they wanted and fuck the consequences. Almost always, those thieves were deprived themselves—a vicious cycle that replays generation after generation.

But if you break the wheel sometimes, *sometimes*, the abuse ends at the last victim.

My shirt comes off next.

Clover makes a miserable sound in the back of her throat. She seems immobile—her arms twitch, but she can't seem to move them more than a quarter inch at a time.

Her body is shutting down. Soon, she'll experience nerve damage in her extremities. Cells will be destroyed as the body draws the last Fahrenheit of warmth to its core organs.

The brain isn't the last to go, but it might as well be.

I want to make a soothing sound, but that could be her trigger. Hell, anything could be her trigger—a smell, a sound, the way someone walks.

In the time she attended my facility, I discovered only two triggers.

First, the most obvious, was the dark.

The night light. Her aversion to going outside at night. The way she kept all her clothes in neat piles on her dresser instead of in the closet.

Honestly, what kid isn't afraid of the dark? I have memories of me as a teen—before I'd become an addict—leaping more than three feet onto my bed so I was sure the hands attached to the monster I knew— I fucking knew—lived under there couldn't grab at my ankles.

Closets? They were an infinity deep, and a decade too long. They could harbor anything from a sadistic clown to a goddamn kraken.

Aliens scared me.

Monsters scared me.

The sight of an empty coat hanging on a coat rack scared me.

But I was a kid. Those things were considered normal when you hadn't hit puberty yet.

What twenty-three-year-old is afraid of the dark? I mean really, *really*, afraid of the dark? To the point where they'd go into hysterics if they woke up in pitch blackness?

Triggers.

They manifest the monsters under our beds into nightmares of solid flesh and bone.

So many people don't understand PTSD. They think it's reserved for the Jews, and the veterans. Those unlucky few locked in their own basements, forced to birth three children to a sadistic, pedophilic father.

No.

It's not that simple. It's not that easy.

No one wants to admit that the smell of lavender sends them into a panic attack.

No one wants to believe that, without the right treatment, sleeping eight hours is a luxury afforded by everyone but themselves.

I kept a diary that I hid so very well. In it, I chronicled my triggers.

Cedar. One of the many complex notes in my father's aftershave, and the only item of furniture we possess that was constructed out of that wood was an armchair he kept in the attic. The one I would have to hold on to as he lashed me with his belt.

Another? Vermouth.

The last? The smell of pennies. In particular, the lucky penny he always kept in his pocket. The one he rubbed when he was anxious, excited, happy, sad, melancholy.

Fine—the smell of his fingers.

Because he'd wrap them around my throat and throttle me, and that's all I would smell for close to a minute before I passed out.

And, when I woke up, I'd often keep smelling it, because my nose was bleeding.

'A little leak,' Mother used to call it.

I will never call her down for it. I would rather have suffered Father being home every damn day than waking up to my mother's empty seat at the breakfast table again.

We never spoke of that day, Mother and I.

We didn't have to.

I'd already sworn never to let it happen again, and I kept my promise. I made good on it.

Father passed away a year ago. For the five years preceding that day, he'd been bed bound, confined to a mental institution here in Mallhaven.

He proclaimed that Satan himself had possessed him.

I agreed, which is why I never bothered to correct the doctors when they prescribed him vast amounts of antipsychotics. After all, who in their right mind would want to be declared insane?

Father died believing the devil had possessed him. I might even be inclined to believe that one day when I'm older and less bitter.

I know for a fact his condition had nothing to do with the crushed Morning Glory seeds I slipped into his Vermouth at night.

Oh, the beatings he laid on me were spectacular. The pain took me into a different dimension—one where I was loved and cherished like the goddamn son of God.

But a healthy man soon became an ill one.

It took less than a month for him to experience his first psychotic break.

CHAPTER FIFTY-SEVEN
CLOVER

What's happening? I used to understand the world around me. Shapes, sounds, colors. Things used to make sense.

They don't anymore.

I've never tripped before. Heroin was my drug of choice, and I never had hallucinations. I had body highs that dulled my aches. Mental lows that made thought impossible.

Everything I ever wanted in a drug and more.

The past didn't exist when I was high.

Neither did the future.

The present was where it was at and that stretched to infinity. I was calm. Warm. Satisfied. Rich. Intelligent. Loved.

Until I came down, and that was when the opposites were undeniably true.

I tried ecstasy once, but it felt like I was having a panic attack.

Meth made me feel like God, and I knew I didn't deserve something that grandiose.

I'm only alive today because of heroin, despite the fact that it almost killed me countless times.

I laugh. The sounds splinter into a kaleidoscope of colors—every one in the rainbow and then some—until I squeeze my eyes shut.

Trust me, Clover.

My eyes open.

Hunter stands in front of me. The fire illuminates him, and burns at his silhouette. His hair is made of snakes, and they're slithering down his neck.

He takes off his sweater.

A bare torso confronts me and demands explanations I'm powerless to provide.

I squeeze my eyes shut. I can barely think, let alone explain myself. Where is the Dark?

All I see is light. Yet I know it's there. It's hiding. Lurking. Waiting for 8:45pm.

I don't wear a watch because I can't.

The mere sight of my wristwatch anywhere near 8:45 would make me fold into myself like an origami hedgehog.

Twice a day.

Twice a fucking day.

I began avoiding clocks, time, numbers in general. Lucky for me, you don't have to be a fucking physicist to get someone into bed. If you don't have money, you never have to do any calculations in your head.

You can't divide zero by zero. At least, that's what I've been told.

His hand is by his buckle.

I'll be deaf if I put my fingers in my ears. But I can't, because I've gone lame.

I whimper, but only because I know I'll be forced to listen to the sound of metal against metal. The whisk of leather against fabric. That penultimate clatter of a metal tongue against wood.

"Trust me, Clover."

And then what? Obey?

According to my body, yes.

Most fucking unfortunately.

My captor has complete control over my body. I don't have a choice but to obey his command. I know his next command will be for me to spread my legs.

It always is.

He's slimmer than I remember.

But I'm fucked in the head, so maybe he's not.

He kneels on the bed. He's still wearing his underwear, but I can see his penis right through the fabric. It's not like it's a chastity belt.

He's not the Dark, but he might as well be.

If I wanted to say no, I couldn't.

If I wanted to move away, I couldn't.

Whatever he fed me has turned me into a vegetable.

Except…

He steps over me.

His weight dips the mattress. I roll an inch against him with no choice in the matter.

A hot arm, warm fingers, slides over my waist and draws me near.

He's the sun.

His touch burns me, sets me alight, wakens me like grass after a forest fire.

If I could have gasped, I would. Instead, I huddle against him.

There's a slab of heated flesh against my back. He's a magnet and I'm iron. When he exhales, so do I.

We're one.

But I'm my own.

He's stolen nothing from me, and for that, I'm grateful as fuck.

Nothing yet, anyway.

CHAPTER FIFTY-EIGHT
HUNTER

Instead of warming her body, she's turning mine to ice. I shiver violently and press tighter against her.

There's a fire.

This cabin is sheltered from the cold, but I'm losing her.

Not only that—she's taking me with her into frozen purgatory.

I deserve nothing less. I know that on an intrinsic level. But I can't help her if we're both in hell. One of us has to live to pull the other through.

I cling tighter to her frozen body. She's shivering. I have to take that as a good sign. An excellent sign, in fact. I can feel the air warming around us as the fire takes root in the logs.

How could I have been so wrong?

I'd calculated every variable I could think of, and still I'd never anticipated this resolution.

Me, naked. Her, naked.

I'm her guide, yet I feel compelled to take advantage of her weakness.

I'm nothing but a predator, like the person—or persons—who broke her all those years ago.

Or I'm not human at all. Neither is she.

At heart, we're all still animals.

We take advantage of the weak.

We prey on the innocent and we sure as shit don't ever make amends for our transgressions.

Clover shifts against me, and I harden. An animal response, no doubt, but that only brings my attention to the fact that despite my degree, despite the honorific of doctor I insist on, I'm nothing but a primate.

She was never my patient, was she?

She was always my prey.

I'd watched her grow fat and complacent in the environment I myself captured her in, so fucking eager for the day she'd break free for the chase.

I have her in my clutches.

Weak.

Vulnerable.

Exposed.

I can do anything I want with her.

Just like Father thought he could do anything with me because I was his son.

He'd made me. He owned me.

Anything.

Fucking *anything*.

CHAPTER FIFTY-NINE
CLOVER

Before, I was trapped in a storm. But that storm stranded me on an island of serenity. The feeling is familiar, yet strange.

My fingers are tingling. My toes, too.

Every inch of me is coming back to life, and it's because of the man pressed to my back.

I'm warm. Safe. But as warm and safe as the defendant in a courtroom.

I have rights, but they're muddy.

There are boundaries, but they're as flimsy as tissue paper.

What I fear the most is yards away from me, and yet I'm supposed to feel safe.

Arms tighten around my chest. They drive those dark thoughts from me. I can hardly breathe, but I don't want air.

I want forgiveness.

I want respite.

My heart starts pounding as it always does this time of night.

It must be close to nine.

Dreadful anticipation overwhelms me although I'm already in the Dark's arms tonight.

But this is different.

Those arms are tight, but safe.

That body warm, but comforting.

I gave no consent, but nothing is being taken.

Instead, all I'm given is heat. Comfort. Safety.

Love.

The fire spills over the grate. By now, I know I'm hallucinating, but that doesn't change anything. Knowing something isn't real, isn't right, doesn't make it change.

Good is good.

Evil is evil.

People wear masks, but that doesn't change who they are underneath.

For the first time in a long time, I let out a sigh of relief. Those hands close tighter around me.

I read once that a boa constrictor does that. It contracts its muscles every time its prey releases a breath. Eventually, the lung capacity of its victim isn't enough to keep the animal alive.

It suffocates with a hug.

That's not what this is.

Hunter's grasp is fierce but not fatal.

I shift a little.

Fuck, I can move!

I'd been trapped in dead flesh. In a doomed body. My mind held captive by someone who'd decided there was no reason to keep fighting.

But now?

I furiously wriggle fingers and toes.

"Better?" The voice comes from behind, and I stiffen at the sound.

I manage a nod, and somehow Hunter feels it, wrapped in his arms as I am.

"You will start warming up."

His voice conveys absolute authority. He's lived this, hasn't he? But that makes sense—a fuck load of it.

This was all too precise. Too carefully planned.

My teeth chatter hard against each other as I reluctantly release the hold on my jaw.

"Did you?"

He tenses against me, and the sensation is both obscene and comforting. I never realized how hard his muscles were. How lithe he was. In comparison, I feel bloated.

"Eventually," he says, his lips right against my ear. "It took a long time, though."

"How long?"

Now that I can speak again, I don't feel inclined to stop. I don't care that he's the trickster to blame for all of this. All I care about is that I'm no longer alone, and not just here in this forest.

Was this what I felt when I brushed his hand in that limo? That, despite our education, our upbringing, our genders, or social status, that we shared something.

We were nothing alike, and yet, we were twins at heart.

He understands me and, now, I understand him.

"An hour." His voice drops. "I'm not sure."

The question that's been on top of my mind for the past few hours surfaces. "What did you give me?"

It's like the question sets Hunter on fire. He grips me so tight I can't breathe, and presses his lips to my earlobe. Every word sends a shudder through me, but he doesn't seem to notice his effect on me.

He commanded me to trust him and I did, because that's what I do.

But this is different.

I want him to command me. I want him to take away the pain. I know he can.

Because if *he* can't, what the fuck's the point of living?

"Did you love your mother?" Hunter murmurs in my ear.

The question sends shards of painful memories spearing into my mind.

My mom, kissing a scrape on my elbow.

The smell of snickerdoodles filling the kitchen on a miserably rainy day.

Her hand around mine as she led me from the principal's office.

Somehow, I always knew I'd be okay. She'd be angry, but she'd still love me.

When she died, I never felt that again. That overwhelming, unprejudiced love.

Which is less than I deserve. After all, I was the reason she died.

A sob wracks my body. Hunter's grip around my waist tightens, but his warmth buffets me.

I *killed* her.

She made assumptions about me that didn't sit well, and instead of talking to her, instead of letting her explain herself...

I told her I hated her. I told her I wished she was dead.

And then I ran away.

Leaving her to die a slow, painful death alone.

For months, Gail let me stay with her. Her own family was defunct —busy lives and even busier minds. Gail had money. She had contacts.

We'd both lose ourselves to heroin's dark, charismatic embrace. And, often, we'd wake up without knowledge of the past twenty-four hours.

I can't count how many times I visited the clinic. Methadone, HIV tests.

I was a fucking regular, and I didn't care.

Because I thought my mom didn't. If she had why would she have told me I dress like a slut? After all, she made it clear that the only way to gain a man's attention was to display whatever pathetic assets you had. Tits, legs, cunt: in that order.

I had all three, and I used them to my advantage from the age of thirteen.

After all, isn't this what men wanted?

Eventually, reluctantly, I'm drawn back to Hunter's question.

Did you love her?

"I never stopped," I spit out.

I grab his wrists, digging my nails into his flesh. "But she did."

"Before she died of cancer?"

The world swims until I blink. Cool tears track the curves of my cheeks.

"She gave me to him like a piece of china."

"Who?"

My breath catches.

Who?

Him.

I will not summon Satan to my bedside by calling his name. Because although Lucifer and I go *way* back, it's not in a good way.

"Doesn't matter. He's dead now."

"How?"

"How?" The word ratchets from my mouth like a missile. "Heart attack."

"Natural?"

"Aren't they all?"

"Deserved?"

"Obviously."

A memory flails like a dying animal in my mind. Hunter's voice. Insidiously probing at the heart of the rotten tooth.

What happened when you were sixteen?

Stuff that would turn your expensive hairdo gray, Doctor most-eligible-bachelor-three-years-running. In fact, forget the fact that I was *ever* sixteen.

I have.

"Then I'm glad." The statement is a seductive murmur in my ear, but I'm not having any of it.

I draw pinpricks of blood from his wrist. Blood that reeks in this intimate, confined space.

"You're just glad we're the same. You're glad you can cure me. That's *all* you're glad about. You don't care about me. You don't give a fuck about Clover Vos."

He tightens his grip around me with each subsequent sentence until I can't speak because I can't breathe anymore.

"You're wrong," he growls in my ear. "I want to help you, Clover. I want to—"

"And what about the other nineteen people in my program? I don't see them here."

His body grows even tighter against me.

"They're not you."

CHAPTER SIXTY
HUNTER

The fire pops. My eyelids squeeze shut on instinct.

In my mind, a wolf falls.

The other nineteen don't matter.

I didn't choose them.

I chose you, Clover Vos.

I chose *you*.

So don't you dare disappoint me.

Don't dare presume this choice was anything but in the interest of science.

Then again, I handled this wrong.

I'm trying to approach her awakening like a scientist when I know better. She needs *a guide,* someone who will show her the way.

Which means releasing her. Which means abandoning her to the ice invading her bones. But just for a moment.

I untangle myself. Climb off the bed.

I feel the need to explain myself. But when I turn to her, she has her head burrowed in a pillow, still nothing but a ball of shivers.

That man—the brute that saved me—he knew nothing about Ayahuasca. I don't think he knew anything about life. Survival was the only thing that mattered to him.

Yet...

When I was with him that night, he stuffed a crudely carved wooden pipe into my mouth filled with the worst ditch weed I've ever smoked. When I couldn't smoke it, he blew it over me, as if we were both partaking in some kind of ritual. It wasn't enough to get me stoned, but the trip changed. It was red before it became green.

When he changed the tune he was humming.

My trip escalated.

He was my guide, whether he knew it or not.

During an Ayahuasca ceremony, shamans blow smoke over their participants. It's used to calm them, to send them deeper into the trip, to unblock them.

The brute did all those things that night.

If I plan to be Clover's shaman tonight, I must perform my duties to the highest standards attainable by mortal man.

Else I would be the only person to blame if this trial doesn't succeed.

I hunt around in my backpack until I find the pouch I'm looking for. It takes me less than a minute to roll a joint. I climb in behind Clover's quaking body, recoiling before I can force my own warm flesh to touch her.

She's carved of ice.

My ice queen.

I press the thought away and light the joint. I hand it to her, but she doesn't take it.

I shake her shoulder.

Nothing.

She's unconscious again.

Shit.

I take a big hit and blow the smoke over her naked back. It puffs between us, obscuring her as if to retain some modicum of decency.

Another hit, more smoke. This exhalation piles over her shoulder like fog over a mountain.

A last hit. This one covers her face, and she coughs so violently that her back arches against my chest.

I extinguish the joint in the candle holder and slide my arms around her, willing her flesh to respond to my warmth.

Instead, my flesh responds to hers.

I should pull away. I should—

She needs my warmth.

She's partially unconscious, anyway. It's not as if she'd know that—

Clover's breath catches in her throat. She fumbles, and I'm convinced she'll begin struggling again. Instead, she finds my arms and clings to me as if I'm the only thing between her and a precipitous drop.

Maybe I am.

I had my share of hair-raising scares when I was on Ayahuasca. The brute got me through them all with his calm presence and—

The humming.

That repetitive, wordless tune.

I put my mouth to Clover's ear and start to hum. I try to ignore how my body is responding to hers. The urge I have to be inside her.

To fill her.

To claim her as my own.

But I don't deserve her. I tricked her, and that alone entitles me to no more than a slap in the face.

Instead of pushing me away, she drags me closer. So I squeeze her tight, and hum harder, until she relaxes against me with a sigh I feel through her entire body.

For the first time today, I'm convinced she'll live through this.

Hell, she might even come out of this cured of her addiction.

But right now, I'd just be happy if she makes it out alive.

CHAPTER SIXTY-ONE
CLOVER

I never thought of my mind as something separate to me. I *was* my mind, my mind *contained* me. But now I know different. My mind is a separate entity. It controls me. Regulates me. Defines me.

Like a good parent, it never wants to expose me to the bad, and it will always encourage the good.

I was never afraid of the dark. But there was no other way for my mind to communicate caution to me.

It would go dark before he came into my room.

Because he would turn off the power.

It didn't matter that my lights were on. My night light made no difference. If he ever found candles in my room, he'd take them away.

He liked the dark.

Darkness hides sin. Shadows breed evil.

My mind simply figured that, if I stayed away from the dark, if I avoided all the shadows then I would never be exposed to sin or evil ever again.

But evil doesn't wait till night. It breeds during the day, overflows at twilight, and takes control at dark.

To fight it means twenty-four hours of vigilance.

My mind's also been keeping things from me, just like any good parent would. The bad, the ugly, the downright evil. Better not to ruin a child's innocence than have it exposed to the real world.

For six years, I've been terrified of the dark when, in fact, I should have been terrified of my uncle.

But he's dead now, so what's there to be scared of? Of course, he isn't the only evil man in the entire world. There are others. Some far, some near.

A life lived in fear is not a life. It's survival.

I can't go around thinking my safety is at stake every second of every midnight hour.

No one can live like that.

Which is why I haven't been living. I've been surviving.

That has to change.

Uncle is dead.

My life began when I was born, and I should never have stopped living it.

In the swarming darkness behind my eyes, this is all so clear I feel like laughing.

I *am* laughing.

Crying.

It all makes sense now.

The drugs. The meaningless sex.

I was stuck in survival mode, even after the monster had been slain.

The nightmare I was trapped in ended at seventeen, but I've been trapped in that shadow world for the past six years.

If it hadn't been for this moment of enlightenment. The brew Hunter commanded me to drink.

Hunter.

If it hadn't been for him, I'd still be trapped.

A powerless child.

An abused teen.

A good-for-nothing slut.

CHAPTER SIXTY-TWO
HUNTER

Eight Years Ago

I have no recollection of falling asleep but when I wake, it's to an invasive beam of sunlight scoring my eyelids. I lie there for a few moments, desperately attempting to gather my thoughts.

There are too many.

Too tangled.

Obscure.

To say the left side of my brain got me this far is an understatement. None of my finger paintings are stored in Hill Manor's attic... because I never made any.

Words, numbers, and the physics of the world were the only things that mattered to me early in life. Art was for people that couldn't cope with reality. Not only could I cope, I planned to strip it bare.

Back then, computers had only just become *a thing*. But in Mallhaven, everything arrives ten years later than the rest of the world. I never had a chance to join the programming revolution.

I could have owned Silicon Valley.

Instead, I'm its slave.

What happened last night was inexplicable, in the sense that no one can explain a Rembrandt to someone blind from birth. There would be no shared vocabulary.

We rely on memory to explain the present. If there are no memories, then we are children to the new.

I felt born again that morning. Not in any religious sense, but as if I'd never thought about color and now had a rainbow to consider. My world, my life, my *existence* no longer made sense.

The brute fed me a rabbit for breakfast. It was stringy, dry, but so extraordinary that I asked for more.

I left just before noon. It was a long walk home, and I only managed to find it by keeping the tallest peak of the Devil's Backbone in my sights as I moved through the forest.

I arrived at Hill Manor at a quarter to ten at night. The Hill Manor slept, but Cervil let me in the back like he always did, with a respectful nod and a quiet, "Can I get you anything, Sah?"

The answer was always no. But that night, I asked him to bring me something to eat, some hot tea, and anything sweet the kitchen had to offer.

I spent every hour until dawn chronicling my experiences in a leather-bound journal as I shoved food down my gullet with the relish of a man stranded the past ten years on a remote island.

Father was gone the next day, and I'd evaded him.

I should have been ecstatic about that. Instead, I was furious.

I had plans to confront him that Monday morning, but instead he'd taken ill on Saturday night. His GP admitted him to Fool's Gold Hospital, an hour's drive from Mallhaven proper.

On the Wednesday of that same week, I visited him.

Strangely, he didn't seem surprised by my presence.

He tapped the side of his bed as if expecting me to take a seat beside him.

I stood instead.

I watched.

I began to laugh. "Do you think you've broken me?"

I will never forget the expression on his face. The confusion. The shock.

Then came the shame.

"You just made me stronger, Father."

I said nothing more to him that day, but I returned once a week to visit him. Every time, I would bring him a soda. He, just like the nurses and the doctors and the hospital staff, assumed it came from the vending machine downstairs.

It didn't.

No one, not even my cantankerous father, noticed the tiny hole in the bottle cap.

All he said was, "It's flat."

"My apologies, Father." Was my simple response.

From then on, I cultivated his madness from the evil spores infesting his mind. They invaded his brain and leeched every trace of sanity that remained.

Just before dementia claimed him, he signed the entirety of his wealth over to me.

The shareholdings of his companies.

I became his power of attorney.

When his psyche finally cracked like thin glass, I became the Hill legacy.

Not Mother.

Not Holly.

Me.

I'm damn sure I'll do good with it. I used every red cent of his fortune to build the Hill Institute, knowing I would mentor patients that had to suffer trauma in their pasts.

Abuse at the hands of their fathers. Their mothers. Their relatives. People in authority, and people that had once sworn to love them.

The Hill Institute became a sanctuary.

I, their guardian.

I didn't—I will *never*—take that responsibility lightly.

SHE'S NOT SHAKING ANYMORE.

Her skin is warm against mine.

We sweat against each other in this tiny cabin. The air is warm, stifling even. At the same time, comforting.

Because, when it's this cold outside, warmth equates survival. Comfort.

I smoked too much.

Which means I'm not thinking.

An intellectual draws conjectures and sifts through data.

Instead, I can't stop smelling her. She smells of the forest.

She *is* the forest. A wayward nymph. A lost soul.

But she's stopped shaking. I was supposed to remain neutral. I'm her doctor, she my patient.

Yet I feel compelled to speak to her, and I can only blame the THC flooding my veins.

I stroke her shoulder, thrilling in the touch of her skin.

"Tell me you're okay." My voice sounds strange; leaden yet echoing.

"I'm okay," comes her weak response. "I think."

"Are you warming up?"

"Yes." A pause. "I think."

"Stop thinking!" I hear the harsh cadence of my words and try to soften my tone. "*Feel.* Do you *feel* warm?"

She takes minutes, hours, *decades* to respond. "Yes. But only because you're warm."

I didn't expect that caveat. What am I to make of it? I understand my body heat might be singularly responsible for keeping her alive but I also sense her words are deeper than what they appear on surface value.

I'm holding her as tight as I can, but I hold her tighter. She's not petite—in fact, she meets me eye to eye in a pair of heels—but in that moment she's a baby bird and I'm a fox.

And this fox wants to crush her bones if only so no other fox could ever experience this moment.

Sweat trickles down her back, sliding between our bodies as if it has some right to be there.

Maybe it does.

It's hot in here.

My thoughts are plagued with the sounds she made the other night. But they had to be fake. She's a seductress. A prostitute—her fee? Safety, comfort, a bed for the night. She'd sell herself to anyone in the right income bracket, which makes me a prime target, and I don't care.

She didn't even know I existed before two nights ago, but I've known her for months. She fascinates me.

Intrigues me.

I want to know everything about her. I want her to know everything about me. The good, the bad, the downright evil.

Don't judge. We all have evil inside us.

It's whether we act on it that will be the deciding factor. Don't think for a moment I believe in heaven and hell. I don't. But I believe in comfort and discomfort. Moral, immoral.

We are no longer animals, but that differentiation insists on us ensuring that, unlike animals, we know when something is right or wrong. Admittedly, those values may never be tested in our lives.

But *we* will.

Repeatedly.

The small things. The life-changing things.

It will *always* be our choice. Even if our minds are diseased...those choices were bred of a diseased mind.

Like mine.

But no more.

Like Clover's.

But soon, no more.

My lips are pressed to the damp skin of her shoulder, and I have no recollection of putting them there. The fire cracks and pops less than two yards away. Its heat strokes me with a physical touch.

She's sweating against me, but still I feel her pressing into me. Against me.

I tighten my grip even more.

"Don't let me go." The words burst out of her mouth like I pushed them out.

"I won't." My promise is ferocious.

"Don't." As if she doesn't believe me.

Can she *ever* trust again?

"You remember, don't you?"

She remains silent. Did I overstep?

I'm glad I smoked that joint. If I hadn't, I'd have been the insensitive, narcissistic Hunter Hill I've forced myself to be all this time, instead of *this* person. A person who's been through this exact same thing—in more ways than one.

Sympatico.

"Let it go."

She resists, not only in the harsh string of words she spits at me, but in her body language. There's suddenly an inch of hot, damp air between us, and she shrugs her shoulders so hard that I'm no longer touching her.

"Never. Why? Fucking asshole. Motherfucker!"

"Then let it out."

She quivers hard. Draws into a ball.

And then she shoves back her head and yells, "Who gave you the right?"

Her voice is raw, her body shaking as she yells out that curse.

I squeeze my eyes shut if only so I won't break down in tears. "No one gave them the right, Clover."

I don't know if she's heard me. If she *can* hear me.

"You are *not* God!" Another violent accusation. Her body jerks as if she's stabbing out her arm. "I didn't deserve that!"

"No one does. No one ever."

My mind sweeps back to the only gospel song I've ever seen performed. It wasn't live, but on YouTube. The male singer up front, a harem of modestly clad, African American women as his choir. He would wave a hand as he sang, and they would echo his every word in a sonorous chorus that made my hair stand on end.

"You never owned me!" Clover yells.

Hallelujah! I chant in my mind, eyes shut and my forehead pressed to the skin between her shoulder blades.

"You can't control me anymore."

Praise the Lord!

"And I'm done being scared of you."

A-fucking-men.

She shakes as she sobs.

"I didn't deserve this," comes her mumbled words.

The choir goes silent, but I feel compelled to grip her tight again, making sure there's not a molecule of space between us.

For the longest time, the only movement in our little cabin is the crackle and pop of the fire on the hearth.

The rise and fall of our chests.

In.

Out.

Breath matched in some furious symphony.

Slower.

Slower.

I'm dipping in and out of consciousness. It's been a long day and weed's always had a sedatory effect on me.

Not yet.

We've still a few miles to go.

It takes longer than I'd thought possible before I bring myself to ask the question. Strangely, I don't want to move forward. I'm content to remain right here.

In this cabin.

During this storm.

Tonight.

But what good would a guide be if I didn't lead Clover out of the forest?

"Are you ready?" I ask.

"Yes."

But she doesn't sound it. Not even a little.

"Are you *ready*, Clover?"

She opens her eyes, and twists to face me a little. I can read the answer from the light dancing in her eyes.

I grab Clover's jaw and wrench her face toward mine. Our lips find each other and latch on; desperate, eager, forlorn.

There's a moment's resistance, but it's fleeting.

Her resistance to me has always been fleeting.

CHAPTER SIXTY-THREE
CLOVER

Fury explodes inside me like a nuclear bomb. It flattens everything—my mind, my emotions...*me*. I'm yelling, but I don't understand the words. They're in some foreign language I've never been taught.

Now there's nothing left but a wasteland and the flickering, uncertain silhouette of a single man.

Hunter.

He walks this wasteland with me. No, since before I even arrived. He knows the way. He can guide me.

A heat haze warps the world, but when he's in front of me I've never been as sure as I am right now.

He beckons me, hands reaching for mine.

"Are you ready?"

The world pitches and yaws around us. Nothing feels substantial enough to support us, but it does. The world is cotton candy, and I'm a dandelion. No matter where I drift, I will never fall through.

Not if I have Hunter by my side.

"Yes." It's a lie, of course. I don't know if I'll ever be ready. But I know I don't want to live a lie anymore. If he can show me the way, if he can guide me toward a life that doesn't consist of an eternal struggle against an unknown enemy...then I would lay down my shield for him. I'd surrender and throw myself on his mercy.

"Are you ready, Clover?"

I don't need to answer him this time. Instead, I close the distance between us, grab his head, and pull him in for a kiss.

An invisible force rips away the wasteland like torn newspaper. I struggle to the surface of my mind and open my eyes.

Hunter.

A warm glow bathes his face. His eyes reflect shards of fire, his lips flickering from a straight line to a faint smile as firelight plays over his face.

I gasp, having just woken from a nightmare six years in the making.

Stagnant memories flood my brain like a burst dam.

I grip Hunter's body as I reel from the weight of those emotions I've kept bottled up.

But, despite his strength, I'm crumbling. My body can't hold this weight—my fragile mind doesn't stand a chance.

"The past is in the past," a disembodied voice informs me.

Fuck you.

"You're here, now. The present is all that matters."

You fucking *asshole.*

"Clover. Clover, look at me."

A shake rattles my teeth together. I force open my eyelids, and my view is filled with Hunter's intense forest-bark stare. "Can you see me?"

I laugh.

Of course I can. What, is he on drugs?

No. *I* am.

Fuck.

"Bring yourself here. Every shred, every molecule. Here. Now." His eyes dart between mine, his gaze so intense that I want to close my eyes to stop his pervasive intrusion into my soul.

"I'm here," I mumble through reluctant lips.

"Again."

"I'm *fucking* here, all right?"

Hunter tightens his grip around me, and I burrow into him as if I could dig a hole that will keep me hidden forever.

I wasn't ready for this.

Could I ever have been? Not for this.

I knew it would be bad. That part of my mind had been shoved into a dark corner, but I knew it was there and sometimes I would want to peek inside.

I would shoot up instead because the constant threat of an overdose was easier to handle than unearthing the secrets I'd hidden from myself.

"You are." Hunter's voice seduces me into opening my eyes again. The world is still unsteady. His face is a moving picture—stern one moment, caring the next. "You *are* here."

But not always. I went somewhere else. That dark nest of festering rage, shame, and guilt that skulked in the back of my mind is gone.

Instead, I have a whole new slew of memories. As if I can't stop picking at the scab on my brain, I start going through them one by one.

Like a projector flickering against the wall of my mind.

First slide: my mother's drawn face days before she died.

I squeeze my quivering lips together, but I can't keep anything bottled up anymore. Hunter touches my face, and as if that was a trigger, all my dirty secrets come tumbling out.

CHAPTER SIXTY-FOUR
HUNTER

A tear flashes down Clover's face, heading for her matted red hair. I brush it away with my thumb. Her eyes flutter. She presses into me, her hand finding mine and squeezing it painfully hard.

"I killed her." The pronouncement emerges via an unsteady whisper.

And, instead of a patient priest, I begin arguing. Because I know you Clover. I know you better than you know yourself.

"You're lying," I whisper back furiously.

Cancer killed her mother—Clover had no part in it.

"I wanted her dead."

"You were a kid."

"So why did I pay for it, then?" Her eyes drill into mine, demanding answers she will not accept.

"This was never your fault. None of it. You did—"

"He was my punishment. The dark—" She cuts off, her body shuddering against mine. "Because I killed her."

"That's not how it works." I put as much authority in my voice as I can, but Clover is still not convinced. Perhaps she never will be.

Unlocking the past is only the first step.

Next, you have to accept it.

It can take minutes, weeks. A lifetime.

And don't get me started on forgiveness. I'm not an advocate.

I cup her face with one hand while she squeezes relentlessly at the other. "It's time to start looking ahead."

As if just the thought makes her uncomfortable, she squirms against me.

I'm suddenly all too aware that the only thing between us is sweaty skin. I'd kept my boxers on, but for some reason I feel compelled to take them off.

But I can't, because she still has my hand trapped in hers.

"I fucked up everything," comes her pitiful moan. "I fucked up my life."

"You're not on your death bed, Clover. You still have your whole life ahead of you."

"But I could've—"

"This is the path you chose to walk. Now you have to choose which direction you go. Backward...or forward."

Her eyes find mine again, sparkling with desperation. "I don't know how."

"Then let me show you."

"Will you?" Hope floods her face, parting her lips and smoothing the deep crease between her brows.

She bucks her hips, grinding her pelvis into me. I harden, and fervently try to stop the memory of how she sounded under me from flooding my brain.

This isn't right. Ayahuasca is never to be misused. What Clover's feeling right now isn't arousal—it's relief. Perhaps, a zest for life that flickered out the same day her abuser first touched her. Now that it's returned, now that she remembers what it feels like.

It was the same for me. I—

"You don't believe in karma," Clover says, eviscerating the thought from my mind. "But do you believe in fate?"

I'm about to say 'no' but the word dries on my tongue before I can get it out.

I don't.

I *didn't*.

I'm a scientist. There is no mathematical formula to explain something as ethereal as fate, or destiny. Pheromones, on the other hand, are triggering chemical responses in our brain. With her so close to me, in this hot, sweaty nest of ours, my body acts on its instinct to procreate with a fertile woman. Once safety is met, a person moves to the next step in the triangle of needs.

Sex.

We're safe.

That's all.

For Clover, she's safer than she's been since the age of sixteen.

Pheromones triggering chemicals.

That's all this is.

Except...

I'm not a mathematician, so I wouldn't be able to calculate the odds of one Clover Vos arriving at the Hill Institute. I'm certain they're staggering.

That's before another variable comes into play. Her particular addiction—heroin. It could have been alcohol, or cocaine, or anti-depressants.

But it was heroin.

That fact alone brought her to my attention.

And, so, the odds grow exponentially.

Her case could have been like the hundreds of others passing through my facility.

It wasn't.

In some inexplicable way, the moment I touched her file, I was aware of how important it was for me to read it. I took it home and studied it there to ensure there would be no interruptions as I processed her for the potential to become my first patient in this radical treatment program.

At that point, I'd never met her. There were no pheromones in play. Not back then.

Only pure conjecture. Logic. Reason.

Yet all of that led to *this*.

The two of us alone in this lean-to, naked bodies twined together like mating serpents.

So no. I don't believe in fate or destiny, soul mates or horoscopes.

But I do believe that, sometimes, things happen for a reason. The evidence is in the way people's lives will coalesce. To an outsider, the events that brought them together seem random. But to a theoretical scientist, the fact that there's nothing there is the singular proof that dark matter exists.

Sometimes, even a scientist has to have a little faith.

CHAPTER SIXTY-FIVE
CLOVER

I've never felt this exposed, this vulnerable before. My skull is split open, and anyone with a pair of tweezers can come pick through my gray matter. The worst part is, I can't close it up again. My thoughts, my emotions, my memories; they're nothing but rice grains spilling on the floor. The more I try to scoop them back, the more they escape through my fingers.

I'm literally losing my mind.

I'm hot, but feel frozen inside.

Stifled, but lonelier than ever.

"Hunter…" I whisper.

He couldn't have heard me, and I don't have the strength to—

"I'm here."

With my eyes squeezed closed, his voice blooms neon yellow flowers in my mind. They fade a moment later, leaving me in the dark.

"Don't stop talking," comes my fervent plea. Nothing more than a whisper, but he hears me.

For some reason, he complies.

"This is wrong."

"No. It's not."

"We can't…You're warm now. I should…" But his voice trails away in the wake of a golden meadow.

"Don't let go." I twist my hand in his hair—the only thing I can think to grab—and put my forehead against his.

He's right—I *am* warm.

I'm so warm that I'm sweating. My fingers and toes have stopped prickling, and feeling is coming back to my arms and legs.

But if he lets go of me, I'll never stop falling. His body is the only thing anchoring me to this dimension. Without him, I'll drift into oblivion.

"Okay." He sounds reluctant. "But just for a little while."

"Forever."

"Clover." He makes an angry sound, and I'm finally able to open my eyes. His face is a blur until he draws back enough for me to focus on him. From his expression, I know what he's about to say isn't going to be pleasant, but then his gaze softens. He searches my face as if he's never seen me before.

"I need you, Hunter."

"You don't need anyone."

"I'll be lost without you."

"You never needed me. You just had to trust yourself."

"And you."

Hunter ducks his head a little. "And me."

In that moment, I have never seen anyone as humble or as proud.

He got me to open up when I was not only a closed book, but one of those old-school grimoires with like locks on it and shit. Chains, to make sure it didn't escape the library.

But, at the same time, all it took was him opening up to me.

I've misunderstood my attraction—my *fascination*—with this man.

Wealthy.

Available.

Powerful.

I only ever needed two out of the three to commit to seducing a man to lend me his bed for the night. Sometimes, I'd get away with a week or two. It all depended on how busy they were, how idealistic their minds.

Idealists, you see, believe that inside every hooker lies a heart of gold. That, sometimes, the philanthropic endeavors of billionaires are not just for show. That, someday the need to help mankind, the whales, the rain forest—whatever fucking ecological or humanitarian disaster was pending—would overwhelm their greed.

I aided in those fantasies. Charity, with benefits. Let Clover stay in your penthouse suite for a week, feed her, buy her some drugs. She'd fuck you every night until your Viagra ran out, and then she'd even let you spoon her.

But not Hunter.

I had no intention of staying at his place. Fucking him, yes. That I won't deny. But he was never a conquest. I merely wanted to unravel him.

Except, he's not the kind of man to come undone after one night in the sack.

I slide my leg between his. It's so easy because we're both lubricated with sweat. It might have been entirely unintentional—which I doubt—but he'd turned this ramshackle cabin into a veritable sweat lodge. With the fire blazing in one corner and the only source of ventilation being the chimney. To say it's hot in here is an understatement.

Firelight paints every surface not hidden in shadow. In the orange light, Hunter's brown eyes take on a demonic cast.

I slide my hands over his hips and tug at the hem of his boxers.

His eyes are so intent on me that it's as if he's reading my every thought.

If that's the case, then he knows what I want. Is he going to chicken out, or is he going to transform into that delicious beast that took what he wanted without any expectation of consent?

Because I won't settle for anything less.

It's his prize, my punishment.

My punishment, because I didn't trust him, and I should have.

His prize because he saved me when he could have given up.

I don't know of anyone who's ever stuck around long enough not to give up, and if he's the first, then he'll be the last. If Hunter wants me, then I'm his and he can do whatever he wants to me.

CHAPTER SIXTY-SIX
HUNTER

This isn't what I wanted.

Let me rephrase—this is *exactly* what I wanted, but not now. Her therapy is proving to be a success—but to be certain, I will need to run a psychological profile on her. I can't do that in this goddamn cabin.

I also can't give her what she wants.

She's fixated on me, and it's no surprise. I opened the door to a hidden part of her mind, and for that she's grateful. Even if she weren't the Clover Vos that slept with wealthy men for the brief respite they offered her, I would never have let her repay the favor like this.

Except...

Maybe it's the weed.

Maybe it's the memories twining over my mind. How helpless, how abandoned, how fucking needy I felt when I went through this exact same episode eight years ago.

She wants—needs—comfort on every level. Emotional, psychological, physical.

This cabin should have provided the physical, but perhaps it fell short. Understandably, to a city girl, a cabin in the woods could never compensate for the penthouse of one of New York's finest hotels.

Bears, bugs, birds that wake at dawn.

She wants more, and I feel compelled to provide her with everything she wants.

Why?

Because I'm only fucking human.

I'm forever throwing myself into my work. When I need release, it's more convenient to take a ten-minute shower. I've never been in a relationship.

Nothing personal.

I'm a busy man.

I've never spent a minute considering who should be my perfect partner in life.

Yet now, in this moment, I do.

I don't even know what my requirements are, but Clover checks every single one of them.

This could be lust, but I'm immune to that.

This could be love, but I don't believe in that crap.

So I'll write this up as some highly explosive mix of pheromones. Obviously, my DNA wants to fuck the shit out of hers, and I'm powerless to stop it.

Perhaps our children will be on the spectrum. Intellectuals to such a high extent that they struggle to communicate with lesser humans like their own parents.

If only.

Again, it could be the weed.

Her flame-red hair.

The stormy irises crowded out by those magnificently dilated pupils.

Or perhaps it's this cabin, wrought in its own plethora of sentimental memories.

It was here, after all, where, for the first time, I understood that I was not to blame for what was done to me. After a lifetime of being informed that I was weak, stupid, useless...I realized I wasn't.

A feeling like that isn't easily dismissed.

Clover gasps and I'm drawn to the present with the speed of a bullet train.

My hand is on her bare breast. The other between her legs.

Yet I have no memory of moving.

Just as she probably has no memory of arriving here. Perhaps she will *never* have a memory of this.

I can't.

I *won't*.

But the carnal appetite building inside me takes no heed of my pathetic morals.

I want Clover. I want her now. I don't care how she feels about it. I don't care what state she's in.

Consent is for the meek.

I stopped being a victim a long time ago. I'm used to getting what I want, when I want it. I bend people to my will, sometimes without them knowing.

I guess we all have evil in us.

Some more than others.

CHAPTER SIXTY-SEVEN
CLOVER

Electric fire rips through me, forcing me into this moment.
Hunter's hand is between my legs.

He's watching me. Waiting. Expecting me to protest?

But he doesn't understand—I *want* this. I need release. Surrender.

Doesn't he realize I can only lose control if I no longer have hold of it?

To say I'm a dominatrix might be overkill, but in the past I liked to order my men around. They liked it too, so don't you dare fucking judge. Those CEO's, those Managing Directors, they spent every minute of their lives ordering people around. Their release was having me instruct them. For them to obey *me*.

I didn't use whips or wear stilettos to bed. Nothing as ridiculous as that. But I took what I wanted. Sometimes, I let them take what they needed, but not until I'd been satisfied first.

Now, for the first time, I didn't want to have to think. I didn't want the responsibility of leading this encounter. I wanted Hunter making the decisions. I wanted him to take what he wanted.

He's making me wet and ready for him, his hand between my legs. I lift my knee to give him better access to my cunt, and he immediately slides his fingers inside me.

I might still have been tripping, I don't know. But whatever he gave me already peaked, and now I'm coming down. Not as hard as I would have if this were ecstasy or meth, but the world still isn't quite right.

I let out a low chuckle.

When the fuck was it ever?

"What's so funny?" Hunter demands, his words brushing my mouth.

"What did you give me?"

"Ayahuasca."

I laugh. "What the fuck is that?"

"The Mother plant."

"That's some Freudian shit right there," I say, unable to control my giggles.

Fingers wrap around my jaw, forcing it apart. Hunter's eyes are a darker shade of red-black when I look at him.

"Respect her."

I manage a nod, but I've obviously pissed him off because he thumps his fingers into me as if he wants to tear right through me. I let out a strangled moan and yank his boxers over his hips. He twists as if he wants to get out of my grip, but I follow him and grab hold of his cock before he can get away.

He hisses at me, eyes fluttering closed as I give his dick a hard pump.

"What's going to happen now?" I ask him.

Because there's always a tomorrow.

It's usually better not to talk about it, but I'm baiting him because I know he's holding back on me. I want him furious, and I don't know why.

Because then I know he'll punish me? Am I still hung up on the fact that I *deserve* punishment?

My head whirls, and it's impossible to find anything solid to grab hold of. I mean, what does this all mean?

I was abused. Now I'm some kind of sexual deviant. Is that normal? Is this how I cope? Or is my fetish someone else's vanilla?

Sexuality is such a fucked up subject, I wouldn't even know how to begin a conversation about it.

"What happens now?" He times those parroted words to another violent thrust into my cunt with his fingers. My world tilts as pleasure spreads tendrils through my entire body. "I'm going to fuck you."

Yes, well, *obviously*.

I force my eyes open and stare at him in open challenge. "And then?"

A flicker of confusion, swiftly replaced with defiance. "You want more than that?"

Before I have a chance to a retort, he bucks his hips into mine. The crown of his dick presses against my cunt, and it's only the width of my hand still gripping him that's preventing his cock from burrowing into me.

It's a struggle to keep my eyes open. It's a struggle to fucking breathe. I want him inside me so badly, I'm salivating.

But this is a chess match. We're competing for something, even though I don't know what it is.

Territory?

Power?

He knows so much about me, maybe he knows that I like to be on top. I dominate while my mates submit.

But Hunter will never submit.

He's a traditionalist in the worst way. He fucks his women, they don't fuck him.

Guess what, Doctor Hill? You'll have to fight to win this bitch.

I refuse to let go of his cock. When his hips buck forward in an attempt to penetrate me, no more than his lubricated tip goes inside me.

I'm wearing a victorious smile, and I know he's going to have to perform some fucking Copperfield magic trick to get me to stop, and the fucker does just that.

He kisses me.

His mouth is my undoing.

My mind tears apart like cotton candy under greedy fingers. I can't resist him, not when I want him this badly. Every inch of my body aches for him and the punishment he will bestow upon me.

He wrenches my legs apart, sliding his knee against mine as a stopper. I'm spread open to him. Vulnerable. Exposed.

And, for the first time, it doesn't feel like an invasion.

This is a parlay.

We're trading, him and I.

My body, my mind. It's his.

In return, he won't destroy me.

Because I know he's capable.

I didn't imagine the chase. His eyes on me. The bunny blood.

He's an animal at heart. A beast that hides under sheep's clothing. Or, in this case, a suit that costs more than I can wrap my head around.

He kisses me hard and deep, like he's mining for gold and eager to excavate every ounce he can find. At the same time, he slips his hand around mine and forces me to pump his cock as if I'm a ten-dollar whore he's paying for a hand job.

I might not be a ten-dollar whore, but I'm definitely a thousand-dollar whore.

Luckily, he has enough cash to go around.

I comply merely because I don't have a fucking choice. But as long as he's kissing me, I don't give a fuck about what he's using my body for.

So I jerk him off against my cunt, wishing he'd fuck me instead but enjoying the fact that—for the moment—I won't allow it.

He slides on top of me, and the chenille throw that probably cost more than a second-hand car ends up on the floor. We're both naked now, gleaming orange in the cabin's voracious firelight, while, outside, a storm rages. But this cabin doesn't leak, and the only howl is the wind in utter despair at the fact that it can't work its way inside.

Because he made sure the cabin was clean. Warm. Safe.

The bed is a firm, orthopedic mattress decked in linens that must be Egyptian cotton, because I have a feeling that's how Dr. Hunter Hill rolls.

A rich hippy. I never thought I'd see the day.

The rustic wooden bed frame might have suited the rest of the cabin. But I suspect Hunter never settles for anything less than a reclaimed masterpiece which a very talented craftsman spent several weeks building with his bare hands up in the Colorado mountains somewhere.

I'm sure what makes him happy is knowing that no one else in the world has the same house, the same bed, the same redhead under them.

Hunter pushes between my thighs. He spreads his legs, opening me to him.

Somehow, he got my hands pinned over my head.

Firelight caresses every defined muscle on his chest, stomach, and thighs. His cock stands proud, a demon in its own right and ravenous to boot.

I'm trapped.

Whatever hedonistic thinking drove me to this point of abandonment evaporates.

I don't take orders—I give commands.

But just like the other night, his eyes twinkle with a sudden debaucherous victory.

"When a girl screams in the woods and there's no one to hear," he croons, putting his mouth by my ear as the tip of his cock brushes my cunt, "does she actually make a sound?"

CHAPTER SIXTY-EIGHT
HUNTER

The analytical half of my brain acknowledges the fact that Clover Vos is crucial to my research and, on those grounds, I can't yet release her back into the wild.

The other half of my brain, the one operating my cock, knows I want to fuck her so bad I can taste it.

I think it's the first time they've ever agreed on something.

The woman I thought a wretched creature of excess lies beneath me, her lithe body twisting in some pathetic excuse for struggle. The orange light paints her pale skin a fantastic hue. I studied color therapy—it's one of the programs I put patients through during their treatment—so I know orange promotes appetite. That's why so many fast-food joints have either red or orange in their branding, their shops, their wrappers.

I could eat this girl whole.

The weed plays a part. I limit my intake purely because I can empty my entire refrigerator after a joint.

Clover's struggles are tiring my arms. It's as if she hasn't been on the run for the past forty-eight hours. Where does she get the energy?

"Enough." My voice sounds strangely solemn in our sacred temple. Outside, the wind beats an impotent fist against the door.

It doesn't rattle, of course. When I rebuilt this cabin, I made sure that, despite all outward appearances, it was perfectly designed. No leaks, no drafts, no rattling doors or windows.

I also made sure it looked as close to the original as I could manage.

Call me sentimental, if you wish.

Clover stills under me, but defiance draws a spectacular scowl over her mouth.

"Either you obey me, or you leave."

She scoffs at me, her mouth twisting into a sneer. On cue, a violent gust of wind drives a hard patter of raindrops against the window. And, obviously, she must remember how horrible it was for her out there. The dirt, the mud...

Which she's still covered in.

I reel back from her, not because the filth disgusts me, but because I'd barely noticed. She looks like a wild woman—a female Tarzan—and all I can think to do is fuck her?

I pull Clover up from the bed with the grip I have on her wrists. We're close again, bodies touching in such inappropriate ways that I almost forget all logic and just fuck her anyway.

But I must do this right.

She deserves it.

CHAPTER SIXTY-NINE
CLOVER

Hunter jerks me up.

Our lips are less than an inch away, his breath puffing warm air against mine. At first, I think this is how he wants to do me, but then he moves back, drawing me to my feet.

The floor is unsteady.

No, wait. That's me.

There's a small rug in front of the fire, and he draws me over to it.

"What's going on?"

"I'm doing this right."

I want to smile, but he's wearing such a serious expression I don't dare. I sink to my knees, and he sets my hands on my knees, positioning me.

The fight I had in me leeches out in the wake of whatever the fuck he's up to now.

I can't get an angle on this guy. The minute I think one thing, he does another. It's like he—

"Can you read my mind?" The question's out, somehow without passing through border control first. "Like...you can, can't you?"

He chuckles, but more to himself than in answer to my question.

Suddenly, I'm convinced that's exactly what's going on here.

Nothing else makes sense.

A hot, rich, *psychic* hippy.

...The fuck, right?

He goes into one corner and comes back with a bucket. As he sets it down, the water inside splashes around like it's all happy and shit.

I recoil, but he catches my elbow and keeps me in place. He studies me and then begins to wash my body.

I won't lie—it's the most sensual thing someone's ever done to me. Perhaps because he's so fixated on my skin. As his gaze slides over me, goosebumps break out everywhere. His gentle touch seems such a stark contrast to the night he pinned me to his mattress and claimed me as savagely as a wolf. Now, he caresses me with a damp cloth, ensuring every streak of dirt has been wiped away before moving to a new area.

He doesn't clean between my legs though. When I glance down at the cloth, I'm glad—it's changed color.

To think I was that filthy.

Ugh.

That's what happens when you live off the land for two days.

He lets the cloth fall into the water and takes it back into the corner. As he moves, the shadows swirl around him as if they're made of smoke and not darkness. I sway, pressing my palms to the floor when I almost tip over.

Ayahuasca. That's what he said he gave me, right?

The name's familiar, but I have no idea what the hell it's supposed to do. Is it like shrooms? I've never gotten off on that hippy shit.

Hot, rich, psychic hippy.

I laugh, because I can't *not*.

This whole thing is so fucking ridiculous.

Or is it?

I won't say I feel clear headed but it's as if I've just emptied my attic from a lifetime's worth of hoarded junk, and I never considered myself a hoarder.

I feel light. Calm, despite the fact that I'm out here in the middle

of a forest with a stranger who forced me to drink some hallucino-
genic substance and just finished washing me.

He comes back with a compact toiletry bag and zips it open.

Wet wipes.

I won't say I'm surprised by them, but when I realize what he
wants to do I push myself up to my knees and attempt escape.

He makes a cooing noise. But I'm not a fucking bird that's flapping
around like an idiot after he startled me. I'm a human being. My life
has meaning.

Where did that come from?

He yanks on my wrist, and I go down. When he catches my face in
his hand, I try to twist it away but he follows relentlessly with that
damp wipe, trying to clean my face. When I realize I'm acting like a
snotty toddler who's an hour late for nap time, I burst out laughing.
My spine turns to jelly, and I lean into him as he cleans my face.

He spends time on my lips, and more around my eyes.

The wipe comes back streaked with black and red. Was I still
wearing makeup? Gail wasn't shitting me when she said her stuff was
waterproof.

Make that river proof, forest proof, and rain proof.

He puts the dirty wet wipe in a brown bag. Then he jerks another
from the container, catches my chin between his fingers, and shoves
his hand between my legs.

It happens so fast that I'm still in the process of gasping when he
swipes over me with that cool, damp cloth. I try to move away, but
then his perfectly manicured nails bite into my flesh.

His eyes bore into me, challenging me to maintain eye contact as
he does his worst.

Where he was gentle on my entire body, he's rubbing my cunt so
hard I'm getting wet.

Which is probably what he wants. He's a veritable gentleman until
he touches my most intimate places, then he turns into a fucking
animal.

My eyes start to flutter closed—fuck, I'm clean already—but he wrenches my head forward an inch as if commanding me to pay attention.

He has his boxers on, and I remember him taking them off, but when did he put them back on?

Hunter tosses the wet wipe into the fire, which consumes it with a hungry pop.

"Am I that filthy?" I manage, despite his fierce grip on my jaw.

"Not anymore."

Fury boils my blood. I shove him away from me and scramble to my feet. The room dips and sways, and I reach for the first thing I can find to steady myself.

The bed.

This fucking place is so tiny. A cage.

My cage.

"Let me out."

"In the rain?" Hunter gets slowly to his feet. His hard-on is so fucking blatant, he shouldn't even be bothering with the boxers.

He must have seen my gaze flicker down because he spreads his hands a little and gives me a dark smile. "If you run, I'll just have to clean you again."

My body trembles at the thought, and I squeeze my thighs together as if that would somehow bring my cunt to order.

It doesn't.

The body wants what the body wants, and my body wants his cock.

CHAPTER SEVENTY
HUNTER

C lover watches me with a disgusted sneer on her face. She has every right to feel that; my self-control is non-existent of late.

It could be the cabin. Its memories.

Or the strange poison she's intoxicated me with.

Unless I've reached some point where I can no longer deny my own nature.

That shouldn't have been possible.

I have made so many difficult—impossible—choices to become the person I am now. I gave up friends, lovers, *life*. How could a sacrifice so great not have been enough?

My hands are in fists, and I struggle to force them open.

All I wanted to do was clean her and look how that turned out. I wanted to fuck her the other night and just look how *that* turned out. I wanted to guide her, to show her the light.

Instead, I've dragged her down into hell with me.

This wasn't supposed to happen.

I'm not this man anymore.

He died. Violently, and at my own hands.

He's in hell where he belongs.

Or did it just take him this long to claw his way back from the Devil's lap?

———

LIFE IS a maze with an infinite number of dead ends, and just as many exits. Very few ever reach the prize in the middle, and those that do, don't always want to accept it for what it is.

I had ample opportunities to change my life. If my choices had been black and white, I always chose gray. Eventually, the gray turned darker and darker, until my only options were two paths, both black as night.

The brute was one of those black paths. I didn't see the brute again after my first ayahuasca experience.

Kane was another of those black paths.

Kane and I met at a time in our lives when we were meaningless to anyone but ourselves and each other.

More specifically—I had money, and I needed heroin. He had heroin, and he needed money.

Sympatico.

It was so easy to believe that our first meeting was serendipitous because back then, I still believed in shit like that. When Hunter Senior threatened to kick me out for the fifteenth time, I left on my own instead.

Kane had a place for me up in the mountains. A farm where I would be surrounded by fellow-minded purveyors of the good life twenty-four-fucking seven.

That first year was idyllic.

Just a few guys, ten weed gardens hidden between the redwoods, and all the weed we could smoke.

I grew my hair out. I never wore shoes. I almost never bathed, except in the small lake close to one of the marijuana gardens we tended.

Weeks went by. The girls came and went. The compound slowly began to change. Other outlaws were moving into the mountains to start their own illegal grow ops, putting pressure on our supply and driving down the price per pound.

That was before I knew our little farm was a drug smuggling compound. Before I knew anything about *The Father*. Before I had any idea who—*what*—we were actually working for. That would all come later, and all at once.

A year after living with Kane and the rest of the crew in the mountains, we were told to start hiring trimmers to help us during the harvest months.

All girls.

The reasoning being that they ate less, drank less, and cost less.

One of the first girls we hired had taken an Ayahuasca trip a month before she'd arrived in Mallhaven. In fact, her guide had told her it was her path to walk.

We smoked a lot of weed the first week they arrived. The story about my own experience came out, and for some reason, Kane latched onto it.

Especially the brute.

I thought nothing about it at the time.

Kane discovered a DMT supplier.

Now, although Ayahuasca tea has DMT in it, mixed with all the other vines and plants, it's not the potent shit you buy off the streets.

It's not the DMT you smoke like crack, flip out, and come clawing back—if it all—half an hour later with only shreds of your sanity still remaining.

I did it once, and it almost broke me. After that, I stuck with heroin.

I DIY'd my rehab for an excruciating four weeks.

Then I founded the Hill Institute, paid for mainly with a trust fund I'd forgotten I had. The Institute turned a profit in its first year—a profit that grew exponentially each quarter as word spread of the luxurious rehabilitation facility tucked away in the redwood mountains of the nowhere town of Mallhaven.

My programs were inspired. Unique. Bleeding edge.

But still patients would relapse. I'd start seeing the same faces as file after file crossed my desk.

I took one Ayahuasca trip after that, but never again. My demons were too plentiful—I feared they'd overrun me the next time.

About three years ago, a surge of sentimentality brought me back to these exact woods where I'd taken my first plunge. I was feeling despondent, as if the carefully crafted programs I ran were a band-aid on a festering wound that would never—*could* never—heal.

I've always had a remarkable, if selective memory. I worked my way back to the brute's cabin.

What was left of it.

The forest had reclaimed much of it by that time. Moss and a few tender trees had sprouted amid the carbonized remains. I stood there for the longest time, staring at the heap of black-burned wood.

I should have been angry. Instead, I was just forlorn.

It took six months, but I rebuilt the cabin as perfectly as I could remember. Better, even.

The brute wouldn't have cared. For him, it was a place to lay his head and ward off the rain.

I COME BACK to the present with reluctance.

No, this is not a cycle of abuse.

I chose to do right, and so can she. It's the Mother plant that's confusing things. Somehow, it's affecting me too.

Or is that the weed?

Can't be—it's never had this effect on me before.

It's her. Clover. She's the one that's shutting down my rational mind in favor of things I can't define.

Dangerous things.

Science is neither good nor evil. It's simply factual or inaccurate. Every neuron in my brain is telling me that the very fact that I'm here in this cabin, with this woman, is simply not the most effective way of conducting this study.

But my body craves her like I craved heroin.

Addicts should never be allowed close to another addictive substance. Too many rehab facilities treating alcoholics have no problem with their patients smoking cigarettes.

Anathema.

An addictive mind can never overcome addiction until it's free of *every* addiction.

Sugar. Alcohol. Nicotine. Heroin.

Clover.

I'm addicted to Clover. I want her even though I've already had her. She's right in front of me, but I'm already missing her.

It's not logical. It's not even possible.

I'm stronger than this. I've overcome worse than this.

I have the scars to prove it.

But I've already had a taste, and it's going to take a lot more than positive thinking to break me from her.

I wrap her matted braid around my hand, yanking her head down and to the side so I can see her pretty neck bend for me.

Her carotid pulses against her fair skin.

Terror or anticipation?

I expect the first. After all, I'm standing over her with a bunched jaw and what I can only assume a fierce scowl on my face. A junkie faced with her worst nightmare. After being clean for so long, who could relapse without hating themselves, the drug, the fucking entire world?

She sinks down until she's perched on the edge of the mattress. Her pupils have dilated to the point that her irises are a sliver of turquoise. She's doe-like in her complacency, a kitten under the paw of a wolf.

Clover spreads her legs. Despite her neck being at an odd angle, despite the fierce grip I have on her hair...

I step forward, claiming that space she's opened with my thighs. Her body arches forward, her naked breasts brushing my stomach.

She watches me. Silent, but with a mouth set in challenge.

Commanding me to do my worst because she's been through much worse than the likes of me.

I touch my thumb to her lips. They're a lighter shade now after I wiped off what was left of her makeup. Her eyes, too. I brush my finger over her mouth, and I can feel her quivering under me at the soft touch.

She doesn't know about my past. She doesn't know of the things I did when the demons took control of me.

If she did, she wouldn't still be here.

If anyone did, I'd be locked away on death row.

But I made peace with the past. I locked that part of me deep, deep down. Until now, I've never even thought about it.

Now I'm starting to worry that maybe, just maybe, I didn't lash down those demons tight enough.

If they were ever to get out...

I must warn her. Perhaps give her a chance to flee. She deserves that much, at least.

Instead, I ask, "Do you really think you can handle me?"

My voice comes out as a grating murmur. Her eyes are answer enough—she stares at me as if she's trying to fry my brain.

She doesn't get it. No one does. What she sees standing in front of her is a mask. A puppet.

I've been able to hold myself back these past years. I've dealt with all my addictions, not just heroin.

Addictions no one except Kane and The Father would ever know about.

Some harbor more evil inside them than others.

As if to impress this on her, I say, "You're too weak."

Clover's lips quirk as she lets out a tiny snort of derision.

"Yeah? Try me."

CHAPTER SEVENTY-ONE
CLOVER

It's been a strange few hours. I'm tripping on something called Ayahuasca in a remote cabin in the middle of the woods with a psychic—psychotic?—hippy. I've just realized that the reason I was addicted to heroin was some desperate need to escape the past.

Shit like that changes you, man.

It's changed me.

I won't call it night versus day, but I'm different. I feel motivated.

But not in a good way.

I feel self-destructive. Like I want to hurt myself, but I don't have the guts.

That's where Hunter comes in.

He can hurt me without trying. In fact, he has to try *not* to hurt me.

Is that ironic? I never could tell.

College was for those losers that had people to impress. Me? I just had to survive and that shit required a whole new skill set. Things like sucking dick and knowing when to fake it.

The only thing left of that Clover is a few grains of dust. Hunter shattered that persona.

I want Hunter to grind me out under his heel.

I know, it's crazy.

Where's my sense of self-preservation, right?

Well, it's gone now. I'd be just as happy if he killed me as if he fucked me.

You think I wanted to see that shit? I'd buried those memories for very explicit fucking reasons. That shit was never meant to see the light of day. Or the light of a fire. Whatever.

Pandora's box.

He wrenched it open without a fucking care in the world.

I'll cure you, Clover, you junkie. You'll be free as a fucking bird.

Thanks for nothing, asshole, because free is far from what I am.

"I'm not!" My voice doesn't echo in the small cabin—it *fills* it.

Hunter's attention diverts back to my face. He'd been staring at my cunt like a bee sizing up a flower he was about to invade for pollen.

"You're not what?" he asks.

I'm seeing shit. I must be. His face isn't the same. There are faint scars on it. So very, very faint, but they're there. I reach out to touch one, and Hunter flinches like I've scorched him. He snatches my hand away from his face and watches me from the corner of his eye. "You're not what?" he repeats slowly, expectantly.

"I'm not free." I toss my head, managing to rip my braid from his hand. "I was, but I'm not anymore."

He laughs, but cuts the sound short. "You'd have preferred living in that void?" He flicks his hand. "Empty. Soulless. The only meaning in your life your next hit?"

"Ignorance is fucking bliss." I hiss the words at him and cut him off when he begins speaking again. "What? You've never wanted to forget your fucking past?"

His mouth is open, but ain't shit coming out.

"Oh, right." I cock my head. "You're a trust fund baby, aren't you? Born with a fucking silver spoon in your—"

He claps a hand over my cunt and gives me a rough squeeze. Whatever I'd been about to accuse him of disappears in a wave of pleasure.

"You don't know shit about me," Hunter says, and for once he doesn't sound like he was born with a stick up his ass. "And you never will, because I've dealt with it. My past is my past."

"Dealt with what?"

"Is this some pathetic attempt to distract me?" Hunter's eyes flash with anger, his mouth turning up in a cruel smile. "Did you honestly think you could throw down a gauntlet, and I wouldn't accept?"

Gauntlet? What the fuck is a—?

He grabs the front of my throat and forces me onto my back. His entire weight is on me an instant later, his cock pressing against my cunt.

Damn, he moves fast. I didn't even notice him taking off his boxers.

I laugh at him. "You think having some entitled asshole taking what he wants is the worst I've been through?"

It was supposed to be glib, a way to rile him up. But now, after those floodgates in my mind were opened, I realize the statement has so much more truth to it than I'd ever imagined.

And then I'm fucking pissed at Hunter for doing this to me. He had no right to interfere with my life. No right to attempt to fix me. Because, face it, I'm broken. I've fallen off the motherfucking wall, and there's no putting Clover Vos back together again.

Christ, now I want to bawl like a baby. What the hell did this shit do to me?

Hunter tightens his grip on my throat before forcing his way inside me.

The thought disintegrates, as does everything else in the fucking world. I expect blackness behind my eyes. Instead, things move against my eyelids. Long, slender, slithering things.

I don't want to look at them anymore, but for some reason I can't open my eyes. I don't know how much more of this hippy drug I can take.

"How long till I come down?" I ask through gritted teeth as Hunter eases out of me.

"Depends." His voice is by my ear, his lips brushing my skin.

"On what?"

"How long you take to walk the path."

I squirm under him, furious at his Cheshire cat riddles. "I'm done, okay? I'm fucking *done*."

"You might be, but the Mother isn't yet."

"The...?" I finally get my eyes open.

Hunter's watching me, a rapt, almost zealous expression on his face. "Why does this feel so wrong?"

"Because you drugged me?" I snap back.

He's inside me again, so I'm not quite as snappy as I wanted, but at least I tried. "Because you're supposed to be my doctor or some shit? Instead you have me holed up in this—"

He has a hand between us, and my sentence dies when he begins massaging my clit.

Jesus, this *is* wrong. Is that what makes it so fucking delicious? Or is that the aya—whatever-the-hell he drugged me with?

But he didn't drug me, did he? I *took* it. I felt I had no choice, but I didn't resist him either. I could have poured out that water bottle.

What would he have done then?

I study his face as he studies mine. Those scars are still there and they're driving me insane. I touch his jaw, running a finger along the barely visible line that runs up to his ear.

He jerks away his head, eyes narrowing. "What are you doing?"

"You have so many scars."

Hunter shakes his head, his mouth going into a cruel line. "You're hallucinating." And then, as if he could no longer stand me looking at him, he pulls out and flips me over.

I have a second to struggle, to protest, before he kicks open my legs and burrows himself inside me. I want to scream, but instead I groan as my back arches. He grabs my braid and jerks back my head, putting his mouth by my ear.

"Where will you go after this?"

I laugh at the question, or maybe at the tone of his voice, or maybe just this entire fucked up situation. This man is obviously several sandwiches short of anything approaching a picnic. So what, am I just supposed to roll with it?

"Home," I say, not knowing why, or even where the fuck that was supposed to be.

Hunter plunges into me again, drawing a gasp. He speeds up, fucking me so hard that I have no idea if what's driving me to the edge is pleasure or pain.

Probably both.

I was always fucked up like that.

I guess, sometimes, if you lie to yourself often enough, you start believing in every made-up thing you invent.

"Yes," Hunter says. For a moment I think it's one of those, 'Oh, God, yes, fuck,' statements, but he doesn't strike me as the type.

I'm close. I think he is too, judging from how hard he's pounding into me. I balance on a hand and start getting myself off with the other. I have good timing sometimes, but if I can't read him, can't figure out how close he is—

"Yes, what?" I manage in a tight voice. Fuck, this feels so glorious. I want to command him to go harder, but I think he's at the peak of violent fucking.

"You *are* going home," he says, his words running together. "With me."

Words have never triggered me into climax before so it must have been good timing.

I come with a throttled groan, bucking fiercely into him. He twists my head, pressing his mouth to mine as he comes a second later, meeting my thrust with one of his own. A sliver of pain tears through me, but it's muddled with so much bliss it doesn't stand a chance.

I'm moaning against his mouth as I ride out my climax with him pulsing inside me, his hips grinding against my ass. He nips at my bottom lip, breath hot and fast.

"What?" I manage, my head reeling.

He twists my hair even harder, pulling me an inch away from him so he can stare into my eyes as he eases out an inch before pounding into me again.

I could be hallucinating, still, but at the same time I'm pretty sure the possessiveness in his eyes is as real as whatever connection there is between us.

He shows me his teeth in a fierce snarl before putting his lips to my ear again. When he speaks, his voice is husky as fuck.

"You are going home, Clover. Home with me."

PART FIVE

JOIN ME

"Red Riding Hood sprang out, crying: 'Ah, how frightened I have been! How dark it was inside the wolf.'"

LITTLE RED RIDING HOOD - THE BROTHERS GRIMM

CHAPTER SEVENTY-TWO
CLOVER

I've always been a light sleeper. I guess it comes with the territory —the last thing you want is someone sneaking up on you when you're incapacitated.

All it takes to rouse me is the sound of Hunter's voice, despite the fact that he's not even close enough for me to hear what he's saying.

My eyes open to a too bright room. I swipe a hand over my face, trying to chase away dregs of sleep as I roll onto my back. A deep groan escapes me. Fuck, you'd think I ran a goddamn marathon, as sore as my body is.

I guess I did, in a way. Clover Vos isn't used to running for her life.

Pushing to my elbows, I strain to make out what Hunter's saying.

I'm on his bed. I vaguely remember getting here—we trekked back here earlier today. He carried me upstairs and put me to bed. He lay beside me for a while, but I must have fallen asleep.

There's a touch of either frustration or annoyance in his voice before he says something that almost sounds like, "Then fix it."

Silence.

The bedroom door opens. Hunter stands at the threshold, staring at his phone as he taps his thumb over the screen. Does he feel my eyes on him? A second later, he looks up.

I expect a smile. Instead, I get nothing. Not even a flicker of change in his expression. Phone still in his hand, he points to the closet door. I follow his finger and stiffen a little when I see a kaftan hanging from the door handle.

"Bathe. Get dressed. I need you downstairs in five minutes."

He leaves without another word.

I slide out of bed and pad over to the en-suite bathroom. There, I hurl violently into the toilet bowl until there's nothing left in my stomach.

Not that there was much to begin with.

I flush the toilet and blow my nose. As soon as I can breathe again, I glance to the copper tub positioned in the middle of the expansive bathroom.

It's full of water. There are things drifting on the surface.

Flowers. Leaves. Bits of bark.

Bathe.

Exactly when did I turn into Hunter's pet? I know I was all sitting up and begging and shit yesterday but…

But what?

But I was under the influence of some hectic shit.

My mind is clear now.

Very, *very* clear.

I test the water with my foot. It's the perfect temperature, which I find hard to believe but can't deny.

Look, I *do* need to wash my hair, and the water feels glorious.

A deep, shuddering sigh escapes me as I sink into the fragrant water.

I drift off and then snap awake a few minutes later.

Five minutes.

I'm sure it's been longer.

I stand and move to pick the flowers from my skin. A square of white catches my eye, and déjà vu floods me. I stare at the folded piece of paper for the longest time before I take it from the top of the tub's bronze faucet.

Don't dry.

Don't clean.

The Clover Vos I know and love would have crumpled that note in her fist, grabbed the closest towel and—

Ah. There *are* no towels. Guess Hunter wasn't taking any chances that I would disobey.

Well, if he wants his carpets ruined, that's his fucking problem.

I pad back to the closet, consider the pale, beaded kaftan hanging from the door handle and snort. I run my fingers over it. The delicate fabric slips like silk through my fingers, light as air. It's not quite opaque—when I slip a hand beneath the fabric, the color of my skin shines through. Wooden beads—some as big as a penny—form an intricate pattern around the neckline.

He's obviously dressing me up for something, but what?

Well, guess what? Not my style, Hunter. In fact, it's so far from my style, I'd rather wear nothing at all.

I smirk to myself as my hand falls away from that sensuous fabric.

Challenge accepted.

The house is so quiet, I can hear birds chirping from the trees outside. I guess Hunter's waiting downstairs, so I head for the only other room up here to snoop around.

It's locked. Not only locked, but there's a keypad next to the door with a number pad.

I try 1-2-3-4, but nothing happens. So I try 4-3-2-1, and then four zeros and then just a bunch of random numbers.

Nope.

I try the handle again, but it's still locked.

Damn.

I'm starting to itch as I dry, and the urge to peel a bright yellow petal from my left breast is almost impossible to resist.

Instead, I take the stairs.

I do hope we're all alone—I'm not exactly one for public displays of nudity. Then again, I almost wish he's having a business meeting downstairs so I can walk past a bunch of astonished suits and be all like, 'You wanted me, Sah?'

Hunter's in the kitchen, his back turned to me as I come down the stairs. It looks like he's cooking something on the massive range taking up one side of a kitchen that's too large for a single person.

But he isn't alone anymore, is he?

You are *going home, Clover. Home with me.*

That bit I remember. Okay, there are a lot of bits I remember and would rather not. Especially all that shit that went down when I was sixteen.

I watch Hunter for a few seconds as he moves around, oblivious to my presence. He's wearing three-quarter shorts the color of dried mud, and a floppy, dark green vest.

There are scars on his shoulder blades. Faint, but visible.

At least, I fucking *hope* they're there. Could I still be hallu—?

"Take a seat."

I flinch. "You sure?" I ask, hooking my hands behind my back and swinging from side to side.

Hunter glances over his shoulder and then does a double take that's so fucking satisfying, I almost want to forgive him. That won't be possible, of course, but it's nice to think a world exists where we could be friends or lovers.

He points a spatula in my direction. "The flowers remain potent as long as they're in contact with your skin," he says, and it's as if—despite the lack of a suit—he's back to being Dr. Hill again.

"Potent?"

He's staring so intently into my eyes, it's as if he's schooling himself not to look at my naked body.

Game. Set. Match.

"Their cleansing properties," he says, but in a distant kind of way. "The floral bath cleanses you from residual negativity after an Ayahuasca ceremony."

I snort at him and walk over to a barstool. It's some kind of shiny white plastic and my damp ass squeaks when I hoist myself onto it. "You call what happened a fucking ceremony?"

I might be imagining it, but I swear there's the slightest flinch in his eyes at my statement.

"You should be hungry," he says, which is Hill for 'would you like breakfast?'

"I'm not."

"You will eat."

Another command. I shift on the stool, pouting when it doesn't make any more inappropriate noises. I glance back the way I came and see a trail of flower petals and leaves scattered on the floor.

Not my problem.

"What if I was allergic to something?" I ask, trying not to sound like a child and probably failing miserably.

"You're not."

Oh, right. Dr. Hill knows Clover's entire medical background, and more.

"How did you find out so much stuff about me?" I ask as Hunter dishes up whatever he's prepared into two bowls.

Dr. Most Eligible Bachelor of Mallhaven's going to have breakfast with me?

What a fucking honor.

He sets down our bowls and slides onto the stool beside me. "The government does an excellent job of keeping track of its civilians."

I stare into the bowl. It looks healthy, smells delicious, and would be the last thing I ever want to eat.

Normally.

My stomach grumbles, and I curse it for being so goddamn self-preserving.

At least it's not raw.

"What is this?"

"A nutritious breakfast." Hunter puts a forkful of it in his mouth and chews as he watches me from the corner of his eye.

"With a dash of horse tranquilizer? Or is it roofies this time? Acid?" When he says nothing, I tip the contents of my fork over into the bowl. "Give me a clue, at least."

I freeze when Hunter reaches over to me. Hating myself for it, of course, but unable to unfreeze until I know his intentions. There's a damp leaf smaller than my pinkie finger still plastered to my upper arm. He peels it from my skin, tips back his head, and eats it.

"Hey! That was mine. It's supposed to be all potent and shit."

"Are you expecting an apology from me, Clover?"

I hate how goddamn officious he sounds right now. "No, but I think it's about time you called me a cab."

He eats another mouthful of his food—Jesus, how can something smell so goddamn delicious?—and sets his fork down with exaggerated care.

"Am I keeping you from something important?"

Asshole!

"Yeah," I say, pushing away my bowl and sliding from the stool. "My fucking life, you psycho."

I turn for the door and then remember I'm naked. Not just that—the only thing for me to wear is that filmy Lawrence of Arabia harem outfit.

No worries, I'll grab something of *his* to wear. But that means going upstairs, and I have a feeling he's going to follow me.

I go upstairs, my hair standing on end as I strain for the sound of him following me.

Nothing.

I fling open his closet, and then take a long, slow step back. Every inch of my skin prickles with fire and ice.

A shadow darkens the door.

I didn't hear him coming closer because the blood roaring in my ears is so fucking loud.

It's not a large closet by any means, but clearly divided in two. Two separate areas for hanging clothes, two columns of shelves for folded stuff.

There are a handful of suits, some still in their plastic baggies. Two pairs of dress shoes. More of the type of clothing he's wearing now though—casual, colorless shit. No name brands.

But that's not what makes my breath stall in my lungs.

The other half of the cupboard is full of clothes too. Dresses, jeans, some nice tops. Bras and panties and socks. More shoes than he owns and two of each kind—boots, sneakers, sandals.

"What. The. Fuck?" I turn to him.

My hair's still wet, coiling against my neck and shoulders. He takes a stray strip and tucks it behind my ear. The gesture is so intimate that I shiver when his fingertips brush my earlobe.

He gives me a smile that's neither warm nor cold, neither cruel nor kind. "Welcome home."

CHAPTER SEVENTY-THREE
HUNTER

I don't appreciate the tone in Clover's voice. I expected surprise, not disgust. She turns to me from the closet, her mouth in a sneer.

"What. The. Fuck."

I'm really starting to deplore her use of bad language. I realize it's how she expresses herself, but I have no liking for it.

"Welcome home."

Instead of understanding, something approaching fear fills her Bluestar irises.

"You knew." She takes a step back, swatting away my hand as her eyes narrow dangerously. "You *knew* I'd come home with you."

I shrug. "Where else would you go?"

Astonishment widens her eyes. "That's it? Because a stray like me has nowhere else, you just expect me to stay? What's next? Do I gotta roll over and let you scratch my fucking tummy whenever you want?"

I frown at her. "You're being unreasonable."

"No." She takes another step back. "This is me being pissed off."

I want to focus on her eyes. I want to take stock of her emotions as they flicker across her face if only in an attempt to understand this strange creature standing in front of me.

But she's still naked. Magnificent in her fury.

My gaze runs over her body, and as if that was exactly what she was waiting for, she darts forward, snatches the kaftan from its hook and bolts past me as she tugs it over her head.

With a nimble twist of her body, she evades my grasping hand.

By the time I reach the top of the stairs, she's already headed for the front door.

I don't bother giving chase. I can lock the door from here. I reach into my pocket for my phone, but realize too late that I left it on the kitchen table.

Clover wrenches open the front door, throws me a victorious scowl over her shoulder, and disappears.

I reach the door seconds later, but she's nowhere to be seen.

My heart thunders in my chest. I press a hand to it, willing it to calm.

No.

Not now.

I was so *fucking* close.

I grit my teeth and go back inside, slamming the door behind me.

She won't get far.

CHAPTER SEVENTY-FOUR
CLOVER

As soon as I'm out of Hunter's house, I head straight for the road. But then I realize he'll be able to see me a mile away, and detour for the forest running alongside.

I almost seize up when those cool shadows fall over me, but I force myself to keep going.

You did this once. You can do it again.

As long as I keep the road in sight, I'll be fine.

I keep to a run, but I eventually slow to a jog. It's that or pass out.

My jog just slowed into a fast walk when I hear a faint, mechanical growl in the distance. I pause, holding my breath so I can hear what—

Fuck. He's coming after me.

I surge into a run, heading deeper into the forest so he can't see me from the road.

As long as I keep my head, I'll be able to find it again.

Please, God, let me find my way back.

Leaves and branches slap and scratch at me like a feral cat, but I've been through worse. The kaftan snags and tears on just about everything, and for a wild second I consider taking it off.

But as little as I want to be in a forest, I know I definitely don't want to be *naked* in a forest.

Bugs.

Mud.

Poison ivy.

I shudder as I run, my brain serving me a particularly vivid flash-back of me ripping a millipede from my hair.

My stomach's cramping.

Fuck, why didn't I eat that bowl of food? My body feels weak. After all, I've barely had anything but drugs for the past two days. After six months of proper nutrition, my body seems unable to cope with starvation.

I can still hear him in the distance, but I think I'm losing him. I slow down, and change direction. I want to loop back to the road so I don't get lost.

I doubt there'll be any yellow arrows this time around. Which mean I'll probably die.

That distant motor cuts off.

Shit, does he realize I've gone into the forest?

I guess he could see far enough down the road to figure out that…

I stop walking.

A fragment of a memory from my time in the forest comes back to me.

I thought you put a tracker on me.

My hand goes to the kaftan's neckline.

More specifically, to the largest of the wooden beads sewn into the neckline. My bracelet clacks against it as I try to rip the bead free.

Shit.

Shit!

That's how he knows where I am. He knew I'd have to put this on so, even if I bolted, he could find me.

I try to tear that big bead off, but it refuses.

Maybe I'm too weak from hunger.

I laugh, hurriedly cut off the sound, and yank the kaftan over my head. I lurch forward, jaw clamped against the feel of the air sliding over my skin.

Well, at least I can tick, 'running naked through a forest' from my bucket list.

Clover: consider your life lived to the fucking fullest.

CHAPTER SEVENTY-FIVE
HUNTER

By the time I get the four-wheeler out of the garage, Clover's nowhere in sight. I open the throttle and tear down my road, glaring through the trees for a sight of the white dress.

As much as Clover thinks I had this all thought out to a tee, she has no idea how far we've veered from my original plan.

Luckily, some things never change.

Like my trust issues.

I park the four-wheeler, yanking my phone from my pants pocket. I open the tracker app and take a moment to orientate myself before heading into the forest.

I'm right behind her, and closing in.

Why did you run, Clover?

I don't want to have to chase you, but you leave me no choice. I need you close at hand to study the effects of your Ayahuasca experience, can't you understand that? If I were to let you leave without knowing you've been cured...

There will be no one to claim your body if you overdose.

You have no mother.

No father.

No siblings.

Gail will never see you again.

I'm *all* you've got.

I'm all you *need*.

Why can't you understand that?

Wait...are you changing direction? Why? Do you think you're heading back to the road?

You're not, Clover.

No. Clover. Fuck! You're going the wrong way!

The tracker slows. Slows. Stops.

I break into a run, but I already know I'm not going to reach her in time.

CHAPTER SEVENTY-SIX
CLOVER

I wish I could say I saw this coming, but I really fucking didn't. I mean, here I am, right, running naked through the forest. I think the worst thing I have to deal with right now is psycho hippy Hunter Hill.

False.

So fucking false.

There's a barbed wire fence and a gap where something tore a hole through it.

Bear.

I dodge through a little gap with little more than a scrape on my left calf.

Where the fuck is the road?

I should have hit it by now.

Nope. Still running.

The forest clears out. I suddenly become *very* aware of how naked I am and how little foliage there is to cover me. Morning sun basks on my skin, and I start slowing down.

I finally take stock of my surroundings.

There are still trees and shit in the way, but I see a building up ahead.

Not a cheery little cabin way too small for seven little dwarfs or any of that shit.

Oh no.

This is a *big* building. It even has like a little tower.

If I didn't know better, I'd swear it was a church.

But a church in the middle of a forest? I mean, come on.

Even if I'd turned around right then…they would still have caught me. But when I see the first humanoid shadow disentangling itself from a nearby tree trunk, I spin around and head back the way I came.

If I'd been an Olympic sprinter, I might have made it. And, if I hadn't run away, I would never have seen Hunter.

He's still following me. Somehow managed to find me. Did he track me by studying broken twigs and shit?

Doesn't matter.

He's too far away to help.

Not just that—as soon as we make eye contact, his gaze flashes away.

To the guy chasing me.

A pair of rough hands grab my waist and throw me to the floor.

Hunter slips behind a tree trunk.

Hiding?

He's fucking hiding.

"Let go!" I yell, kicking and squirming like my life depends on it.

Well, it probably fucking does.

I got a brief glimpse of the grunt on top of me. He's dressed in dark clothes, a bandana over the lower half of his face. Hair unruly, and—from the stink—as recently washed as the rest of him.

He scrambles to his feet, hauling me up with a hand in my hair. I scream, but hoarsely because he knocked the wind from my lungs. I try my best to see if Hunter's manned up enough to come and help me, but I see nothing but dark shadows out there in the forest.

"You shouldn't be here," a rough voice grates into my ear.

Not the best thing to hear when you've just trespassed. But if he'd said something along the lines of 'I like my girls with a little fight' or something, I swear I'd have said my prayers and hoped I died of syphilis sooner rather than later.

"I'll leave. Please. Just let me go."

Logically, this argument should have worked gangbusters.

It doesn't, and I'm done debating the subject with him when my captor clamps a hand over my mouth and drags me toward that tall white building I'd so erroneously thought a church.

Because, of course, it could only be an abattoir, a crack house, or the headquarters for a human trafficking ring.

Where the fuck was Hunter? Would he send for help? Or did he fear that I'd rat him out about everything that had happened up to this point?

I won't.

If you can hear me, if we're somehow cosmically entwined after those herbs you made me drink...please.

Help me, Hunter.

MORE MEN ARRIVE the closer I get to the church. No, I can't argue the fact anymore. There's even a little bell in the tower.

I don't know what's freaking me out more—the fact that I'm naked, or the fact that none of them seem to care. I sincerely doubt that I've somehow ended up in a naturalist retreat that caters only for gay, brawny men.

Look, it's possible, but highly implausible.

The building's wooden doors creak when one of the bulkier men drag it open.

Thank God—ironically?—that there isn't a service going on. I doubt anyone in this congregation is on the normal, law-abiding side of Mallhaven's population.

Inside, the church looks like I'd expect. Judging, not from personal experience, but from movies and shit of course since I've never been inside one. Stained-glass windows throw shafts of colored lights onto rows of empty pews. There's a pulpit at the far end—just as empty. Some flower arrangements that look more feral than pretty.

There's something wrong, though.

It's not the fact that this place is utterly silent.

Creepy, yes. Wrong? No.

Is it the guy dragging me down the aisle?

Again—creepy, but not it. After all, I did cross some rudimentary barbed wire. I could—*possibly*—truly be trespassing here.

There's something I'm not seeing. Something—

"Father."

Who's he speaking to? There's no one here.

A small arched doorway leading off the stage—or should I call it an altar?—opens to admit a dark-robed figure.

Ah. There you go. There's the fucking strange I was looking for.

This is no church. Well, not in a holy way. I scan the place around furiously, trying to find another piece of this twisted puzzle.

When I find it, it's so blindingly obvious I almost roll my eyes.

The stained-glass windows don't depict Christ on the cross. There are no virginal Mary's up there, glowing with their inexplicable pregnancy. No three wise men.

Okay, honestly, I don't have a fucking clue what goes for normal church doctrine.

But an enormous man with the head of a goat is *probably* not it. Unless he's being slaughtered by like, an angel or something.

Nope.

Beastie's positioned right above the pulpit. One hand's up and making some weird occult symbol, the other is stroking the head of a blond woman who's either weeping in his lap or going serious deep throat on his dick.

The robed figure draws closer. I try to cover myself because this is the first time I feel eyes on me. Eyes where they shouldn't be, like if you happen to spot a vulnerable naked young lady in the middle of— oh, I don't know—your satanic church?

A stray beam of red light flashes over the man's face. I thought he had his hood up, but it turns out he's got long, dark hair that hangs just past his shoulders, and a neatly trimmed Jesus beard.

There's a zealous gleam in his eyes as he works at a button at the top of his robe.

I swear, if he's naked…

But he's not. He's wearing a plain, long-sleeved t-shirt and faded jeans.

The robe swirls around him as he plucks it off, and then it's around me and my captor is no longer holding me by the scruff of my neck.

"What is the meaning of this?" his dark voice demands.

Oh, thank God, and not even ironically. This was all a mistake. His ignorant grunt is obviously really stupid. I surge forward, so fucking glad that I've discovered a sane person that I don't bother with sorting out my legs first.

As I trip and fall forward, I grab for the first thing I can to stay upright—and that happens to be Father's neckline.

Eyes such a pale blue they almost don't have any color latch onto me. Dark brows contract. The man jerks my hand from him with such aggression that I yelp in pain.

"She was inside," grunts the grunt.

"No, I wasn't!" I hate the fact that my voice is much higher than it should be, but now's not the time to worry about coming off weak. "I mean, I didn't know—"

"Where are her clothes?" Father says through perfect teeth. But not to me—he's talking to his fucking grunt.

"Wasn't wearing any, Father."

Cold eyes flicker to me. A scan takes in every pore on my face. "You're trespassing, girl."

"I guess I missed the sign," I manage, my words muffled how tight my jaw is. "Now, if you'll just let me—"

"You're not going anywhere." The man called Father grabs my wrist. "Hunter knows the rules."

My mouth is open to protest, but what the fuck am I supposed to say about that? So, instead, I gape up at the Father as blood drains from my face.

He *knows* Hunter.

Is that why Hill didn't dare chase after me? Why he went and hid like the yellow-bellied fucking coward—

"Father!"

I spin around at that familiar voice. Hunter stands silhouetted in the church's doorway before striding up to us.

Father rips me to the side, taking a step forward as if expecting Hunter to take a swing at him. "You know the rules."

Hunter's dark eyes spark with anger, but his voice comes out smooth as silk. "She doesn't."

"That's not how this works, Dr. Hill."

Honorifics? I gape from Hunter to the priest, eyes so big they feel as if they're going to fall out.

Hunter holds out a hand for me. "She's mine. Return her to me."

His?

If I weren't getting such a hectic vibe from Hunter, I'd have said something snarky.

Look, I don't believe in things like soul mates and spiritual connections and all that shit. I just don't. Call it cynicism, or experience, or whatever the fuck you want.

But right now, *somehow*, Hunter's mentally commanding me to go with this. To swallow whatever pride I have left and trust him.

Trust him.

Trust him?

Trust *him*?

Doesn't he get it?

"I don't belong to anyone," I spit out, wrenching my wrist free from the priest's grip. I almost want to take off the robe around my shoulders, but then I'd have to stalk out of here naked.

Doubt I could hold my head up if that happened.

Instead, I grab it around me with all the arrogance I can muster, turn on my heel, and walk straight into the grunt that dragged me inside here in the first.

Rats.

"So not one of yours, then," the priest muses smugly. "See yourself out."

"She's not—" but Hunter cuts off without finishing his sentence. Then he glares at me like this is all my fucking fault. I scowl back at him a second before I'm herded after the priest.

Wait, what?

"Hey, let go!" I start struggling, throwing Hunter a pleading look over my shoulder. "Hunter!"

But he just stands there, tight-lipped and eyes dark as a thunder-storm, not making a move in my direction.

"Hunter!" I yell, more in confusion than anything else.

Why the fuck won't he help me?

What the fuck is going on?

I whip my head forward.

And where the fuck is this priest taking me?

CHAPTER SEVENTY-SEVEN
HUNTER

My chest is so tight, I can't even breathe. I watch the High Priest of the Messianic Church of Solomon drag an incredulous Clover down the aisle.

But Father is right; I know the rules.

I should accept the fact that Clover is gone. I should be getting to work finding a new test subject.

A new trial.

More data for my study.

That's all that should be—

"Please!" My voice echoes strangely in the massive church. "Father, please!"

But the priest doesn't even pause mid-step. Clover looks at me over her shoulder, face the color of milk and her hair glowing as a stray beam of light glances off it.

"Father!" I take a step forward, but his crony is blocking my path. I grit my teeth, my heart thundering like a herd of wild horses in a chest banded with icy iron chains.

"She belongs to me!"

The priest stops. Clover's eyes are wide, but there's not a trace of fear in them.

If she knew where he'd been taking her, she'd have been fighting him tooth and nail. But she probably wouldn't fight him until it was too late.

"I can't lose her."

The Father turns to me, Clover spinning around with him. He's got her by her upper arm, but with such a tight grip that even when she tugs at his fingers, he doesn't loosen his grip.

"The other one is dead," the priest says.

Confusion flickers over Clover's face, and I can't blame her. But there's no time for explanations.

"I know." I step closer, holding a hand up to the Father's crony so he doesn't tackle me. I could take him easily, of course, but I know there are twenty, thirty more of the Father's men roaming nearby. "Her name is Clover. She's mine. She belongs to me."

Father cocks his head at me. I've almost never seen him wear anything but the patient smile of a Buddhist monk and now is no different. He watches me from behind implacable eyes. "Which is what you claimed about the other one."

Fucker.

My lips squirm; tongue battling my jaws. "MJ." The name comes out as a strangled, angry sound. "Her name was *MJ*."

"Yes." That beatific smile remains completely unchanged. "I remember now."

I hold out a hand. "Please." And then, because it was the statement that seemed to have the most impact on him, I say again, "Clover belongs to me."

The priest regards me for a few seconds before walking back my way. Clover's frowning so hard, I can only hope she doesn't decide to say anything stupid.

Or anything at all.

I wish then, more than ever, that I knew this motherfucker's name. But I don't think anyone does. If he was even born of a mortal woman, I'm sure the Devil himself destroyed those birth records.

I don't believe in God, it's true. But I know for a fact the Devil exists if only because of this man standing in front of me.

The priest's colorless eyes flicker over my face as if searching for some hidden meaning in my expression, which I keep as neutral as possible.

"Blood for blood," I murmur, hoping the words will only carry to Father's ears.

Clover's eyes narrow to slits. Her mouth thins. But she doesn't say anything, and for that I could kiss her.

For that I *will* kiss her.

Father lifts his chin, and slowly releases Clover. She slips to the side, moving as slowly and fluidly as a cat without making eye contact with the priest.

I suppose anyone in a ten-yard radius can feel just how volatile this situation is.

I beckon Clover with my fingertips, and she comes to my side. I grab her arm—not unlike Father had just been holding her—and start backing away.

"Blood for blood." Father's voice feels like skeletal fingers walking down my spine, but I ignore the feeling and give him an abrupt nod.

I can't stand looking at him anymore. As it is, a plethora of ghastly memories I've successfully dealt with years ago flood my mind.

Turning, I urge Clover close to my side and whisper a furious, "Don't say or do anything. Just follow me."

"But—"

"What the *fuck* did I just say?"

Her mouth clamps shut with an audible click. We're almost at the door when the Father's voice reaches me.

"It was good to see you again, Dr. Hill."

CHAPTER SEVENTY-EIGHT
CLOVER

Holy fucking mother of Christ. Hunter's walking so fast it's all I can do to keep up while holding the edges of the priest's robe closed. I know they don't seem to care, but I still don't want the cluster of men we have to walk through peeking at my private bits.

We're through the group of thugs, but I can feel dozens of eyes on my back as Hunter heads back to the forest. I break out in goosebumps, and not in a sexy way.

I jerk at the unexpected bellow of a voice when someone calls out. "We can take ya back."

Hunter lifts a hand without looking back and tightens his grip around my shoulders. "Don't look back."

"Or they'll charge?"

"Very likely."

I guess the embargo on silence is ended. "What the fuck? What the fucking fuck?"

"Shut up and keep moving."

"You're going to call the cops, right?"

"The...what?" In his astonishment, Hunter looks at me before catching himself. We surge forward, slipping through the hole in the barbed wire fence. "The cops?" he demands, releasing me and staring at me as if I've gone stark raving mad.

We're out of sight of the church and the priest's bodyguards, but Hunter doesn't stop. When he notices I have, he waves an angry hand at me. "Keep up."

"Ain't nothing good happening in that place," I say, stabbing a finger toward the distant church. "We gotta call—"

"We ain't gotta fucking *nothing*," Hunter snarls at me.

I'm so shocked, I'm not even pissed off at his sarcasm. He comes back for me, grabs my wrist, and hauls me through the forest after him. "Now keep up!"

"What, you didn't notice the fucking devil in that stained-glass window?"

Hunter falters and turns a confused face to me. "Devil…" he murmurs. Then he barks out a brittle laugh. "That's their—" he waves an impatient hand "—nature god or something."

My eyebrows skyrocket to my hairline, but Hunter's pulling me after him again, not bothering with whether I want to be going in his direction or not.

"Try Satan!" I whisper furiously. "And what the hell was that about blood for blood?"

Hunter's grip flinches around my wrist, but he doesn't answer me.

"Hunter!" I rip my hand free and tuck my hands under my armpit so he can't grab them again. "I'm not going anywhere until you—"

"It's not my story to tell!" he yells.

Birds take flight, and several smaller mammals plunge away through the forest.

He's angry. Or scared. Or a little bit of both—it's so fucking hard to tell with him.

"Now, are you coming with me, or are you going to wait for them to come after you?"

"But they—"

Hunter throws up his hands. He starts off, ripping foliage from his way with reckless abandon. I hesitate for longer than I should. Seriously, how can Hunter be worse than whatever the fuck was going on at that church?

I follow him, of course.

It's not as if I have a choice.

We eventually make it back to the road leading to his cabin, what feels like hours later.

Hunter climbs on his four-wheeler, starts it up, and looks expectantly at me. When I don't immediately climb up behind him, his shoulders sag a little like I've just exhausted the last bit of his patience.

Which I probably have.

"Fine," he says, opening the four-wheeler's throttle, so he has to shout over the sound. "Walk back to town wearing just that." He lifts his fingers, eyebrows twitching in annoyance, and makes to pull off.

"Wait," I grumble, stomping over to him and sliding up behind him with ill grace.

He pulls off so fast that I almost topple over backward. Instinctively, I grab his shirt and cling to him as he tears up the road. The wind whips my robe behind me, and I have to laugh because I can imagine how ridiculous the pair of us look.

If there'd been anyone within a one-mile radius to see us, they'd have been pissing themselves laughing.

I struggle one-handed with the robe and manage to draw it over myself in some semblance of modesty and narrow my eyes so the wind will stop drying out my eyeballs. Eventually, I just tuck my head behind Hunter's back, pressing my cheek to his shoulder blade as I watch the forest stream past in a jade blur.

I close my eyes, wishing I could push out the sight of the priest's feverish gaze.

Hunter parks close to the front door of his house and waits for me to climb off before he does.

Neither of us says a word when he opens the door and stands aside to let me in.

This time, I don't hesitate.

I need clothes. I have to call a cab. None of those things are going to happen if I stay outside like the stubborn bitch I am.

Just like before, his home is utterly silent. If he has servants working here, they obviously only come during the night or something weird.

It wouldn't shock me in the least if they were all robots.

I start upstairs, freezing when he follows me.

"Privacy?" I snap, dragging that odd robe tighter around me.

A whiff of something puffs up from the robe, and my mouth twists. That priest didn't strike me as the kind of person that wears cologne, but what else could explain the scent of cloves and oranges I'm smelling? Some kind of herb, I'm sure. Rosemary?

Fuck it, I have to get out of this thing.

Hunter holds his hands to the side, looking down at himself and then up at me. His clothes are grubby from our dash through the forest, sure, but it's not as if he's naked.

"You can't wait?" I ask as I carry on up the stairs.

"Clover—"

"No!" I spin around on the landing, stabbing a finger that almost gets him in the eye.

"No?" He frowns at me as a look of incredulity grows on his face.

He's two steps down, so I'm towering over him. Which I quite like, I'll have to admit.

"You don't get to *Clover* me. If it weren't for you, then none of this would have happened." I rear back a little, not finding the right words to express the last few days in anything that would make sense.

I storm into his bedroom and rip open the closet door.

Yup, just as I remembered.

Hunter follows me into the room and then slows down.

I point at the closet. "What *the fuck* is this?"

He opens his mouth.

I swear to God, if he's about to say something sarcastic like it's a closet, I'll beat the shit out of him.

Well, I'll try. He's pretty fucking strong for a geek.

In a surprising show of self-preservation, Hunter instead closes his mouth. He walks up to me, so close and with such intent that I think he's going to push me up against the wall and do nasty things to me while I pretend to protest.

He doesn't. He maintains the very frankest of eye contact as he reaches past me, pulls out a fresh outfit for himself, and goes into the en-suite bathroom.

"Hunter!"

The fuck he's not going to explain this shit to me. If anything, I deserve—

I rush after him and then skid to a halt. He has his shirt off already, and he's busy kicking off his sneakers. He glances over his shoulder, but doesn't catch my eye.

"I had everything planned out," he says quietly. His socks come off next—a feat accomplished solely with his toes, which is pretty fucking impressive—as he unbuttons his shorts.

"Right down to my bra size?" I say through my teeth. "How long have you been watching me?"

"Since you began the program."

"Really? Just six months?" My stomach twists at the thought and I'm not sure if it's in a good way or not.

Six *fucking* months.

And here I thought I was just being paranoid as fuck when I felt eyes on me.

Watching me while I ate.

While I walked the halls.

While I...

"While I slept?"

"Sometimes," Hunter says, voice completely devoid of emotion. "But not always. I also need to sleep."

I swallow hard. Not just for his confession, but because he's taking off his shorts. His ass isn't as pale as I'd have figured. Makes me wonder if he goes outside in the nude sometimes. Maybe skinny dips in the forest...

Seriously, Clover? Get your mind out of the fucking gutter.

I shift my weight and force my eyes up even though he's not

looking at me anymore. He turns on the shower's faucet and doesn't even bother testing the temperature before stepping inside.

"So what...you saw me, thought I'd be perfect for your little experiment, and that was that?"

"Trial," he says, but absently.

"Whatever! You *experimented* on me. You...You can't just do that. You can't spy on people and..." I wave a hand toward the unseen closet. "You can't just lay out my entire future like I don't have a fucking say in it."

"So, you want to be an addict for the rest of your life?" He grabs a bottle of something and begins lathering his skin.

Holy fucking shit; he's making it impossible for me to concentrate.

"Yes. If I want."

I don't, obviously.

"Because it's *my* choice, not yours."

"Then you should leave," Hunter says, working that lather into his hair as if he's been in the Amazon jungle for a week, not just a brief sprint through his back yard.

Back yard.

That church wasn't exactly in the middle of fucking nowhere, was it?

Yes, fine, they had like a fence and stuff, but...

I take a step back, absently gripping the robe tight against me. "Those freaks are on your land."

Hunter ducks his head and spits out a mouthful of water without replying. He turns to me, not seeming to care about the fact that the soap suds sliding down his body hardly provide any cover for his junk.

"That's quite a leap."

"Not even a little. Someone like you doesn't just own an acre of land." I sweep out a hand, almost losing grip of the robe. "You probably own this whole fucking mountain. Which means they're on your property. And since no one does anything without your permission..."

He watches me for the longest time, running his hands through his hair as if he can't wash out the last bit of soap. Then he turns off the shower and steps out.

Eyes, Clover. You just keep looking at his eyes. Son-of-a-bitch is doing this on purpose.

"What does it mean?" I ask, forcing my voice to steady. "Blood for blood. Tell me what it means."

I don't actually *want* to know, but I also don't want him getting out of answering me.

He grabs a towel, slings it around his waist. "I'll call you a cab."

Without thinking, I snag his lower arm and tug him around to face me. "Who are they? What are they doing on your land? What the hell happened—?"

He slams me into the bathroom wall, cutting off the question as he crushes me with his body and pins my hands on either side of me.

"This isn't your concern," he says coldly, his eyes flickering over mine as if to impress the seriousness of the situation on me. "Shut your mouth, get dressed, and get the fuck out of here."

"You're letting me go?" The words are out before I can think them through.

The snarling anger on Hunter's face disappears in an instant. He stares at me, lips parted, and then turns his head to bark out a laugh. When he looks back at me, bitter mirth twinkles in his eyes.

"Are you fucking kidding me?" he asks, pushing harder into me. "You *ran* from me. You accuse me of keeping you here without your consent. You all but *beg* me to let you go, and now...?"

I tug. He seems to have forgotten how hard he's gripping me but I won't show weakness. I simply turn my attention away from where my wrist bones are grating against each other.

"I want to know what's going on."

He shakes his head hard enough to splatter water on my face. "You can't have it both ways, Clover. You want to leave, so fucking leave."

Goddamn my curiosity! He knows all this shit that's happened is eating me up.

Hang on. This may be my paranoia speaking, but did he plan *this* too? Did he know I'd run into that strange church? Did he plan on the fact that I'd be so curious to find out what was going on that I'd stay... if only for closure?

"What stops me from going to the cops?"

A risky move, sure, but I know he's not going to kill me, else he'd have done it already. I mean, I'm not exactly the nicest person in the world and I've been grinding his balls nonstop since I've arrived.

Come to think of it, he's actually been pretty fucking patient with me.

That doesn't count in his favor, of course. He still dragged me out here and set me free in his stupid maze like a rat on coke.

Exactly like a lab rat high on coke.

His eyes crinkle like he's going to laugh again, but instead he just shrugs a little and takes a small step back. "Go, Clover. Tell them what happened. Tell them what you saw."

He releases my hands and rakes his gaze down my body. With him stepping away, cold air slides over my skin. The robe has flared open and isn't shielding me from his eyes anymore. I shift a little before I can stop myself.

No biggie. He's seen me naked. Twice. Three times.

Fuck, plenty of times, possibly.

I narrow my eyes at him. "In the shower?" I whisper.

He blinks, frowns, and then closes his eyes as he lets out a sigh. "What purpose could me watching you in the shower possibly have served?"

I cock an eyebrow, and my eyes dart down to his loin-cloth-cum-towel. "You tell me, Doctor Hill."

I was hoping for a laugh, something to diffuse the situation, but he rips his hands away from mine, opens his mouth, but leaves the bathroom without another word.

I stay behind, rubbing fingers over my wrists where he bruised me.

There's absolutely no reason for me to stay. And I *will* go to the cops—especially after he dared me like that.

I snort to myself.

I mean, does he honestly think I won't—?

I pause in the process of slipping off that horrid robe.

He *knows* I'll go to the cops, if only to spite him.

Which means he knows nothing will come of it.

Does he own this fucking town or something?

Dr. Most-Eligible-Bachelor Hunter Hill, owner of Mallhaven.

Okay, maybe not an owner, at least a majority fucking shareholder. He's probably a pillar of the community. No one would believe he's hosting a satanic church on his land.

There's a mirror inside the shower, and the steam from Hunter's session has cleared out. I catch sight of my reflection as I step inside.

The tiles are still wet and it reeks of Hunter. Crisp, pine-like freshness. Wood. A touch of something sweet.

I haven't noticed how much I've filled out these past six months. I never used to have such pronounced curves. But that's not what's making me stare aghast at my reflection.

I'm covered in scratches and bruises.

Streaks of dirt paint my arms and legs.

My hair—although still pretty clean—is tangled and unkempt.

No one in Mallhaven will listen to some out-of-towner talking shit about their Dr. Hill.

I have to get cleaned up. Have to get my facts sorted out, then maybe...

Maybe I could fuck off out of Mallhaven and never come back.

That's all I wanted, right? To be left alone.

Independence.

Except, Clover Vos was never really independent, was she? She may have been a strong, smart woman, but without a job, without a hope of ever getting a job, she quickly learned to depend on men to give her what she needed.

Money.

A place to stay.

Some pseudo-excuse for love.

But that was the old Clover. I'm reborn. Free of addiction. Except, what if I'm not? What if all that shit Hunter said is true? What if I can never—?

I. Am. Free. Of. Addiction.

I push back my shoulders and lift my chin, daring my reflection to defy me as I turn on the shower.

CHAPTER SEVENTY-NINE
HUNTER

I should be calling Clover a cab. Instead, I'm staring into the forest beside my house. It looks like rain. Not unusual—Mallhaven likes its gloomy afternoons in summer as much as its snowy mornings in winter.

Blood for blood.

Sometimes, I wish I had it in me to believe in something spiritual, if only so I didn't feel compelled to explain every second of every day with rationale.

Everything that could have gone wrong with this trial went wrong. I had all the data I needed to make the correct decisions, and still I erred.

Clover should never have gotten close to the Messianic Church of Solomon but she ended up right in the Father's bloodstained hands. I expected her to be eager to be rid of her disease. Instead, she fights me every step of the way.

Change is difficult, I understand. But no one can be ignorant enough to turn aside a cure for their ailment and yet it happens all the time.

Bare feet slap on tiles behind me and I half-turn to face Clover as she walks into the kitchen.

"I was just about to call a—" I begin, lifting my cellphone and unlocking the screen.

"Whose story is it?"

I face her and then lean back against the counter, phone in one hand and gripping the lip of the granite countertop with the other. I watch her for a few moments, willing her to take back the question, to move to a different line of inquiry…

Any-fucking-thing but this.

She's wearing one of the dresses I picked out for her. Well, I say picked out, but it was nothing but an hour of autonomous online shopping based on her dimensions and whatever would be suitable for the climate here in Mallhaven over the next six months.

See, Clover? I didn't have your *entire life* planned out.

Just the next six months.

Here.

With me.

I know nothing about fashion, or dresses, but I have a feeling she specifically chose this dress. The pale fabric skims her breasts and hips in a very sensual way.

Then again, maybe I didn't just click 'add to cart' without a second thought.

I can remember the picture they had for this dress. Some stick-thin fashion model with more cheekbones than seemed natural had this hanging from gangly shoulders.

But the fabric looked soft. Silky, even. There were no distracting slogans, or embellishments.

Seeing this dress on Clover, it looks as if it was tailored for her. It sets off her hair in a blaze of red and the cream fabric melds seamlessly with her skin. Her eyes are a darker shade of gray; almost the color of the clouds gathering in the sky outside.

Clover shrugs. Light glides over the fabric and I have an overwhelming urge to touch it, despite the fact that I would never consider myself a tactile person.

"You said it's not your story to tell. So, whose is it?" She dares me to answer, but my tongue cleaves to the roof of my mouth instead. "The priest? Who?"

Reluctantly, I speak. "Kane. Kane Price. You don't—"

She cuts me off with a wave of her hand. "You got his number?" She lifts her chin. "Call him."

I squeeze the bridge of my nose, inhaling what is meant to be a soothing breath. I'm suddenly in desperate need of a joint, and I never smoke during the day. "It's not that—"

"Tell him I want to know." She takes a step closer as I look up at her with exasperation. That fabric flows over her thighs like pouring cream.

"I told you, you can't have it both ways."

She stops. Considers me. And then puts her head to the side. "You own this town, don't you?"

I frown, open my mouth, and then let out a laugh instead. I push past her to go to the couch, my fingertips thrilling as they brush over the smooth fabric draping her waist. "I don't own Mallhaven."

"So what then? You're the mayor or something?"

I throw her an incredulous look over my shoulder, but this just seems to convince her even more. She stalks up to me, hands in fists at her side. "You don't care if I go to the cops, 'cos they won't do anything, will they? You own them. You own this town. They'll take one look at me and throw me in the fucking loony bin."

I'm busy rolling a joint. That was my mistake. Obviously, she wants my attention on her.

She's always been an attention seeker, Clover Vos. Even during withdrawal, she'd become so melodramatic that I'd order Michael to lock her in her room until she came to her senses.

Sometimes it would work. Sometimes I would have to send someone in to sedate her.

And then I realized she was getting off on the buzz of whatever sedative I gave her.

Playing me like a pawn.

Clover grabs my wrist and tugs it hard enough to jar the half-rolled joint from my palm.

I rush to my feet, but she's already put herself out of reach by taking two quick steps back.

A fast learner, Clover. But I've had a long time to study her where she's only known me for a few days.

I step forward, moving slowly so I don't scare her off.

"Mallhaven's corrupt police force?" Another step. "Yes, they would probably commit you if I told them too." She's so caught up in what I'm saying, she doesn't seem to notice I'm drawing near.

"So everyone knows about the satanic church right next to your fucking house?"

I look away as I laugh.

When I lurch forward, I'm too close for her to escape. I grab the front of her dress in a fist and haul her against me.

"All these question…you've decided to stay?"

She wriggles against me, her mouth squirming as if she can't quite decide what she wants to say to me. She eventually lets out a frustrated, "I want to know what the fuck you're involved in."

"I'm not involved in anything." The words come out through my teeth, but that's purely because of how pissed off this woman makes me. I don't consider myself short-tempered to any extent, but Clover has a way of rubbing me the wrong way.

And the right way.

With her this close, all I'm thinking is how good it feels when our naked bodies slide against each other.

Which is probably exactly how she played out this encounter in her mind.

Which is why she chose this dress.

Which is why she's not pulling away but instead arching ever so slightly into me.

I inhale her scent, and it fills me with an agonizing flicker of electric fire.

My fingers slide over her satiny dress, describing each of her curves with a slow, steady hand. Her eyes flutter, but don't close. Her lips tighten, and then part. Her spine curls so her stomach and breasts are flush against me.

She must feel my hard-on, but doesn't react.

Not yet, anyway.

"Give me six months." I hear my voice, understand the words, but I still can't believe I was the one that spoke them.

She's unraveling me. Invading my psyche and laying bare things that should never again have seen the light of day.

"I've already given you six months," she murmurs, her eyes narrowing in challenge. "Why the hell do you want more?"

"Six months. That's all I'm asking."

She studies me. First my eyes, then my nose, my mouth. There, her gaze is a physical touch that wreathes a phantom caress over my lips.

"Room and board?" There's the slightest curve to her mouth, but it could also just be the melting shadows as dark clouds occlude the remaining light from the world.

"Whatever you want," I hear myself saying.

A coy light gleams in her magnificent eyes. "Tell me about the church."

She puts her hand on my chest, arches her fingers, and urges her nails into my skin. The shirt's fabric is thin enough for me to feel her digging her claws into me.

I slide a hand into her hair, tangling those silky strands around my fingers and gently arching her neck. "Anything but that."

Annoyance twists her mouth. Her lips part, and I already know she's primed to begin arguing with me.

An impossible feat if I'm kissing her.

She stiffens, recoils like a snake. But I already had a hand around her waist and it takes hardly any effort on my part to drag her against me.

I've never been this confused in my life.

The urge to shove her away is as strong as the urge to draw her close, and she's partly kissing, partly biting me, as if she can't decide how she feels either. Our breathing synchronizes, buffeting each other with every forceful exhalation as I struggle to pull her to the couch and she fights to stay standing.

I hook my leg around hers. She collapses, and I have her under me a second later.

My hand is under her skirt, but she's clamping her legs closed so tightly that I can't get an inch above her knees. I grasp her breast instead, breaking our kiss as I let out a sigh. Fuck, but she feels so good in this dress. So sensual, so feminine. I wouldn't call her a tomboy—I wouldn't even know where to begin to make that classification—but until I saw her wearing a dress at her graduation ceremony, I had no idea Clover Vos cleaned up so good.

Then again—she spent her time as a high-class hooker before she arrived in Mallhaven. Did I honestly expect her to walk around in torn jeans and a baggy shirt?

Fuck, yes.

But only if it was *my* shirt; skip the jeans.

I bite her chin, nibble her lip, try to force my hand between her legs.

"Tell me," she whispers, the words slurred by our mingling mouths.

"It's not my story to tell."

She lets out an irritated growl, and grabs a fistful of my hair. It hurts when she tugs it, but I barely feel it.

Woman, you don't know what I've been through. Yanking on my hair won't do shit. Kneeing me in the stomach isn't going to set you free.

"Tell me."

I pull away from her, blinking furiously to clear my vision. She flutters her eyelashes at me, but I have a feeling she's reeling as much as I am.

"You'll stay," I repeat slowly.

She writhes under me. My cock stiffens painfully inside my pants, and I grind it against her.

Clover gives me the faintest of nods.

Her hands slide between us and begin working at the button on my pants.

I put my forehead against hers, lifting myself on one elbow as I stare into her eyes. She touches her mouth to mine.

"I'll stay," she whispers, her lips brushing mine.

My button pops open. Her hand glides behind my underwear, gripping my dick and squeezing me so hard I groan against her mouth.

"But only if you tell me."

I shove my hand between her legs. She's not wearing underwear, despite the fact that she has dozens of pairs upstairs.

What is it about the blatant challenge in her eyes that makes me want to crush her under me? Could it be that every other woman I've ever been with has been both docile and submissive—to the point that, even if I wasn't paying for her affections in some way, they were all just prostitutes?

With Clover, I feel as if I have to *earn* her body.

Her lust.

Her complete abandon when she comes.

I have to take it from her, and she won't let it go without a fight.

It makes me feel dirty. Uncouth. A grunting savage with no concern but my own selfish pleasure.

But if that were the case, she'd be screaming for help. She'd be crying and batting me with her fists.

Instead, she's fixated on driving me insane as she deftly avoids my touch.

Her mouth twists away from mine, and she pumps me as her thighs clamp together.

Enough.

She wants to know what that church is doing on my land? She'll know soon enough.

But it won't be me telling that story.

If she understood what it meant, contacting Kane, she would never ask me again.

Kane would never be as gentle as I am with her.

I grip her chin and wrench her mouth toward mine. For a second, her lips are a hard, impervious line. But I sink my fingers between her jaws, forcing them open as I invade her mouth with the ferocity of a wild animal.

Fuck, maybe that's *exactly* what she wants.

CHAPTER EIGHTY
CLOVER

How can someone this repressed, obsessed, fucking distressed have so much passion inside him?

I feel like a boat tossed on an angry, never-ending sea as a storm whips the waves into a froth.

Hunter's lips ravage my mouth. His tongue forces its way between my teeth as if he doesn't even think for a second I'd bite.

I've got his cock in my hands, but I could be squeezing his arm for all the response I'm getting.

God, it's so fucking hard. So smooth. I want it inside me so bad I'm tempted to hitch up my dress and shove it in there myself.

But that's not how we play this game, is it, Hunter?

Oh no.

I make you fight for it.

I'm not sure if that pisses him off or turns him on, but he turns into a fucking champion when I do.

I have never been fucked with this much intensity before in my life.

A wolf in a suit.

An animal that talks and even has a Ph.D. in whatever the fuck Hunter has.

But that means nothing when it's just me and him. He wants in, I keep him out.

It's a fight I know I'll lose, but that doesn't stop me from trying.

I will *never* stop fighting.

If Hunter doesn't know that by now, then he's pretty fucked.

CHAPTER EIGHTY-ONE
HUNTER

Clover makes an angry sound when I finally get her legs open an inch. I shove my knee between her thighs, making sure she can't slam shut like a prison cell.

Fabric rips under my fist.

My eyes flutter open to the ruins of her dress. The angry red marks on her shoulders and arms.

But instead of pain, or fury, I see only lust gleaming in her eyes. Her mouth parts, and I know she's about to call my name.

Which will be my undoing.

I slap a hand over her mouth, and use the other to drag my palm over her cunt.

She's wet and hot as the jungle in midday.

I can hardly keep myself back from sinking into her.

But something as exquisite as this creature quivering under me deserves more than a five-minute fuck on my sofa.

I want her begging me to end her suffering. I want to hold back until I can't anymore, until I destroy her just to come.

Her back arches. Breasts still clothed in cool, silky fabric presses into me.

She bites my fingers, and I pull away my hand with a hiss. I drive my mouth against hers, distracting her as I gather my shirt. It takes me less than a second to rip the fabric over my head. I stare at her as she bucks and arches under me, unable to lower myself over her glorious body.

Instead, I grab the front of her dress and rip her up to me. Our mouths crash into each other, and I turn so my legs can slide off the side of the couch. She straddles me so easily it has to be instinctual, but getting her dress over her head seems to be another matter entirely.

I tug it free. A twist at the last moment traps her hands in the fabric, and I use those satin manacles to keep her hands behind her as I graze my teeth over her breasts.

Her skin is as silky and as smooth as the fabric of her dress. I lavish her nipple with teeth and tongue until she moans and arches into my mouth.

That gesture grinds her cunt against my dick.

It's already as stiff as it's going to get, but she's so fucking wet all it would take is a shift of my hips to fuck her.

As if she knows, she begins sliding her hips back and forth. Dragging her cunt over me. Lubricating me.

Clover ducks her head and puts it by my ear. "Never once?" she murmurs, her lips sending a wave of shivers through me.

I groan as she drags her wet cunt over me.

"Never?"

"Fuck," I mutter, nipping the side of her neck hard enough to leave a mark. "Never what, Clover?"

"You didn't watch me in the shower? Not once?"

"No." I fist my hand, keeping her hands trapped in her dress so I can grab her jaw and make her look at me. She stops grinding me, but at just the right spot because the tip of my fucking cock is right against her cunt. All I have to do is lift my hips, and I'll be inside her. Owning her. Making her scream my name as I fuck her.

"Never?"

I've known for a long time that Clover isn't just any run-of-the-mill addict. Her past forged her into brittle steel. She knows nothing about compassion, or kindness.

Or love.

Fuck, neither do I. I was never given the chance, was I? Every time I thought I could love, the devil tore that prospect away with blood-drenched claws.

I've seen shit no one else has. I know things no one in their right minds would want to know.

Clover knows nothing.

She thinks I'm a scientist. Maybe a good lay—but she's had so many, I find that hard to believe.

But I'm just a scientist like Clover's just a junkie.

We have so many fucking layers, it would take someone a lifetime to peel them all away.

Fuck it—I'm not getting any younger.

Neither is she.

If anyone deserves to be there when that last layer is peeled back, it's her.

CHAPTER EIGHTY-TWO
CLOVER

C hrist, this man can tease like the fucking Joker in Batman, can't he? I'm balanced on a razor edge of sanity and pleasure. Every time I look into his eyes, I wobble.

Sanity.

Pleasure.

I can't have both, but who the fuck would even hesitate to choose pleasure?

Sanity is for those that can afford it.

I'm poor as fuck.

After all, sanity does nothing when you're surrounded by pain. But pleasure is pleasure, whether you're on the spectrum or not.

Sorry, not fucking sorry.

He must know how close he is to being inside of me. Else why would he be looking up at me with such zealous expectation?

This started out as a contest of some kind. He had something I wanted, and I knew what he'd take as payment.

Something I've been giving away since I was thirteen.

My body.

It's not me, after all. I'm my mind—nothing more, nothing less. My body is just some vessel that sends me signals now and then.

Hot.

Cold.

Pain.

Pleasure.

Pressure...

...nothing.

That's the extent of my body's influence over me. I learned early on that I didn't even need to be present all the time.

I think Buddhists do it.

Buddhists and psychopaths.

They disassociate.

Mind is no longer attached to body.

That's what the dark taught me.

That's what life taught me.

My body is what everyone else sees, but I'm not my body.

Not even close.

My body changes and grows while I'm stuck inside, equally slave and puppet master.

I came downstairs thinking I could tie him around my little finger.

Instead, he has me so entranced, I don't even see the strings on my puppet body anymore.

If this was a game, he's won.

If this was war, then he's busy rewriting history just the way he fucking wants.

Because right now I don't care how long he's been watching me. I don't care that I've only been part of some experiment. I don't care that he's part of something so demonic, I can't even wrap my head around it.

I. Don't. Fucking. Care.

Why? Because, right now, the shattered thing that I used to be is whole.

He glues me back together.

Even if it's just so he can break me apart.

CHAPTER EIGHTY-THREE
HUNTER

The day grows dark. If I weren't a man of science, I'd say something sinister stirs outside. But it's just a thunderstorm. Just a thunderstorm.

The fact that I have this goddess on my lap, spread and waiting for me to defile her has nothing to do with the weather.

Why would it?

We're mortals, Clover and me.

Our sexual attraction would never have an effect on the weather. What we do in the privacy of this glass-walled house of mine has no bearing on the outside world.

How could it?

But our gazes lock. Our bodies meld. I can't tell where I end and she begins. I couldn't give less fucks, because I no longer feel the need to define myself.

Just like I never felt the need to define Clover.

I lied to myself.

To her.

She was never a test subject.

Never just a mentee.

I saw myself in her. My addiction. My pain.

Our betrayal.

I'm no anarchist. Clover's probably never put graffiti on anything in her life.

But we both abhor authority in the same way that we both fight against its control.

Even now, neither of us will submit to the other. I mean her no harm, and she knows it. But she's been betrayed so many times she can't tell good from evil.

I don't just want to cure her, I want to teach her how to trust again.

If I can't accomplish that, then no one can.

CHAPTER EIGHTY-FOUR
CLOVER

I'm kissing Hunter.

No, he's kissing me.

Fuck it—maybe we're kissing each other.

Somehow, it doesn't matter anymore. Which I can't wrap my head around, because it always—it *always*—has.

There's always an instigator.

A dom.

A sub.

The person on top.

The person below.

But right now, it doesn't feel like we're competing in a race.

We're both in the same fucking canoe, and our little boat keeps spinning, because we're rowing against each other.

Left versus right.

Up versus down.

Neither of us will submit. We can't both dominate.

Maybe we're just too similar and, in this world, only opposites attract.

Something we both know. Something we're both trying to fight.

Unless I stop fighting.
Or he does.
But will he?
Or must I?

CHAPTER EIGHTY-FIVE
HUNTER

C lover and I both stop moving.
We both stop fighting.

I have her face in my hands. She has her hands in my hair. Our mouths are less than an inch apart.

We're both panting, and our breath paints warmth on each other's lips.

It's noon. We're on some dusty, sun-drenched street in the middle of fucking nowhere. Hands hovering over our pistols. Ready to draw. Ready to decide the outcome of this duel.

I buck my hips, and she lets out a breathless "Fuck," as I spear into her.

Her core clings to me, refusing to let me ease out. She fists her hands, sending a spark of pain through my scalp.

I grab her throat in one hand, slide the other between our bodies. We watch each other like soldiers across No-man's-land as I stroke her clit with my thumb. She rocks into me with her hips, driving my cock even deeper inside her.

A groan escapes me, in spite of how hard I'm clenching my jaw.

I grab her hip, forcing her to ride me again as I squeeze her throat.

Fury sparks in her eyes, but instead of wriggling free she grinds herself harder against me. Her cunt—scorching and wet—coats me with her arousal.

Her breath is coming as hot and fast as mine. Lips open, beckoning my mouth like a flower beckons a bee.

I sit forward, crushing my mouth against hers as I thrust so deep into her that her entire body stiffens in response.

Spreading my legs, I force her thighs further apart. I swipe fingers over her clit until she bucks into me, and then slide my fingers around her ass, gliding fingertips along the seam where we meet.

I'm barely moving now. She's pinned on my cock like a witch to a stake, and I wouldn't have it any other way. I feel her undulating over my dick as her body responds—either willingly or not—to my invasive presence.

She stretches so deliciously tight around me that I can barely pull out the inch I need to ram back inside her.

Our lips come apart, and she gasps, "Hunter," into my ear.

That sound unhinges something in my brain.

"Fuck," I groan, grabbing her shoulders so I can pound her hard enough to illicit a pained moan.

She throws back her head, and I work hummingbird kisses down her neck as she rides my cock with every buck of her hips.

I grab an ass cheek in each hand and open her even further, staring down so I can see how I'm fucking her drenched cunt.

Her hands are on my shoulders, her thighs so wide apart they're almost forming a straight line.

I can see every inch of myself disappearing into her.

"Touch yourself," I grate.

She doesn't even hesitate.

Her fingers circle her clit with languid indolence. I groan watching her, knowing she's teasing herself as much as she's teasing me.

When I look up, she's staring at me. As much as I want to keep watching us fuck, her eyes trap mine.

I slow again, and her jaw juts as she releases a long, staggered sigh.

"Come with me," I murmur.

Her lips tremble, and I feel her fingertips brushing my shaft as she begins working her clit faster than before.

But I don't speed up.

I keep to the same tantalizing pace as before. This way, I feel every inch of her when I slide in, and every inch of her when I ease out. She clamps tightly around me as if daring me to slow even more.

It's agony.

Bliss.

And something more. Something I can't comprehend.

Being inside her feels *perfect*. Her skin touching mine is so familiar, we could have been fucking each other for years, not days.

I never want this to stop.

This feeling.

This closeness.

This union.

I want to tell her that. I want to tell her *everything*.

But I can't.

I made a promise, and promises are something I hold sacred.

"I'm close," Clover whispers. "I'm so fucking close."

She has such a dirty mouth on her.

I love it.

"Hunter." Concern wreathes her words. Because she doesn't know how close I am, or because she can see something in my eyes that she's not sure of?

Hunter.

She may think she's only staying for six months, but she'll never leave.

Never.

"You're mine," I murmur, the words straining as I attempt to keep my composure. "I'm never letting you go. You know that, right?"

Those Bluestar eyes watch me, her lips parted and trembling as she slowly begins to rock against me. Not faster...but *harder*.

"What if I run?" she asks, her gaze flickering over my face.

I lean forward, driving a deliciously tortured moan from Clover. I put my lips against hers, but I don't kiss her just yet.

"You run, and I'll just hunt you down. Every fucking time."

CHAPTER EIGHTY-SIX
CLOVER

I can't take this anymore. Every nerve ending in my body is on fire. Doused in ice. Prickling with electricity. I can feel the air sliding over my skin. I hear raindrops spattering against Hunter's glass walls.

There's hardly any light left in here, but for once, the shadows don't look as dark and menacing as they always do. In fact, the low light blurs them, so I can barely tell where they end or begin.

I can't be sure just yet, but I don't think the dark will ever scare me again.

For one, I know I'm not going to be alone for a while.

Six months.

Hunter's promise echoes in my mind as he fills me with every inch of himself. I'm ready to burst, ready to plunge down that cliff with him.

But something's different.

I thought he was intense before, but it's like he's trying to capture my entire essence just by fucking me this slow, this intentionally.

It's driving me mad, and setting off chain reactions inside me I've never experienced before.

I'm a fucking snowflake, unique and cherished and everlasting.

I know—I just fucking know—that if we were to be apart for too long, I'd melt.

The world is a desert, and he's my glacier.

I'll just hunt you down. Every fucking time.

My lips quirk at that, and his gaze darts to my mouth as if he's trying to decipher my thoughts.

I begin rocking into him, forcing him to fuck me, if not faster, then at least harder. I could come any second now if I apply just the right pressure on my clit.

I've never orgasmed any other way, but I'm an expert at it.

"Look at me."

My head snaps up. I was watching him fuck me, thrilling over the sight of his cock sinking inside my cunt.

"Stop touching yourself."

My mouth opens, but all he does is give his head the smallest shake. I lift my hands and grab onto the curve between his shoulders and his neck.

He grasps my hips, forcing me back and then pulling me forward.

My eyes flutter as that slow friction builds to something hot and fantastic in my core.

Also, I kinda feel like I have to pee.

But that can wait, I'm sure.

I squirm around his cock, but a slap to my rump stills me.

Fuck, this feels good, but if he doesn't let me touch myself, I'll never—

"You're perfect," he says.

My eyes go wide. I want to laugh, want to start listing all the things that make me far from anything approaching perfect, but I can't.

Because I can see he believes it.

He thinks I'm perfect.

He *knows* I'm perfect.

I groan, my body trembling as hedonistic bliss wreathes its way deep into my core.

"What are you doing to me?" I whisper furiously.

"I'm fucking you," he says.

"No, this...this is different." I hear the panic in my voice.

Something's wrong. My body's on fire, but my skin is ice cold. I have no control over myself. I'm moving in ways I've never moved before. My hips are fluid, my spine bending like a supple leather belt.

"You're mine, Clover," he says this through his teeth. The possessiveness in his voice sends a hard shudder through me. I dig my nails into his shoulders, struggling to get my body under control, struggling to keep my eyes open.

"I can do whatever the fuck I want to you."

"Hunter." His name comes out in a sigh, and his lips part around a deep-throated groan.

"Let go. *Be* mine." He swipes a tongue over his lips, and it's possibly the most erotic thing I've ever seen in my fucking life.

"Come with me."

My body is incapable of disobeying his command. His fingers dig into my hips. He holds me still as he thrusts into me, drawing a gasp from me.

Again.

"Hunter." It's a desperate plea, because something's roaring toward me and I don't have a fucking clue what it is.

It doesn't scare me, not with him here. What scares me is the fact that I can't look away. I want him to drink me down, consume me whole, take everything and leave nothing behind.

He thrusts into me. "Come."

I grab him so hard, I can feel blood under my fingertips.

Blood for blood.

My body spasms, gripping him so hard that I can feel his cock throbbing as he empties himself deep, so *fucking* deep, inside me.

"Let go," he says.

Am I hurting him?

But then I realize I'm holding back. I'm stifling my orgasm so I can maintain some modicum of control.

Clover Vos would never allow herself to be unaware, unprepared, vulnerable.

That's when bad things happen.

That's when the dark comes for me, and shreds my soul with its ragged nails.

"Hunter!" I speak his name like a curse, a revelation, a prayer.

Such a look of absolute adoration floods his face that even if I wanted to, I can't close my eyes. I come hard and slow, just like he's fucking me, and it's the most glorious thing I've ever experienced.

He keeps thrusting into me, drawing out my climax until I'm a shivering mess.

I sob and clap my hands over my mouth in shock.

Hunter smiles at me, slides as deep inside me as he can, and drags me down for a kiss. He flips me onto my back on the couch, staying inside me as he softens. Then he just keeps kissing me until I'm so light headed that the room spins around me.

He draws back, our heated panting mingling as our lips brush against each other. With a swipe of his hands, he clears strands of hair from my cheeks and cups my face.

"You can run," he whispers, his brown eyes as deep and dark as the shadows in the forest. "But I'll always catch you."

We both know I will run. It's in my nature. I'm a bunny, and he's a wolf. My instinct will be to race away from the predator that flickers in his eyes.

After he's caught me, he'll bring me back to his den and make him mine all over again.

Maybe, one day, I won't run anymore.

Maybe, one day, he won't chase after me.

I can only hope that day won't be any time soon.

CHAPTER EIGHTY-SEVEN
CLOVER

Birds chirp me awake. I push onto my elbows, completely disorientated. But then I feel the silky sheets under me, and the gentle cast of light coming through a nearby window reels back my mind.

Fuck, what time is it?

I'm still aching inside, and my body feels so deliciously heavy with muscles sore from tensing.

I don't think I've ever been fucked as hard as I was last night. We moved to the room at some stage; how, I don't remember. I think we even fucked on the stairs.

I do know that we came to some kind of agreement. That we made some weird, veiled proclamation to each other.

Like, I think we're a couple now.

I laugh as I wipe my hands over my face. My hair's an absolute mess and it's going to take at least half an hour to brush it out.

"What's so funny?"

I jerk, gripping the sheet to my naked body before my scrambling brain can inform me that it's Hunter asking the question.

He has a tray in his hands. Two cups of coffee, a small plate with some kind of bread on it.

"Nothing," I murmur, and reach out grabby hands for the coffee. "Mmm."

He holds the tray for me to take my cup and perches on the edge of the bed.

I poke one of the slices of bread. I smell vanilla or something wafting from it, and it's been smeared with butter. "What's this?"

"Your new favorite snack," he says, breaking a corner from the slice I touched and bringing it to my mouth. "At least, that's what Esli will insist."

"Esli?"

"My cleaning lady."

I watch him warily for a second before I open my mouth. His fingers brush my lips as he sets the morsel on my tongue, and he sends a shiver through my body as he swipes his thumb over my bottom lip.

I chew once, roll my eyes to the heavens, and let out a lingering, "Mmm."

His mouth twitches into a smile.

"Eat up," he says, standing with his coffee cup in his hand. "We have a guest arriving shortly."

I hastily swallow. "A...guest?"

Who the fuck? *What* the fuck? If I hadn't only just woken up, I'd have given him a tongue lashing he'd still be punishing me for a week from now.

Hunter turns away, but doesn't leave just yet. Instead, he stares out the bedroom window as he takes a sip of his coffee. When his gaze touches me again, a cold ripple shimmies down my spine.

"You said you wanted to know." He shrugs a little. "I've tracked him down. He's agreed to come through." Hunter twists his wrist, and I realize for the first time he's wearing a button-up shirt and smart slacks. Not quite a suit, but with that watch on his wrist...?

"Kane," I say, dredging the name from the bottom of my memory river with some difficulty. I break off another corner of that delicious bread and shove it in my mouth. "Your...?"

I leave the sentence dangling, but Hunter seems to have no intention of completing it. He points to the closet. "Wear something nice."

He leaves then, giving me a faint smile on the way out.

Blood for blood.

I guess it's too late to tell him I don't want to know.

Fuck, who'm I fooling? I *want* to know.

And...I kinda have this feeling he's been waiting a long time to tell someone.

To tell *me*.

CHAPTER EIGHTY-EIGHT
HUNTER

My phone vibrates in my pocket. When I take it out, my hands are trembling ever so slightly. Shit, I can't believe I'm this nervous. I tap on my phone's screen and, half a mile away, the gates to my premises swing open.

I haven't seen Kane in over five years.

And to think, we were best friends. Well, I thought we were. Looking back, maybe I was the only one who thought that. Regardless, I swore an oath, and I refuse to break it.

I'll admit, I'm shocked he even answered my call. No. I'm shocked his number was still the same. After everything—

Fuck it, there'll be enough of that when Kane gets here.

Movement catches my eye. Clover, making her way down the stairs. A red-haired beauty in that dress, cheeks flushed with health, and an inquisitive gleam in her eyes.

My mouth goes dry.

I suddenly want to take this all back. Calling Kane, telling Clover I'd reveal everything.

She thinks she knows me...but after this, will she even be able to look at me?

A car pulls up to the front of the house. It's nothing stylish, a sand-colored Jeep probably three years old. Something I expected Kane to be driving.

What I didn't expect to see was the woman who climbed out beside him.

"Fuck."

Clover comes to a halt at the bottom of the stairs. Then she hurries up to me and grabs my wrist. "What?" Her voice is deep, demanding.

"It's…It's Ziggy."

Clover remains silent, and I glance down at her in surprise. At hearing a name like that, I would have expected a snarky comment from her. But perhaps she senses the tension of the moment. She's a surprisingly intuitive creature. I suspect that's how she lasted as long as she did. She turned that talent to her advantage by picking weak men to prey on.

Ziggy looks toward the house, but with the sun at its current angle, I doubt she can see through the glazing. She shades her eyes and then looks to Kane as he climbs out of the driver's side of his Jeep.

My chest constricts.

Fingers brush the back of my hand. I jerk, glancing down at Clover as she pries my cellphone from my grip. "You're gonna break it," she mutters, as if she can't stand the thought of me damaging something as expensive as this piece of tech.

I lick my lips, lift my chin, and head for the door.

Kane ambles up to the path leading to the front of my house, eyes veiled by a pair of shades. He's smoking a cigarette, the filter right at the juncture between palm and knuckles as he plucks it from his mouth for an exhale.

I worshipped this man.

He was my best friend, my mentor, perhaps even a foster father. He's pushing forty, but it's as if he hasn't changed a day. The lines around his mouth might be deeper, but he still walks with the casual authority of a man who suffered through Armageddon and came out the other side unscathed.

Ziggy's wearing heels, a mini skirt, and her brown hair long and loose.

Just how Kane always liked it.

A torturous pain squeezes at my heart as I think of M.J.

Warmth buffets my side. I look down. Clover is at my side, blue-gray eyes turned up to me and her face devoid of mirth. She slides an arm around my waist, squeezes me, and says, "Thank you."

I let out a short laugh. "For what?" And then I clear my throat because my voice is rough and thick.

"For letting me in."

CHAPTER EIGHTY-NINE
CLOVER

My heart's beating so hard, it feels like it's gonna come right out. The guy walking up to Hunter's front door doesn't look that intimidating. Dark hair, shades, an arrogant sway to his hips. He's older than Hunter, maybe six or seven years, but I don't think age is what's weighing him down.

The girl at his side is pretty enough, but she's clinging to him like he's the only thing keeping her afloat.

But Hunter's tensing causes wave after wave of panic to crash over me.

Who is this Kane guy? What the hell happened to him and Hunter eight years ago that can bring such a strong, determined man like Hunter to his knees?

Hunter pushes me away to go and open the door. His eyes are glazed, like all he can see right now is the past. He opens the door, and Kane flicks away the cigarette he was smoking.

The two men stare at each other, Kane almost a foot shorter than Hunter, and then Hunter sticks out his hand. Tension makes the air sticky with anticipation.

Kane steps forward, knocks away Hunter's arm, and wraps him in a hug.

Well, I guess I'm about to find out.

The Blood for Blood series continues in
The Binding Ties.

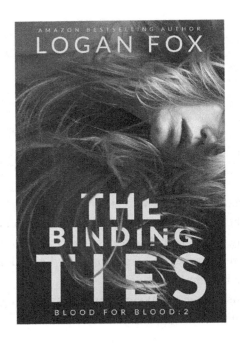

https://smarturl.it/ldfox-tbt-Books2Read

ABOUT THE AUTHOR

L. D. Fox writes deliciously dark and twisted stories for people that, like her, enjoy reading it.

Having grown up on names like Graham Masterton, Dean Koontz, James Herbert, Stephen King, Robert Jordan, and Terry Pratchett, her stories are an eclectic mix of the sadistically twisted, the epic, and the darkly comedic. She strives to create characters that are as immersive as the worlds she raises around them. Expect more than your average amount of plot twists, superb dialog, characters you'll either love or loathe, and a book hangover that's guaranteed to last at least few days, if not longer. She doesn't hold any punches - nor should she, for that's what she expects in the books she reads and what she offers to her readers in return.

She hails from the four-seasons-in-a-day suburb of Johannesburg, South Africa. She's so busy writing she doesn't have time for much else except the occasional indulgent Netflix binge. She loves hearing from readers, so don't be why to contact her and tell her what you thought of her writing.